Brass Bed

"More fun than pillow fighting naked! Jennifer Stevenson's *The Brass Bed* kept me up all night and left me smiling in the morning. I can't wait for the sequel!"
—VICKI LEWIS THOMPSON,
New York Times bestselling author of
Talk Nerdy to Me and *Over Hexed*

"Jennifer Stevenson's *The Brass Bed* is hip, hot, and highly imaginative. I want the sequel. (And I want the bed.)"
—HARLEY JANE KOZAK,
author of *Dating Dead Men*

"Supernatural, sexy, tender, smart-ass, surprising, and funny as hell."
—NALO HOPKINSON,
author of *Brown Girl in the Ring*

"An out-and-out winner—fun characters, rollicking story, and fantastic sex! Stevenson has harvested the beautiful metaphors of her past work, putting them to excellent service in this wacky tale. If Jasper Fforde wrote sizzling sex scenes, they would read like Stevenson's *Brass Bed*. Bravo!"

—MINDY L. KLASKY,
author of *The Glasswrights' Apprentice*

"Once you get into *The Brass Bed,* you won't ever want to get out."

—PHIL and KAYA FOGLIO, Studio Foglio

The
Brass
Bed

Jennifer Stevenson

BALLANTINE BOOKS • NEW YORK

A Ballantine Books Mass Market Original

Copyright © 2008 by Jennifer Stevenson

Excerpt from *The Velvet Chair* copyright © 2008 by Jennifer Stevenson

Smoking pigeon illustration copyright © 2008 by Julie Griffin

Published in the United States by Del Rey Books, an imprint of The Random House Publishing Group, a division of Random House, Inc., New York.

BALLANTINE and colophon are registered trademarks of Random House, Inc.

This book contains an excerpt from the forthcoming book *The Velvet Chair* by Jennifer Stevenson. This excerpt has been set for this edition only and may not reflect the final content of the forthcoming edition.

ISBN 978-0-345-48668-4

Printed in the United States of America

www.ballantinebooks.com

OPM 9 8 7 6 5 4 3 2 1

CHAPTER

 1

On a sizzling Monday afternoon in July, Jewel Heiss was serving a ticket on a convenience-store owner on Walton Street near Michigan Avenue, watching the smog over Lake Shore Drive turn pink, and trying to stake out The Drake Hotel across the street at the same time. Her boss had sent her to watch his wife, who also happened to be her best friend.

The Swiftymart owner whined, "Every time you come here, you ticket me. This is persecution. I'm gonna call the city." He led her out the front door, looking over his shoulder at his Gold Coast customers paying too much for sliced cheese.

The guilty ones always attacked.

Jewel smiled sunnily. "Every time, your scale still isn't fixed. Fix it and keep it fixed."

Sweltering in her polyester pantsuit, she hoped the pink stuff would abate before she had to get on the Drive. The pink was one problem da mayor's admirable anti-magic Policy hadn't been able to wish away.

The Swiftymart owner sweated and lit a cigarette, the dumb ass. She backed away. Sure enough, a pigeon swooped down out of nowhere and snatched the lighted cig off his face. The store owner screamed, "I hate birds!"

"Look, there's one!" A gaggle of tourists aimed cell-phones and cameras at the pigeon. "They really do smoke! That's so cool! Man, Chicago is seriously—"

Mindful of Policy, Jewel spoke up. "They don't really smoke, you know. They just eat the tobacco."

She watched the pigeon carry the cigarette to the gutter.

Stakeout was not Jewel's bag. Stakeout was for cops. An investigator for the Chicago Department of Consumer Services, she rated a badge but no gun. The scariest things in her arsenal were a clipboard and a thick book of tickets.

She tore off a ticket now and handed it to the Swifty-mart owner. "That scale is condemned. If you're found guilty, it could be a five-hundred-dollar fine. Get the scale fixed and you can call an inspector out to re-verify it."

"My customers don't complain." He backed into the shelter of his store doorway and lit another cigarette, cupping his hands around it this time.

"Sir, your store is a repeat offender. You know, it can be worse." In her small way, Jewel made the world a decenter place.

"Are you always this cheerful?" he said with loathing.

"Yep." Smiling down into his weasely little eyes from five-foot-eleven she said, "Fix it."

"Ooh, look, it's trying to pick up the filter end!"

The Swiftymart owner sent her a resentful look and mooched back into his store.

Jewel turned to the least fun part of her job, administering The Policy. "It is not smoking. It wants the filter for nesting materials."

"Ohmigod, it just stole that guy's cigarette," said another tourist who was slow to catch up.

The pink stuff over the Drive had thickened. Something out there caught Jewel's eye, a streak of iridescence over the fog. Groovy. Something new she wasn't allowed to talk about.

"Pigeons don't smoke," she said, quoting lame Policy guidelines. "They're attracted to additives in the cigarette paper."

"No, it's trying to smoke."

The iridescence formed a teardrop shape and then suddenly shrank, as if something were sucking it down into the pink fog.

"That pigeon is smoking! Wow! Get a picture of that!"

Jewel was about to quote Policy again, but even she could see that the pigeon had the filter end in its beak and seemed to be puffing away merrily. Another pigeon waddled over to it and stuck its pointed head into the cloud of secondhand smoke. She sighed.

Just then her quarry emerged from the Drake and wobbled languidly toward a cab. Nina looked fucked and happy. Jewel's heart sank.

Her best friend was guilty as hell. Ed would blow a blood vessel.

She plunged across traffic. "Nina, wait up!"

Nina Neccio's trim figure jerked around, her handbag flailing guiltily. "Don't scare me like that!"

"Going north? I'll share." Jewel hated the suspicious look Nina shot her. This was going to be awful. Nina's hair was flat at the back. *Pillow head. Oh God.* "I need a drink," Jewel said truthfully. It wasn't even two yet, but she was stressed to the max.

"I'll buy you one," Nina said in her gravelly voice. She was wearing tan fuck-me heels, a little beige knit suit over her size two chassis, and no lipstick for once. *Kissed it off?* Jewel wondered.

Nina towed Jewel into the Coq d'Or on the ground

floor of the Drake. When they were seated in front of two tall margaritas, she looked resentfully at Jewel. "Ed sent you."

"He's worried."

"I knew it. I knew that son of a bitch couldn't let me have some fun. What does he think, I wanna stay home and make lasagna for the rest of my life?"

"You're having an affair. My best friend is screwing around."

"I am not. Do you think I can smoke in here?" Nina craned her neck after the waiter and lit up. "I am totally not." Her hands moved jerkily. Her dark expressive eyes looked everywhere except at Jewel.

"Bull." This was icky. *Oh, Ed, can't you fix your own marriage?* "You are."

Nina blew smoke. "Not."

"Ed found the credit card charges." You had to persist with Nina. She was as slippery as pup shit and capable of out-shouting Jewel with one vocal cord. "Three hundred and fifty dollars each?"

"I am not having an affair."

Jewel pushed. "Do you *want* him to find out?" Was this the North Shore wife's buildup to divorce—run up a huge credit card debt and then file? She gazed sorrowfully at her friend. "I love your lasagna. I love your kids. What happens to Sunday dinner?" She shook her head. "Oh, Nina."

Nina sucked in smoke. "He's my sex therapist."

Jewel tossed a hand. "Quibble."

The waiter showed up with fresh margaritas. Nina held the cigarette down below the table's edge and flirted at him with her eyes.

"Ashtray, madam?" he said pointedly, setting one next to her margarita.

"Nice butt," Nina said, stunning Jewel. She brought the cigarette up and dragged again.

The waiter smiled and left. Nina craned her neck after him. She said, "I have never even seen Clay with his clothes off." Jewel's certainty was shaken. "Now, the hunk in the bed, that's another story. But I think even you might argue on my side, if you were there."

Ed should have come. "No wonder you've got new spring in your step. Is this why you've been losing weight?"

"This is the truth. I go in there, I have a drink with Clay, our clothes are on. He's not my lover, I swear it. He's my sex therapist."

For five years now, Nina had effortlessly pushed Jewel's buttons and mothered her and driven her crazy and girl-talked her through homesickness, lovesickness, shopping crises, and guy crises. Jewel didn't handle Nina. Nina handled Jewel.

"Tell me you're not having sex," Jewel begged.

"I've never seen the other guy either." *Okay, now we come to it.* "For all I know, I made him up in a dream. It's the truth. I can't lie to you. It's the plain truth."

Jewel wanted to say, *Ed's hurt,* but that would get her farther into the middle. "I am so disappointed in you."

That should have signalled the beginning of a fight. But Nina just squinted at her and smoked. "I like your makeup today. Did I buy that for you?"

"Don't change the subject."

"It wouldn't hurt you to try this, you know."

Jewel rolled her eyes.

"You haven't had a boyfriend in six months. For you, that's an emergency." Nina tapped ash into her empty margarita glass. "I worried about you when you were dating that creep, the one who liked to choke you during sex. Before that, it was whosis, did it in restaurants. For screwing in restaurants you can get arrested, but that other guy! I don't want to see you dead in a ditch."

"Neither do I," Jewel said tightly. "That's why I dumped them." This was not a good moment to get drawn into a discussion of her hyperactive libido.

"Yeah, eventually you dumped him. After a while," Nina said. "You love the kinky shit. I worry." *I worry too. That's why it's been six months.* "Here's Clay's cell number." Nina pressed a card into Jewel's hand. "Don't rush, no pressure, think about it, will you?"

She sat and smoked and eyed Jewel.

"Nina, this is not about who has worse judgment when she sleeps around. This is about you and Ed. I need you guys," Jewel pleaded. "I don't want you to divorce."

"He's Italian, he'll get over it." To Jewel's shocked face, Nina said, "That's the quick way to say, He's Italian, for years he screwed around with pretty girls at the department, and he knows payback is inevitable. It's marriage. He's not a hundred percent dumb. When you turned him down, he brought you home for me to play with."

"I'm glad he did," Jewel said, blinking. *Ed made a pass at me?* "Nina, he's upset. He asked me to—to—"

"Snoop."

Jewel slapped the table. "And look what I find! This is worse than an affair. Girlfriend, your husband busts bunco artists for a living. You're paying a con man three-fifty a pop for fake sex therapy. It doesn't take Dr. Ruth to figure this out. If you're so mad at Ed, wouldn't the real thing be better?"

Nina drew herself up, stubbing out her cigarette with a much-diamonded hand. "This is not about Ed. It's about me. I am fifty-five. I've only ever had Italian-husband sex, which believe me is nothing to write home about. I can't speak for what he does with his girlfriends." She jabbed the diamonds at Jewel. "And I. Deserve. To enjoy. My-self."

"You don't have to *pay* for it!"

"What, Ed told you to find me a cheaper lover?"

Jewel threw her hands in the air. "*No!* I'm—"

Nina leaned forward. "Look," she said, in a coming-off-the-crap tone. "We talk. Clay gives me the key to the treatment room. I go in, I take a nap. That's it."

Jewel's voice rose. "This mope drugs you and screws you in your sleep!"

"Nope." There was no spin in Nina's tone. "You look good with a light green eyeliner. Next time I'll take you to Arden for the full makeover."

"What about this other guy?"

Nina sighed. "I don't think he exists. I think somehow Clay hypnotizes me and something in that brass bed, it's gotta be that bed because it never happens at home, I dunno, but it's like I imagine the best lover in the world and then I dream about him. *Boy*."

"He's a con artist."

"He's no phony. I know." Nina's palm came up. "I thought so too. I must have been drunk the first time." She leaned forward. "But he's not. It's real. You gotta try this, I'm serious. Someone with your problems, he could be the answer."

"I'm not having sex with your 'sex therapist.' Ew."

Nina's eyes flashed. "I do not have sex with him. It's—oh, I can't explain it, you'll just have to see him yourself."

"Oh, I'll see him," Jewel said grimly. "Criminently, Nina. What have you gotten yourself into?"

Jewel would have preferred to call Ed and run a background check on Nina's so-called sex therapist before phoning him in his upstairs suite. She would have liked even more to have had some means of collecting a sample of whatever drugged beverages he was sure to offer her. *Maybe even wear a wire.* But Nina was standing at her elbow, daring her to get help for her unquenchable sex drive, so it seemed simpler to visit him now while Nina could vouch for her. Plus, that way she could forestall any little professional advice Nina might offer this clown about Jewel's messed-up-ness.

"I'll handle this, all right?" she said to Nina for the fourth time.

"Of course. I'm referring you."

"Thanks, but can you refer me from farther away?"

What am I doing here? The department cross-trained everybody, and everybody agreed: Bunco was not her gig. Jewel sucked at undercover, which was why she spent so much time busting Swiftymarts for selling short weight.

But she was sure she could hack it if she tried. She was sick of the routine stuff, sick of administering The Hinky Policy. She wanted a big case. Ed would owe her one, if she could pull this off.

"Yeah, hi," she said into the house phone, "can you connect me with Clay Dawes, Suite 807? Thanks." Putting her hand over the receiver, she turned to Nina. "Can I ask you something?"

"Anything."

"Has he ever pressured you to agree to treatment?"

Nina shook her head.

"Has he threatened you? Has he cited authority? Does he claim to be a medical doctor or an accredited psychotherapist?"

Nina kept shaking her head. The list of prosecutable material facts was leaking out of Jewel's memory as the phone rang in her ear.

"How about—oh, hi," she said into the phone, trying to come across as breathy and gullible, but sounding drunk to her own ears. "My name is Jewel Heiss, I was referred to you by a friend of mine, Nina Neccio? I'm downstairs with her right now."

The guy at the other end of the line sounded like a pothead, so slowly did he drawl.

"Hel-lo, Jewel, friend of Nina. What can I do for you?"

"Um," Jewel said, sweating, feeling her margaritas, and regretting them, "she recommended a, a service you offer involving a bed. A brass bed."

Holy kazoony, it sounds like I'm propositioning him. No wonder nobody ever brings a complaint against him. How embarrassing is this?

She thought of Ed, staring at charge after charge for three-hundred-fifty-dollar sex therapy sessions, and her resolve hardened.

The guy calling himself Clay Dawes drawled, "I totally understand, Jewel-friend-of-Nina. Why don't you come up and we'll talk about it?"

"Love to," she said, and hung up. "You better not be

setting me up for any shit," she told Nina. "I will totally kill you."

"You won't regret this," Nina assured her.

"That's a comfort."

The elevator dinged.

Clay Dawes turned out to be a hyper-blond. He looked like a surfer bum from Margaritaville in his Hawaiian shirt and chinos. He smiled at Jewel with thirtysomething crinkly blue eyes as he swung open his door. She tried to look dignified and sexually nondesperate.

"I'm not used to doing this," she said haughtily. *God, I sound drunk.*

"Of course not." She couldn't tell if he was pooching his lips out to keep from laughing at her or if he had naturally kissy-face lips. "Can I offer you a glass of wine?"

"I don't take drugs from strangers," she said sharply, then remembered to act gullible. "Maybe later."

He didn't react. "Let's sit down." He led her into an olde worlde living room full of gold-legged furniture and sat down across a coffee table from her. "Nina's one of my clients, so I can't talk about what the treatment has done for her. You probably heard it all from her anyway." His drawl was not Southern but a nasal, boy-next-door, easygoing voice that said, *I've never been bent out of shape in my life.* "Girl talk." He smiled wryly. "I can't advertise the treatment. I don't have to."

She swallowed. *What have you done to my Nina?* He was sitting too close. Her palms prickled with a sense of danger.

He looked at her seriously. "You know the fee is three hundred fifty dollars." She nodded. "I suggest we run your credit card and then hold off before you sign for the charge. After the treatment. No satisfaction, no fee."

That's some little guarantee, she thought. Silently, she presented her credit card. He touched her fingers as the card exchanged hands and she felt a little zing.

Don't let me breathe liquor fumes in his face.

He swiped the card. "This can be a difficult moment for my clients. I hope you won't mind, I'll keep talking until you feel ready to ask me something. Will that be all right?"

She tightened her lips. She felt her eyes getting bigger.

"The treatment was designed in the late eighteenth century by a guy who believed in electricity. In those days, electricity was the new Viagra. Of course he only offered it to men." He made a face and rolled his eyes, and Jewel felt her own eyes rolling, too. "He was treating impotence in men. The client takes a simple nap. The treatment does the rest."

He leaned forward. She began to lean forward, too, and stopped herself.

"I want to make it clear right now that ninety-nine percent of my clients are not really frigid."

The word flopped out between them. She sucked in a gasp. *I may be as kinky as a split-rail fence but I am not frigid.*

I need therapy. But not from this guy.

"They're nice normal women, maybe married but somehow still lonely. They're sexually dissatisfied. That's different from frigid." *Betcher butt, beach boy*, she thought. "Usually it's not their fault. Their husbands may be no good in bed. But, as women will, they blame themselves."

She felt a stab of guilt, what was *that* about? He couldn't know that she was feeling, well, horny. Her margaritas hung in her throat, making her breath tequila-hot, and she was glad he was doing all the talking.

She knew she should ask him point-blank if he could

cure her frigidity. It wasn't going to happen. *I so suck at undercover.* She fantasized that he might be dumb enough to blab a material fact. Then she could ticket him without going a step further.

"I won't ask you to talk about why you're here. That's too hard in the early sessions," he said.

It was like he could read her mind, slathering on all the guys-R-jerks sympathy and saying she was too shy to talk about sex. She looked deep into his eyes, faking dumb.

"Part of the success of my work is being able to empathize with women, sexually speaking." He drawled so slowly that every word sank into her like a big dollop of codeine syrup, soothing her nerves and numbing her common sense. "But the miracle is the opening of the human heart that comes with hope. With hope, these women feel ready to take a risk on treatment. And that openness to risk helps create the success they're paying for. There's no healing without risk. That's what hope is for."

Why did her heart jump every time he said "risk?" The pupils of her eyes shrank and the room dimmed.

She cleared her throat. "How fake is that? They're paying you for something they do for themselves."

He smiled wryly again. Maybe that wry thing was part of his mouth, all plump poochy lips and dimples. "That's the spiritual aspect. It's me showing you the door and then getting out of your way. Because sex, good sex, involves a person's soul."

What does that make me? She felt weird about herself.

"Well, a *woman's* soul," he said, and did the poochy-smile thing again. "No proof yet that men have souls."

She couldn't help laughing. *This is scary. I've got to get out of this room, I'm turning into a mark.*

She said, "Don't you think women just want to have sex

sometimes? If your customers are, like, desperate housewives, maybe their problem isn't soul sickness. Maybe
you're trying to read too much emotion into their sex
lives." Thinking of Ed screwing around on Nina, she
hardened her voice. "Maybe they don't want to have to
consider their husbands's feelings. Maybe they don't want
to have to be sensitive souls. Maybe they just wanna
fuck." *That came out loud.* "The healthy animal thing."
She lifted her chin, thinking longingly of 4–H days back
in Wisconsin. "It's perfectly possible for a woman to
enjoy healthy sex without emotional involvement."

He leaned back in his chair, acting relaxed, but she
was sure that was phony. "Oh, I don't know. Sometimes
love is so risky, sex is a cop-out."

How dare he say "cop" to her face! She leaned forward. "I'm not here about love."

He chuckled, and she was grateful for her rush of
anger. He said, "You know, this conversation is word-
for-word the conversation I have with every one of my
customers."

Oh, great, now she was a mark *and* frigid. Had he figured out who she was? *He's messing with my mind and
I'm helpless to stop him.*

Narrowing her eyes, she said, "So far you haven't
proved you're anything but a smooth talker."

He spread his hands. "Look, if I were trying to con
you, there are a lot of things I could say." *You've already
said them.* The hands came out, pushing at her. "But
since you don't trust me, I'll give you the key and let you
test the treatment for yourself." He laid a hotel room key
on the coffee table between them. "I just hope it's not
too much for you."

Now there was a god damned twinkle in his eye.

The thing was, if Nina wasn't involved, if she didn't

already know he was a fake—well, she might have been tempted.

She pulled herself up straight, breathing deep. "Oh, no. No, I will not. That proves your operation is a con, that double-bind crap."

"Really?" he said in that slow voice. "And why is that?" All of a sudden she knew that he knew that she was waiting to bust him. They both knew he had an invulnerable line of bull and that only made her madder.

She sputtered, "If this 'treatment' doesn't work, you call me frigid. And if it does, I'm supposed to let you off the hook. Tell me this," she said, roostering up. "How exactly *will* I know if it works?"

He smiled a self-deprecating smile that pooched his lips together. "Oh, you'll know. It's unmistakable."

She snatched the key. "I'll be the judge of that."

He murmured, "Word-for-word." Her head filled with hot rage. He stood and pointed to another door.

She marched past him and stuffed the key in the lock, yanking open the door to his "treatment room."

He said, "I'll knock in three hours."

She slammed the door in his face and threw the dead bolt.

CHAPTER 3

With her back to the door Jewel thought, *That went well*. He might guess she was the law, but he'd let her in, and she wouldn't come out until her three hours were up and she'd caught his accomplice red-handed.

With the door between them she admitted that she had stepped into every one of his verbal traps. She had to think outside the box of his con. If only she didn't feel so damned drunk.

She went to the bathroom and rinsed out her mouth. *What the heck, he can't drug the tap water*. She drank from her cupped hands, not trusting the white-paper-capped glass. The water tasted like chlorine. That made her regret again that she hadn't brought a sample bottle. *Went off half cocked*.

Her heart still beat too fast, as it had every time he'd said "risk." Whether it was his line of bull or the plain fact that he was a con artist selling sex, he'd pushed every single one of her kinky little buttons. She felt swollen and slippery and pissed off.

Thinking of Nina's "hunk in the bed," Jewel checked the windows. Locked. She dead-bolted the hall door. Checked the closets for hunks and secret doors.

No secret doors. No hunks. Her personal parts throbbed.

There was no furniture in the "treatment room" besides a big brass bed, a breakfast table and chair, and a hotel night table. The bed looked like a museum piece, high and pouffy, with the coverlet turned down and piles of fat pillows against the brass rails. She walked around the bed, looking for hidden wires. Underneath, it was just a bed—some leaf springs, the mattress.

The wires could be hidden up inside one of these brass tubes. She should have waited, should have gone back to the office and fetched a voltmeter and a few other tools. Next time.

There'd be no next time if she could bust his butt today.

When he'd grabbed for her credit card as soon as she'd stepped inside the door, she was sure she would get him today. Now, not so sure.

She gave in to temptation and sat down on the bed. Pint-sized Nina probably had to climb. *Ew. Don't think about Nina in this bed.* Nina had been in this bed less than two hours ago.

Jewel's feet hurt so much they tingled. She tingled all over. *Battle nerves*, she kidded herself.

Sheets were clean anyway.

She let her pumps slide to the floor and swung her tired feet up onto the coverlet.

Nice coverlet. Four-hundred-thread-count Egyptian cotton sheets. The goose-down pillows—she sank back—grabbed her and held her, safe, seductive, tempting her to let go.

Her brain skittered around. She thought about Nina's messed-up marriage and her heart bled for Ed, a thing she wouldn't have thought possible. She had to nail this smoothie. How dare he suggest his treatment was too much for her! *Treatment my ass*, she thought, picturing his smug smile melting into dismay when she walked out of here three hours from now with a sheaf of citations in his name.

But she couldn't imagine a happy ending for Nina's problem. Jewel felt drowsy with sheer frustration.

She pulled her watch off and set the timer for two-and-a-half hours. *I'll doze. Let the tequila wear off.*

She lay back again, letting the pillows engulf her.

If Clay actually knew so darned much about what women wanted, he wouldn't be so annoying. Why did some guys think a woman had to be pissed off to be aroused? She'd like to show him what it felt like. Not in the least sexy.

She stood in the staff room, pointer in hand. Clay posed naked before the whiteboard while she pointed at the crinkly laugh-at-you eyes, the smug pouty mouth, the shaggy blond bangs that screamed *I don't have a job*.

He didn't get it. He smirked and made Mr. Buff poses.

Nobody was listening anyway. Except the hunk at the back.

I must be dreaming. No buff guys ever came within a thousand miles of the Department of Consumer Services. She looked across the conference table at the hunk's un-believably beefy shoulders and the set of his noble head, like the head of a particularly elegant horse, all dark masculine strength and grace.

He looked right at her. *I'm definitely dreaming*. With all the perky size-five investigators in the room, he was look-ing at a six-foot, size-eighteen, dairy-farmer's daughter?

He'd be wasted on the size fives. Here was a man big enough for her.

He stood up and beckoned to her. Man, oh, man, was he big. The size fives disappeared, along with the Supervisors in Charge of Talking Slowly at Meetings and the doughnuts and coffee. Good thing, because he was reaching across the table and dragging her by the shoulders into his arms. She was startled at how warm and real his hands felt on her shoulders. In a dream you expect something vague.

Nothing vague about his kiss. Masterful and hot, and yet his lips were cushiony.

She reveled in the dream kiss, letting her back melt against him, letting herself droop across the conference table as if her bodice were being ripped away by a medieval knight, a hunky, half-naked medieval knight who kneaded her bare breasts with strong, hot hands, oh, man, oh *man*!

"Where did you come from?" she murmured when his mouth lifted from hers.

"1811," he said, which she could have told him wasn't medieval at all, it was one of those dumb periods where America was almost at war over something so dumb nobody remembered anymore, and the clothes were awful.

"Not that you need clothes," she murmured. She reached over her head to stroke the veined curve of his pectoral muscle, silky smooth yet hard.

"Do you want me?" he said, a little formally under the circumstances. His hot, lusty, black eyes turned anxious.

"Sure."

That didn't seem to be the right answer. "That's it?" he said, more anxiously. "Sure?"

"If you want twelve lines of unrhymed iambic pentameter," she said impatiently, "ask me in the morning."

What was his problem? He was the one who had beckoned to her, stripped her half naked on the conference table, and stuck his tongue down her throat. "Can we get back to the conference table?"

"Very well, Miss—you are single, aren't you? What's your name?"

"Jewel, and yes, I'm single. The table?"

He sighed. "I'm Randolph, but everyone calls me Randy." He reached for her hand and drew her up to him. His fingers brushed her forehead. "Close your eyes. Tell me all about yourself."

His touch was everything she remembered from the staff room: a licking flame, a single wailing electric-guitar note dragged across her nerves like a sexual wake-up call, an undertow of lust that sucked her back into dreamland, back into his arms. "That's more like it," she said, and fell deeper asleep.

They flew out of a broken corner in the window and circled the hotel from above. "I'm afraid of heights," she said. He made her hold on to the edge of the giant rooftop flag and, while the wind snapped and flung her around like a kite-tail, he blew in her ear like the lake breeze, he ran cool like rain all over her body, he called like a gull, *here I come*, he entered her like lightning and lit up every cell in her body at once and she screamed and laughed and begged for more.

"Are you aroused because you're afraid, or afraid because you're aroused?"

"Oh, who knows," she said crossly. "That Jewel girl. Kinky as an old fence."

He held her from behind in strong arms, letting her look down, down on Lake Shore Drive and the beach with its lacy fringe of surf. Her heart hammered. "Be gentle with her," he murmured against her neck, making her shiver. "Even I didn't know I could do this. I could learn so much from your imagination. Pity you're only here for three hours."

Gentle, she thought. *I am never gentle with myself.* "Learn from her? That girl hasn't got a clue." She felt his belly warm against her naked back, felt the wind, stiff and cold up here, making goose bumps along her arms and legs. Felt his cock against the backs of her thighs. "She wouldn't believe if you stuffed her clothes up the chimney. She wouldn't believe if you autographed her pussy."

He flew her back into the staff room, where they put the conference table to excellent use, and then she remembered some wack stories from a mythology book, and he proved that you could, too, have sex with a giant swan. Screaming the whole time, she drove her hands into the feathers on his breast, searching out and clinging to the bony parts, while he pounded the air with his wings, hovering, entering her with each downstroke. He could reach everywhere with that long neck. The airconditioning chilled her butt and his feathers slid over her front, making her think of slipping away, of falling, so that she yanked herself harder onto his weird poky member, trying to hold on with her pussy muscles. He hissed in her ear through his beak, "You love it. You love it." She thought she would never come, and then she did, and they fell from the ceiling to the bed with a thump that knocked the wind out of her.

She opened her eyes. She wheezed, trying to suck air.

Long white feathers showered up, then fluttered down.

The black-eyed hunk lay on top of her. His elbow stuck in her gizzard. He was sweaty and stinky. She got claustrophobic at his nearness.

"Get off me!" she wheezed.

Randy sat up on top of her, one hand on his chest. His eyes bugged out. He held up the hand, turning it and staring at it, and then he looked at her.

Get away from me! She couldn't say it. She couldn't breathe.

Finally she sucked in enough air.

She screamed.

He screamed.

He vanished.

The weight lifted off her pelvis. She sat up, panting. "Where—" No Randy. Just a scattering of unnaturally long, white feathers all over the bed and the carpet.

Then the feathers melted away.

She flopped back down on the bed and stared at the ceiling. Ten feet up, over the table by the window, hung an oddly ugly chandelier. She squinted. "That looks like my pants. My God." She sat up again. Her hair was plastered to her with sweat, and she stank of sex. "I'm naked. How did I get naked?"

The alarm on her wristwatch went off. She squeaked.

In thirty minutes, the con artist Clay was going to knock on the door, and she had to be ready to cite him.

Trying hard not to think about how they got there, she retrieved her polyester pants from the breakfast-table chandelier, her matching jacket and shell from the top of the drapes, and her bra and panties from cornices on the crown molding twelve feet in the air. She found only one shoe.

Totally demoralized, she went to the bathroom for a shower.

The second shoe was in the sink.

In the medicine-cabinet mirror, she saw bright red writing all over her face.

She screamed again.

She lifted her hands to her face. "What—what—wha—" The writing was backwards. Panicked breathless, she squinted at the mirror.

Beside her right eye was written in small, neat letters, AND HERE.

"And here? And *here?* What—wha—" It was written beside her mouth. And at the hollow of her throat. And—she tipped her face to one side, staring walleyed out of the corner of her eye—under her left ear. AND HERE. What the—? And here what?

It wasn't her handwriting, either.

She whirled to the full-length mirror on the back of the bathroom door. Another scream escaped her throat.

Her body was written on, all over. Not quite her whole body. Her breasts, in a circle around her nipples, and the soles of her feet, and a line of writing that ran up the inside of her right leg and disappeared from view. She stood up quickly and banged her head on the sink.

She swallowed. Had Clay snuck into the room and scrawled all over her while she lay dead to the world, dreaming of—

"Oh no!"

Dreaming of a Viking-sized hunk with hot black eyes like a Doberman sailing over the back fence.

Speaking of Dobermans at the back fence. She recalled more of her dream. He'd bent her over the table and done something else that reminded her of dogs, did it until she howled and wriggled and yelped and whined and begged. She throbbed with leftover bliss.

And when they were both too tired to move anymore, she had suggested that he should sign his work.

They'd lolled naked on the conference table. They'd taken turns with the overhead-projector markers.

Swallowing hard, Jewel turned hesitantly and looked into the mirror over her shoulder.

There, on her behind, in huge, smudgy red letters, she read—backwards—RANDY on her left butt cheek, WAS on her tailbone, and HERE on her right butt cheek.

That answered that question.

She fell against the door with her hand on her throat. Her brain was full of musk and smoke and erotic dizziness.

One fact seemed to penetrate the haze. "I can't walk out of here like this."

Stupid with afterglow, she licked her hand and rubbed the writing on her cheek. It smeared.

"Oh, thank goodness. At least we had sense enough to use the overhead markers and not the Sharpies," she said, forgetting that the conference table was in a dream. *Get that through the woodenhead, Jewel!*

Right. Whew. Just a dream.

Feverishly she jumped in the shower and worked bath gelée into every corner. She was dragging on her clothes when Clay knocked at the door.

"Time's up."

"I'm fine," she called. She gave up trying to find her knee-high nylons. She shoved her bare feet into her pumps, grabbed her shoulder bag, and hurtled through the door into Clay's sitting room, trying not to look fucked to a fare-thee-well.

Surfer boy wasn't smiling. Her self-control was shattered. She felt totally unprepared to deal with him the way she should.

"Everything go okay?" he said soberly.

"Fine," she chirped. "Except I failed to stop your accomplice from sneaking out of the room."

"I don't work with anyone. It's just me and the treatment," he said, looking puzzled and uncomfortable.

"He got away." It was humiliating that she had fallen for the con, whatever the hell it was. But after all, that was why she'd come. *And come and come.* She shook her head, trying to get her mad back.

Clay said, "Some of my clients hallucinate partners while they're undergoing treatment."

"I'm fine," she said again.

"Would you like your money back?" he said gently. He held up the credit card slip.

When she didn't speak, he held up a pen. And smiled a tiny little kissy-face smile. She grabbed the pen away from him, signed with a slash, and walked to the suite door on wobbly legs.

To her back, he said, "Some clients find one treatment is plenty. I'd call that a success for both of us."

He sounded so genuinely satisfied that she risked meeting his eyes. "What do you get out of this, anyway? Besides too much money?"

His eyes crinkled and his lips pursed and his dimples showed. "I guess I like making women happy."

"I'm not happy," she lied.

He said awkwardly, "I like you. Even if you look mean."

"I'm meaner than I look."

She shut the door in his face.

Clay remade the brass bed in the treatment room and went downstairs for an early cocktail in the bar. He met another lonely socialite within the first five minutes. His patter was in top form. She practically begged him for a treatment. It was a sign. He had her upstairs inside of an hour.

He took his time sweet-talking her. He tasted the wine.

After Jewel's accusation about drugs, that wasn't paranoid, it was smart, he told himself.

The client melted like warm butter. Smiling, he ushered her into the treatment room, heard the lock click, and leaned his back against the door.

An hour and forty silent minutes later she came out, glowing the way they all did, patted him on the cheek, and left.

Cautiously he went into the treatment room. Nobody under the bed. No unlocked window.

Still his shoulders wouldn't unknot.

Putting fresh linens on the bed, he felt an urge to see Nina's big friend with the razor eyes and the Gibson Girl figure in the polyester body bag. Maybe it was the smell of his recent client's activities on the sheets, but the thought of Jewel Heiss made him schwing like the Washington Monument.

Get her back in here, he thought, the words loud in his head.

"I don't have her phone number," he said. The pressure in his groin increased. "Down, boy. Jeez." The last thing he needed was a cop sniffing around here.

CHAPTER

4

At eight o'clock Tuesday morning, the pink haze still hung over Lake Shore Drive and Jewel was stalled bumper-to-bumper in the left lane, surrounded by a thousand filthy-tempered motorists. She couldn't hear herself think for the honking. The AC was out on the Tercel so she had the windows open. Heat shivers wiggled off the asphalt. Her thighs stuck to the upholstery in spite of a layer of fresh polyester.

She had stopped by the deli at Walton and Mich to make sure that wonky scale was out of service. Then she'd tried a shortcut by taking Lake Shore. Bad idea.

Every driver in sight was flipping somebody else the bird. Three lanes away, Buzz, her favorite homeless boy, was threading his way between hot, throbbing cars, lugging his backpack, smiling into the drivers's windows, flourishing whatever cheap junk he had to sell today. The people in the camper with Michigan plates, one lane over, were asking loudly, "Why is the smog pink here?"

"It's the new additives in the gasoline," the tourist wife said.

"I'm sure that's what the papers said," the tourist husband said.

Additives, schmadditives. That was Policy talking. Everyone knew it was really road rage that made the pink.

Jewel was too freaked out to get mad. She couldn't believe she'd had sex with that guy. In her sleep. That part would not be in her report to Ed this morning. *I know I'm a—a healthy animal, but this tops anything I've ever, ever done.* She felt unsettled, light-headed, and a little bit cranky.

On the Drive's right shoulder, a black BMW sedan roared past three stalled lanes. Two seconds later, a cop car followed.

Whatever hallucinogen Clay Dawes had used on her, it was a dilly. *Next time I'll take samples of the tap water.*

The thought of a next time made her hyperventilate pink smog.

With the AC broken she couldn't shut the window, so she turned on the radio.

"—*More comfortable when you consider the facts*," said a woman's soothing voice. "*Statistically speaking, only two cars out of our half-million commuters get lost every day*—"

It was the "Ask Your Shrink" call-in show. Jewel cranked it up. The doc was like a canary on drugs in a coal mine. As soon as trouble reared its head, she was the first to say, "I don't smell anything funny, and neither should you."

"*There's no proof these people don't return to their homes the same day, or soon after, perfectly safe and sound. You're much more likely to get hit by a drunk driver. We are as safe on the road today as we have ever been. Relax. Be serene. Relax.*"

"That's crap." Jewel squirmed on the sweaty vinyl seat.

The Fifth Floor thought highly of "Ask Your Shrink." Jewel herself thought the doc was mental, but her show did seem to help keep panic down. Da mayor set great store by low panic levels.

"*Your Shrink is ready to take calls from listeners.*"

Jewel hit speed dial. "Yeah, hi, Doc, this is, um, Ruby, I'm stuck on Lake Shore in traffic."

"*You did the right thing to call me, Ruby,*" Your Shrink intoned. "*Breathe deeply. Put your road rage behind you.*"

"Actually I'm not mad about traffic. No more than usual." A shouting match erupted between two drivers jockeying for the space in front of her. "It's this guy I'm seeing."

"*You can tell Your Shrink anything.*"

She doubted that. "There's something, I dunno, something hinky about him."

"*Hinky. Can you be more specific, Ruby?*"

"Weird. Uh, he can, like, do stuff."

"Ooh," Your Shrink said in an *ah-hah* tone. "*Stuff.*"

"I don't mean stuff like *stuff*, hell, I can do *stuff*. I do more stuff than anybody. I mean stuff nobody can do. I mean, really nobody." As usual Jewel felt like an ass talking to Your Shrink, but it beat confiding certain things to Nina, who not only knew too much already, but would use it against her. "He's got hinky powers."

The screaming motorist jamming the left side of the spot in front of her leaped out of his car. He ran around his hood and punched the hood of the car jamming the right side of that spot.

"*Ruby, Ruby,*" Your Shrink said. "*There are no hinky powers. Only the powers of your wonderful, purely human imagination. Perhaps you are so in love, you have created—*"

"I'm not in love with him! I don't fall in love with guys I f—uh, date!"

"*You've created ideas about this perfectly ordinary fellow.*"

Typical Ask-Your-Shrink thinking. Why had she bothered to call? "Sure, yeah."

"*These ideas have power only in your mind, Ruby. Stop thinking about them and they will disappear.*"

"Great. Thanks." Jewel thumbed the phone off and threw it on the seat.

"*Call back any time, Ruby,*" Your Shrink urged from the radio.

Jewel turned the radio off. The guys from the two cars jamming the spot ahead of her were now outside their vehicles, trying to strangle each other.

Her head pounded.

The pink descended until she couldn't see three car lengths ahead.

Breathe.

Her cellphone rang. She snatched it. "Heiss."

"So how'd it go?" Nina's voice was full of glee.

"How'd what go?"

"C'mon. Did you ask Clay for a refund?"

Jewel opened her mouth and breathed pink smog shallowly, trying not to smell it. It smelled like car exhaust. "No."

A cop car squeaked up beside her between the left rail and the outside lane. The homicidal commuters separated at last, shouting curse words at each other.

Nina crowed, "I knew it! Now tell me that's adultery. I dare you."

"Tell me how many treatments you've paid for." Jewel wasn't about to discuss the mysterious disappearing feathered hunk.

The duelling commuters got into their cars and crammed themselves into line ahead of her. The cop car crawled away.

Everywhere, cars changed lanes like burnt-petrochemical-farting snails, honking like the end of the world.

"I started twice a week in May," Nina said. "I'm up to four times a week."

Jewel sat up, scorching her shoulders on the vinyl. "What?"

"It'd be more, only Ed hasn't been working weekends."

"Nina! That's fourteen hundred dollars a week! No wonder Ed's having kittens."

"So how'd it go?"

"Nina, that's outrageous. He's conning you!" Not smart to get madder when she was stuck in the pink.

"But you liked it. You didn't ask for a refund."

Jewel dodged the question. "I'm a fraud investigator, Nina. You don't spook the suspect before you have enough evidence to bust him." She caught up with an abandoned car spang in the center lane. The pink stuff was so thick, she could barely see two cars ahead. She felt herself hyperventilating.

"You did like it."

"He has an accomplice who sneaks into the bed after the drug takes effect." Behind her, drivers laid on their horns. She put the phone down a moment. "Think—serene—thoughts," she panted to herself. She didn't feel serene. She was starting to panic. She picked up the phone.

"What drug? He's never given me anything," Nina said, diverted. "Did you pay extra for a pill?"

"I don't know how he administers the drug. Not yet."

"But did you enjoy yourself? What happened? I know you loved it because it's right up your alley," Nina said.

Now Jewel could only see one car ahead. "Listen, would you keep talking for a minute? I'm deep in the pink and I've got traffic to get around."

"You're afraid of that stuff? As much as you drive?"

"What's with the kids?" Jewel countered, frightened as the sounds of honking and yelling faded. "Talk to me."

So Nina babbled about her daughter's latest piercing and what Ed said and what her sons said and what the guidance counselor said and where Nina told the guidance counselor to stick it, and Jewel clung to the phone with one hand and the steering wheel with the other, trying to think serene thoughts.

The bumper of the car ahead of her got harder to see. She was alone in the pink.

Something dark loomed up at her open window.

Jewel shrieked.

"Buy a nice—well, hello, officer lady." A zitty teenage boy's face appeared in front of an immense backpack.

"Buzz!" She dropped the phone. "You scared the crap out of me! What are you doing out here? You could get arrested!" Jewel had been trying hard not to cite him for two years.

"Aw, cops are busy with traffic."

"I don't have a doughnut today. I'm sorry." The kid was so scrawny. "Did you talk to the admissions office at Lane Tech?"

Buzz smiled like sunrise. "Been meaning to. Then I got this great business opportunity."

"Oh, Buzz, no. You need an education."

He hefted his clinking backpack. "It's a chance to raise tuition money."

"Lane is a city school. It's free."

"Okay, book money."

"Are you eating? You look thin." Sheesh, she sounded like Nina. Actually, Jewel enjoyed fussing over Buzz. He didn't try to get too close, and he was the hardest-working runaway she'd met in five years.

The phone was quacking. She put it to her ear. Nina said, "Is that Buzz? What's he selling today?"

"Nina, I have to hang up now—"

"No, I'm dying to know," Nina said. "He sold me some bath salts that turned my fingernails and toenails blue. I didn't need a manicure for weeks."

Jewel laughed in spite of herself. "I should bust his butt right now," she said, and Buzz vanished into the pink behind her. The car ahead pulled out of sight. Jewel crept forward, alone in the pink, her skin prickling. What if she never drove out of it?

It happened. Two commuters out of half a million every day.

Serene thoughts, my ass.

Yet for a moment she remembered clinging like death to the giant flag flying over The Drake Hotel, flipping and twirling in the wind, while the guy with the black eyes drizzled kisses like rain all over her weightless body. A long sigh eased out of her.

A whiff of fresh air passed through the Tercel. The camper in the next lane reappeared, and the Drive opened out in front of her. Jewel hit the gas.

"—Next time I'll ask Clay about this drug. Sounds like he's holding out on me," Nina was saying.

Jewel sucked in smoggy air. "There should be no next time."

"You ask too. We'll compare notes."

I'll bring handcuffs next time. Fourteen hundred dollars a week! "Yeah, yeah."

"My boys are home, gotta go, ciao, honey. Say hi to my hubby."

With relief Jewel exited Lake Shore, parked in the lot on Peshtigo, and walked across Illinois to Wolfy Shekel's, a high-end yuppie grocery. *Tomorrow I walk to work.*

She bought a green apple and a chunk of aged Stilton cheese, crossed Illinois again to the Kraft Building, and took the elevator to the Consumer Services staff room.

Ed was already handing out assignments for the day. He pointed to the front row. Jewel slid into a seat next to Digby.

"Hey, sunshine, who ya doin'?" Digby whispered to her. "Rotation day. Want to come home with me and call cabs?"

"Hey, yourself. Not today," she said, though he smelled deliciously like apple pie. *Must be on bakery duty.*

Ed seemed like himself. Jewel listened, thinking about his credit card statements and wondering which of her coworkers had been strong-stomached enough to do the nasty with her balding, paunchy boss. *If it's true, he must be amazingly discreet.*

Ed said, "All investigators listen up for where your division is moving. Deli-duty teams move to Internet fraud. Sayers, you team with Finbow, he'll train you. Maxwell Street teams move to deli duty. Cab-fares division moves to immigration assistance. If it's been more than two years since you did immigration, there's a briefing at ten o'clock. Immigration, you'll do cabs. Child support, condos, home repair, you rotate do-si-do around in a circle so's you're all doing something different. Vehicle-repair division, stay put until we clean up that business in Beverly. Target investigations will meet in the chief's office today for a special briefing on that identity-theft case. It's going critical. I'll need everybody we got."

Jewel's heart leaped. Something hot must be brewing.

"Except you, Heiss, you're off deli for now. I want your pet street vendor nailed." Jewel groaned. "Latest is, he's been selling genies in bottles. Get him. Okay, everybody, training and refresher schedules are posted on my door. Any questions, see me afterward."

Digby leaned closer to Jewel and whispered, "Cabs sounding better every minute, huh?"

"Hey, Hinky, grab me one of them genies."

"You get enough bottles, Sayers," Jewel said.

"You still need a partner," Digby said. "C'mon, Jewel. I need your sunny face to cheer me up."

Digby was a nice guy and not lousy in bed. She'd dated him about a year ago. He had taken *no more* like a gentleman, but he never stopped asking.

"I don't think so," she said. "Why don't you ask Britney? She's dying for some on-the-job training."

"I'm not kinky enough for you," Digby said mournfully.

"Sadly, that's true." Why she couldn't date anybody nice more than three dates had her baffled. Instead, it was guys like Chad the Choker, not only a safety hazard but also intolerably clingy.

Digby leaned closer, crowding her. "C'mon. We had fun."

Jewel stood up. "You could have twice the fun with Britney. She'll go to at least six dates," she said, recklessly committing her friend.

"Heiss, see me in my office." Ed. Out of the frying pan.

Jewel followed the boss. "Digby better get laid soon or the poor schmuck's gonna suicide," she said as she closed Ed's door. You had to talk tough with Ed or he treated you like a girl.

Ed looked gloomy. "Just get that guy with the genies off the expressway. Things are bad. Da mayor has been noticing."

"I hate it in the wack ghetto, Ed. Give me a real case. I

want to chase grifters who cheat little old ladies out of their gutter-fixing money. I want to bust crooked lawyers for screwing over Mexicans who don't understand our immigration laws. I've worked in every division in the department. You used to give me sensitive stuff. Now it's all this hinky shit."

"The hinky shit is sensitive. It's the most sensitive shit we got. Fifth Floor goes ballistic when it gets into the papers."

"I'm sick of administering The Policy."

"The Policy is in place for good reason. Nobody wants another Pittsburgh."

"I'll do gas stations again," she pleaded. "I feel like I'm losing my edge."

He shook his head. "This is your job. It was bad enough when we hadda look out for terrorists and crookit Homeland Security bozos, now we got this shit. The city needs you."

"Why am I the one stuck with it?" Like everybody else, she'd been pulled from regular rotation for half a dozen hot cases over the past five years, and went back into rotation when the investigation ended. "I found that guy who was Kinko-ing drivers' licenses, didn't I?" He grunted. "Why me?"

" 'Cause you don't freak out like the rest of these sissies."

"Fab," she grumped. "I worked on the taxi medallion bust, didn't I? Got a lot of good press for that one."

"And I'm grateful," he said ungratefully. "This is the new world, Heiss. It's too bad I can't get you a partner yet." Like that would make the hinky cases more fun. "Find this genie salesman and I'll try to get you something better."

Her heart quickened. "For real? Can I get in on this new identity-theft case?"

He looked shifty. "Maybe. If you lock up that other thing."

She felt the next question coming. *I hate this.*

He seemed to sense her discomfort, because he moved behind his desk. His brown eyes looked soft and vulnerable. "Well?"

"I haven't found out anything yet." *I hate this.*

"Monday is one of her days."

"I know, but I didn't see anything." She sweated into her polyester. Was Ed guilty? Nina wouldn't flat-out lie.

He fidgeted with his clipboard. "You two are close."

"I'll try again today."

The phone rang. He picked it up but he kept his eyes on Jewel. "I'm busy," he told the phone. *Girlfriend?* she wondered, her hackles going up.

She watched him. If he looked to the right, it would be Nina. If he looked left, girlfriend.

"So what," he barked. "You have to call me for that?" He looked right. "I don't care what you pick," he said roughly.

Did he always talk this mean to her and I never noticed? Jewel felt bad for urging Nina to talk to him.

He hung up. "What." Jewel didn't answer. "Keep watching her. She's up to something." Jewel watched the boss color up. "Quit looking at me like that." He flounced into his chair. "Go get the genie guy. And follow my wife."

I guess this means no Sunday dinner with the Neccios. But he'd hinted that he might give her a real case.

When she came out of Ed's office, there was Digby, lurking. She revised his score from *gentleman* to *clingy*. Time for an intervention.

"Did Ed assign you a partner?" Digby said eagerly.

Oh yeah, I want to spend six months fighting you off.

She said confidentially, "I've been telling Ed you need to get laid."

His eyes lit up. "You were? Can I call you sometime?"

"Fuggeddaboddit." She whispered, "Your trouble is, you're too timid. And you don't take hints. I had to drag you off by your hair."

Britney and Merntice came into the staff room for coffee.

"You did," he said, sighing down to his Sansabelt slacks.

"So now I'm gonna do you a favor." Raising her voice and her right hand, she said in a throbbing voice, "Take that, you sex fiend!" and slapped him.

"Ow!"

"And keep your spurs away from me!"

At that moment Ed walked out of his office, took one look, turned around, and went back in and shut the door.

Merntice chuckled and shook her head.

"Digby, she hit you! Ohmigod!" said Britney, bustling over. "Are you bleeding?"

Digby looked baffled. "You hit me!" The love light was definitely dimmer in his watering eyes.

"Good boy." Jewel patted him on the head. "Your ball," she told Britney.

"You poor baby!" Britney cooed. She glared at Jewel. "What did that vicious slut do to you?"

As she left Jewel heard Digby tell Britney, "You have such gentle hands."

Merntice followed Jewel to the restroom. "Think that's gonna work?"

"I hope. He's been a pest, and yet I feel guilty."

"You hard on your dates, girl. You got a problem."

Jewel sighed. She was about to go have more sex with a con artist's contortionist-slash-hypnotist-slash-escape-artist accomplice. Looming over Merntice, she looked her in the eye. "You're right."

That shut Merntice up.

If I were half as good at picking 'em as I am at damage control, I wouldn't need to slap anybody. She wished she could call Nina. *I need girlfriend talk, stat.*

What the hell, she called Nina anyway.

But Nina's cell was busy, and her home line only took a message.

CHAPTER

5

Jewel met the girls at Dick's Last Resort for a late lunch. Lolly, Merntice, and Merntice's granddaughter Tookhah had already ordered.

Jewel's intervention with Digby must have been the talk of the office. Everybody turned to her as she sat down.

"You finally dumped him," Lolly said, chuckling.

"I dumped him last year. What is it with men? Swear to God, in high school they only wanted to hit and run. Now I can't get rid of 'em." Jewel sat next to Tookhah. "Moom over."

Tookhah sighed. "Give the lady space," she said, but she moved to the far end of the bench and put her purse between them.

"Thanks, Too," Jewel said. "Gimme fries, I'm dying."

"Fries are coming," Merntice said.

Britney showed up, glowing. "Jewel! That was awesome! Gimme five!"

"You got a date with Digby finally?" Jewel said, slapping Britney's palm. "I hope he hates me."

"His cheek is still red," Britney said cheerfully.

Jewel felt guilty again. "He was so clingy. Like Chad."

"Chad?" Lolly stuck her tongue out and grabbed her own throat with both hands. "The Choker?"

"Another clinger. Wasn't enough for Chad to get kinky with ropes in bed. He wanted to 'extend it into our relationship.'" Jewel snorted. "What relationship? I told him, 'We had sex. Get over it!' Plus he wanted to cuddle all the time."

She made a face. Sex was sex and she wasn't fussy how she got it, but when it was over, she liked to have her space back.

"You can slap him again tomorrow. He smiled at me," Britney said. She giggled like a girl. "He let me touch his face."

"Brit-ney's got a cru-ush," Lolly sang.

Jewel said, "Brit, can I borrow the handcuffs? You won't need 'em with Digby."

"They're in my gym bag," Britney said, looking disappointed. "You're really done with him?"

"So done. Take him," Jewel said. "Maul him. Make him happy and get him out of my hair."

"Guess you better start bein' lousy in bed," Merntice said around the straw in her Coke.

"Yeah, yeah." Jewel hunkered down over the menu.

"Admit it, you felt sorry for him," Tookhah taunted.

"Jewel's a ho with a heart of gold," Lolly said.

"He sits too close," Merntice said. "I've seen it."

"Uh-oh," Tookhah said. "Space invader."

Lolly said, "Nobody invades Jewel's space."

"Yeah, yeah." Jewel changed the subject. "So who's phoning taxis next week?"

Tookhah was drinking iced tea. She waved a hand.

"I envy you," Lolly said. "I'm inspecting taxis at O'Hare again. Two years ago, I got stuck at O'Hare for six months. Six. I'd rather do gas stations."

"Ugh," Tookhah said. "The measuring can leaks in your trunk no matter what you do and the smell stays forever."

"What's the best rotation?" Britney said.

"Calling cabs," Tookhah said. "You write up the dispatch call, you wait, you take a little ride to your partner's house or maybe around the block until your phone rings. Then you sit on your butt until the next cab comes."

"Nuh-uh. Give me food. Deli," Lolly said. "And the Maxwell Street jobs."

"I like 'em all," Jewel said.

Britney opened her dumb-blonde blue eyes. "Even Hinky Corners?"

Jewel made a face. "Not so much."

"Ed says you're gonna do it forever," Britney blurted, and then turned color when Jewel stared at her. Since when did Ed tell the secretaries his career plans for the investigators?

"Sooner you than me," Lolly said. "Hinky Corners is a career killer." Jewel transferred the glare to her. "Well, it is," Lolly added defensively. "You never know when Fifth Floor will blow a gasket, and then you're on the evening news in a really bad way. Plus, I'm scared of that shit."

Merntice spoke and everyone's head turned. "Sayers had to take a leave after he screwed up his last hinky job."

Britney spoke for them all. "Ooh, what happened?"

"He ain't sayin'. But he turned in three weeks's worth of insurance claims for psychiatric visits." Merntice would know. She did all Ed's typing and she handled investigator personnel files. "The other guys sometimes stick stuff in his locker to fuck with his head."

They waited, but Merntice retired back into her Coke.

"Well, I like home repair and auto service," Tookhah said, flexing her manicured talons. "It takes a while to make your bust, but oh, the satisfaction. People who fuck over little old ladies really annoy me."

Lolly sang out, "Red alert, Tookhah's blood sugar is low!"

"Give her fries," her grandmother said.

"Here's your darn fries." This was Dick's famous anti-service. Tourists actually paid for it. Their waitress slapped down the bucket o' fries and scowled over her pad.

"I wanna be an investigator," Britney said, staring into her Green River soda.

"Someday," Jewel said. "Hang in there."

"Screw someday," Britney snapped, and Jewel raised her hands placatingly. "I want it now."

"You gonna order lunch or what?" the waitress said.

"I'll have the Vienna red hot with everything," Tookhah said, "but no bread."

"I'll have it in a bun—naked!" Britney said.

"Slut," Tookhah said.

"Slut," Lolly said.

"Cheap ho," Jewel said.

"Gimme two double dogs and slather 'em with that brown mustard," Lolly said.

"Ew," Britney said. "Too slippery."

"One big bratwurst is enough for me," Merntice told the waitress, smiling tolerantly at the youngsters. Merntice always made Jewel feel like Mom was watching, and then she'd say something that raised goose bumps.

Lolly said, "Say, I finally found out what Jason likes."

"No!" Tookhah said.

Britney sniffed. "Jason doesn't like anything. Does he, Jewel?"

"Wouldn't know. I never fucked him," Jewel said.

"Word. He does it in roller skates," Lolly said.

"What, *in* roller skates?" Tookhah said. "Ick. You people are such sluts."

"You didn't know this, Jewel?" Merntice said. Merntice seemed to know that Jewel never lied about her sex life.

She shrugged. "He asked. I said no. Too messy."

"There's a cleaning service for that," Britney said.

"*You* said *no*?" Tookhah said, incredulous.

"I do now and then," Jewel said, nettled.

Lolly said, "No, you dummies, he wears roller skates. To bed. I thought he was gonna break my ankles, kicking and thrashing in those things."

While the others discussed Jason's kink, Jewel examined her conscience. *Am I the only person at this table who feels guilty about what she does with men?*

Lolly dished on Jason, her eyes bright. Tookhah narrowed her eyes as if critiquing a fish story. City girls, pretending, daring each other to be tough. Britney was the only relaxed slut in the bunch. Britney's dumbness made a virtue out of stuff that troubled Jewel's conscience.

Jewel thought of her hot dream in Clay Dawes's treatment bed and wondered if she'd picked up a fever. Or maybe she ate some pumpernickel with LSD mold on it. She could still feel swan feathers tickling her thighs, that corkscrewy swan's thing sticking into her.

Maybe it was only dumb if you were actually doing what other people lied about.

She shouldn't let it bother her. Wasn't like her folks would ever know. Jewel felt that painful spark in her throat and chest.

She leaned forward.

"Did I tell you, I dreamed I did it with a bird?" All heads turned toward her. "A giant swan."

Back in the office, Jewel beat the keyboard, trying to fend off Nina when she didn't want to, and trying to think of a professional way to say "lying scamming self-impressed wannabe-seducer of vulnerable housewives" in her notes on Clay Dawes.

"You can't leave me alone here tonight," Nina pleaded on the phone. "Ed won't be home for supper. He's being impossible."

He was impossible all day, too, Jewel thought. Ed had left an hour ago, looking guilty when he met Jewel's eyes. "I bet. Maybe I shouldn't get involved."

"So you'll come for supper tonight," Nina said.

"Nina, I think—"

"Yeah, but you don't mean it. There's nothing but Thai food in your fridge. Aren't you sick of cold pot stickers?"

"Nobody could ever be sick of pot stickers." *Seemed to be aware he was under suspicion,* Jewel typed, *but made only a slight effort to maintain his*—line of bullshit? She stared at the screen.

"I'll make that Gorgonzola ravioli you like."

Jewel groaned. "You want to butt in on my investigation of your sex therapist."

"So we're on the same page. Great. See you at six."

Nina hung up. That meant the third degree plus Gorgonzola ravioli. Could be worse.

Jewel stared at the report. It wouldn't make Ed happy. Sighing, she erased it with a keystroke.

She shut down her terminal and drove up to Sauganash.

The cicadas were droning their midsummer song on Peterson Avenue. The farther she got from the lake, the louder they sang, harmonizing with lawn mowers, ice-cream trucks, kids yelling and running in sprinklers, and the occasional fire-truck siren arriving to put out a blaze in somebody's tinder-dry gutter where a pigeon had dropped a lighted cigarette. Sauganash was homey in a way she'd never known on the farm. Jewel's heart felt hollow.

She would get mildly snockered with Nina and girl-talk for a couple of hours.

But when she arrived it seemed Nina wasn't alone at all. Ed's Fender was audible, twanging angrily in the basement. Jewel cocked her head. The Stones. "Things are different today." Anger management, Ed-style. Her heart sank.

Nina's daughter breezed through the kitchen looking like a gang rape waiting to happen, grabbed a fistful of bread sticks, and ran out. "Wash your face!" Nina howled from the kitchen as the kid banged out the front door. Jewel could hear the racket of video games in between Ed's plonky, rageful "and if you take more of those." So the boys were home, too.

In the kitchen, Nina came at her exposed flank. "What do you hear from Nathan the Napkinfucker?"

Jewel put place mats down on the tablecloth and then set the plates on them. "Nothing, thank goodness—"

"He was cute. Apart from pulling you under the table-cloth, I mean. Here, taste this dressing, it's too sweet, isn't it?" Jewel opened up. Nina stuffed a spoon into her mouth, saving her from having to answer. "Did you ever do it in a movie theater?"

Jewel swallowed. "I haven't seen Nathan for eight months. I told you last—"

"Don't you think he was a little off? I always thought so. That thing about wanting to have sex in five-star restaurants. Why restaurants? Why not a nice, warm car with a big back seat?" Nina was twenty years older than Jewel. She could find Jewel's sensitive spots without breaking a sweat. "Did you ever suggest that to him?"

Jewel sighed. "Nathan was into risk. Which wine-glasses? Frankly I was grateful for the restaurant thing. I always got half a decent meal—"

"Only half? Was it the first half or the second half? Me, I can't have sex on a full stomach. I don't know why, I've always been like that. Don't use those—the gold comes off the edges." One of Nina's little ways was to interrupt an answer to one highly personal question with another, nosier question. It could be the result of being a sort of cop's wife for twenty years, but Jewel thought it was just Nina.

Nina seemed edgy tonight. "Another terrific place is—"

A bellow from the basement interrupted her. "Can we have some beer down here?"

Without drawing breath Nina yelled back, "I'm coming, I'm coming," and went to the freezer. "The thing I love about you is I can talk about these things with you."

"Beer, Nina!"

"Shut up, it's coming!" she screeched. "Jesus Christ."

Quicker than thought, Nina put a frosty glass on a tray, opened three cold beers, put the church key in the drawer and the bottle caps in the garbage, swept a wayward drop of beer off the counter, and hustled downstairs with the tray.

Jewel folded napkins and laid out silverware, feeling the mixture of raging hunger and nervousness that meant supper with the Neccios.

"The thing I love about eating here," she said aloud for the sheer pleasure of knowing that Nina could and would hear her, even while in the basement bitching about the mess the guys were making and taking their orders for antipasto snacks, "is the yelling."

"That's because you're an orphan," Nina said positively, sweeping back up the basement stairs. "Would you look at this dip? What do they do, put their feet in it?"

"You know, he never yells at work," Jewel said, lying only a little. Ed never raised his voice to anyone who ranked him.

"An Italian male is king in his castle. You remember that. The sex doesn't last, but what else is new," Nina said bitterly.

Jewel sent her a worried look. Things were heating up at Palazzo Neccio. "He can probably hear you."

Nina held up a finger. "Ah, but he doesn't want to. Thank God, I can talk to you. I think I'd go out of my mind otherwise. What about this casserole, I only made it yesterday, do you want to take some home? I'll wrap it up."

"Ohmigod, the potato thing?"

"Please, I made a double batch, I've got enough Tupperware to whack Ed up in quarts and freeze him," she said with relish. "It's made with real cream and butter and sweet onions. You'll be doing me a favor."

"Deal." Jewel found it was better to use short sentences around Nina. At least she'd stopped bugging her about—

"About sex," Nina resumed. "Your problem is, you don't commit. Slice these tomatoes."

"No." Jewel took the knife and tomatoes to the cutting board. "My problem is not commitment—"

"It doesn't get better until you commit to breaking him in. Wear down his resistance to what you want. That doesn't happen without marriage. You don't have ahold of his balls, you don't have a chance. Not so thin," Nina said, peeking over Jewel's elbow at the tomatoes. "More chunky. Yeah, like that. This risk thing, I worry about you."

Jewel worried about herself. "I dunno if Ed likes you having hold of his balls."

"Oh, please. If I stopped, then he'd worry." Nina swallowed. "It's like I got four kids, not three." She blinked rapidly, and Jewel felt her heart squeeze.

Don't cry, Nina! "I don't think about 'breaking them in' when I think about partners."

"Not that you have a partner. With your job, you need one," Nina said.

"Are we talking about a work partner or a life partner?"

"Doesn't matter, you did all the guys at the office already. Except mine. I don't notice it's cramped his style any." Nina sounded depressed again.

"Keep it down." Jewel glanced at the basement doorway. "I skipped more than Ed."

"If your mother was alive, she'd worry about you."

Jewel rolled her eyes. "Whereas if I worry about you, I'm wasting my time?"

"No, I love it, but I'm saying you've had, what, two weirdo boyfriends inside of a year?" Jewel watched in fascination as Nina ran a damp paper towel around the edge of the cake plate. The chocolate cake would look pristine until the last piece was eaten. "That Chad scared me."

Jewel gave up pretending she was slicing tomatoes and stuck her finger into the frosting. "Me, too. Ohmigod. Cream cheese?"

"Sour cream and brown sugar. My point is you didn't get rid of Chad until a month *after* you found out about the choking thing."

Jewel flushed. "It was okay at first." It was more than okay. Then her common sense had kicked in.

Nina pointed with a spoon. "That's what I'm talking about."

"Hey, I stopped."

"You need professional help."

"Oh, brother." Here it came. Jewel gave up. "Gimme a piece of that cake. If I'm going to be lectured—"

"I'm not lecturing you, I'm concerned." In eighteen seconds flat, Nina cut cake for two, poured two cups of coffee, and assembled cream, sugar, forks, spoons, and clean cloth napkins on the table in the breakfast nook. "Just put the spoon in the saucer. That's why," she said, lowering her voice and sitting down, "I referred you to my sex therapist."

"Nina."

"You need it more than I do."

"Nina."

Nina looked at her. "What."

"I cannot tell you about this case."

"You're the case, doll."

"I can't talk to you about what"—Jewel swallowed—"goes on with Clay Dawes." *And his little friend. Big friend.* "It's a case. I can't talk about it." Although she really, really wanted to talk about it. *Did he turn into a swan for you? Did you fly out the window through a hole the size of a quarter?* This shit was seriously cutting into her girl talk.

Nina looked at her shrewdly. "Can I ask—have you filed any paperwork?"

"Not yet."

"Has anyone filed a complaint?"

Jewel bit her lip. "No."

"What does a man have to do to get fed around here?" Ed said from the basement doorway. Jewel went limp with relief.

Supper went downhill from there.

Ed started with grousing about the ravioli. "What is this crap? I thought we were having chicken tonight."

"Jewel was coming over. She loves my Gorgonzola ravioli."

"The fucking cheese police from Wisconsin."

"Ed, your language." The twins, Ed Junior and Matt, ducked their heads over their plates.

"We don't eat enough cheese, they come down to the flatlands and put fucking blue cheese in your fucking ravioli," Ed grumbled sotto voce. "Stuff costs a fortune. Where's your daughter? I put good food on the table, she should eat it, it's expensive, this blue-cheese crap."

Matt turned his head to Ed Junior and whispered, "Cheese police," and Ed Junior broke up in silent yuks.

Jewel wished she hadn't come. Then she took another squishy, salty, cheesy bite of ravioli. Bliss.

"How's your week going at work, Jewel?" Nina said in a pointed tone. "You investigating some big-shot chisellers? Or persecuting innocent fun, like Mr. Killjoy here?"

Ed cleared his throat. "I ever tell you how we got the old Kraft Building back, Heiss?"

"No," Jewel said gratefully. "Before my time."

Ed stuffed two of the despised Gorgonzola ravioli into his cheek. "That's right." He bolted down the ravioli and drank wine. "First time the city tried to stick the depart-

ment for the hinky shit." Nina swung her head around
and he said, "Stuff. They sold the whole block out from
under us, moved us downtown, and razed the building."

Jewel said, "All I ever heard about was a humongous
lawsuit over who owned the land."

" 'Cause the douche—developer disappeared up in
smoke without a trace. Shareholders went class-action.
The city won because we paid to tear it down an' the developer hadn't finished paying for the land. Then we
hadda pay to move. Again. And parking's worse than ever.
But here's the thing." Ed paused, fork in hand, looking at
Jewel. "This goes no farther."

"No, sir."

"Six months later, it came back."

"Yeah," Jewel said patiently. "I work there."

"Betcha don't know this, smarty-pants. The Kraft Building that came back, it was the one they built sixty–eighty
years ago. Not the one they tore down."

Jewel poured more cheese sauce on her plate and
chewed her squishy, blue-cheesy ravioli. Heaven. "Great
sauce, Nina. How? You mean, it came back like new?"

"Exactly. Including the old cop shop downstairs, the
old staff room and Consumer Services offices upstairs,
the old furniture, the old files, the old friggin' water
cooler."

"Is that why stuff keeps happening at the building?"

"What stuff? Who's been talking?"

She waved her free hand. "Nobody. People talk, Ed."

"Women," he grunted.

"Like opening the fridge sometimes and finding a
Coke bottle from, like, the fifties," she said. Ed must be
seriously rattled, or he wouldn't be talking about this.
"Only it's that new diet chocolate-caramel-cherry Coke
flavor."

"That was so cool, when the Kraft Building came back," Ed Junior said. "It shimmered for hours and hours first. I must have seen the clip a hundred times on the Internet."

"You weren't supposed to see that," Ed said heavily. "Da mayor din't want coverage."

Ed Junior rolled his eyes. "It's my screen saver, Dad."

"Boys, you can go if you're done," Nina said.

That started a chorus of whining about dessert. Nina got up to serve the chocolate cake.

"Coverage on hinky stuff was tight back then, too, huh?" Jewel said to keep Ed distracted. *This is what you missed being an orphan. Six-way digs across the table and getting stuck in the middle.* " 'Chicago is da city dat woiks?' "

"Got that right," Ed said, wiping his lips. "Look what happened to Pittsburgh. Mayor panics, calls in the feds. Fuckin' government thinks it can fix anything with a strip of yellow disaster tape. Like they 'fixed' New Orleans." He snorted. "Cordon off the joint and let the looters take over. Fu—fri—freakin' gangs run Pittsburgh now. Our mayor won't put up with that." He watched cake plates move around the table without landing in front of him. "I still live here," he said to the air. "I still pay the bills. All the bills."

Matt grinned at Jewel and silently mouthed, "Cheese police."

Jewel put her own slice of cake in front of Ed. "Good for da mayor." She watched Nina hesitate with the last plate of cake in her hand, and made pleading puppy-dog eyes until Nina broke down and put the cake in front of her.

Nina sat down to her cake. "Jewel, didn't you find some old-timey handcuffs in your locker once?"

"Uh," Jewel said.

"You said you thought they were magicked up from when the cops were using those lockers," Nina said. "Unless it's Chad the Choker's handcuffs I'm thinking of."

The twins sputtered.

Jewel split a dirty look between them and their mother.

Ed finished his cake in one bite and blundered out of the room, rattling the wineglasses on the table in his haste.

Wednesday morning, Nina stood on a ladder in the front hall, cleaning the chandelier with rubbing alcohol and a Q-tip, squeezing the phone between her ear and her shoulder.

"How about day after tomorrow?" She was practically begging. Normally it wasn't so hard to throw money at Clay. She had never thought of him as a con artist before Jewel said all those awful things about him, but now, god dammit, he was acting fishy. "I got the whole week open. I'll take any time. What have you got?"

"Uh, I'm a little backed up right now, Nina."

"Aw, come on. You can squeeze me in tomorrow."

" 'Fraid I can't." He didn't sound easygoing today. "You're my best customer. You know I wouldn't stall you for no reason."

She didn't know any such thing. The thought that he might want more money made her feel a little queasy. She had to have that treatment. Ed wouldn't even talk to her on the phone.

"Tell me you're not raising your prices."

"I'm not raising my prices," he said soothingly, and it didn't comfort her a bit.

"Sure you are. You deserve it. Go ahead. So, an extra fifty, and I'll be there tomorrow afternoon."

"No can do, Nina. If I could, I would—"

"A hundred, and I'll be there in an hour."

"Let me get back to you, okay?" Clay sounded tense.

He hates me. If he hates me he won't work with me anymore. "Don't hate me."

"I don't hate you. I promise."

"Seriously. Whatever I did, I apologize."

"It's not you, I swear." He was talking fast for once.

"Did you run out of drugs?"

"Did I—drug—what?"

"The pills, the stuff. Whatever you put in the wine before the treatment. I'd pay extra for some of that all by itself."

"Nina, I don't use drugs, and if I did, I wouldn't give you any without telling you."

"My husband's a fraud investigator, you know."

"We don't always have a glass of wine."

That was true. Most days she just handed him her charge card, ran for the treatment room, threw the bolt, and jumped into bed.

He said, "Look, give me a day or two to—"

"I don't have time!" The way Ed was acting, she was liable to buy a gun if she couldn't blow off some steam pretty soon.

Clay's tone told her the conversation was over. "I'll call you the minute I'm up and running again." The connection quit.

"It's Jewel," she said to the dead phone, the light bulb finally going on. Ever since she had let Jewel in on her big secret, Clay had been stiff-arming her. "What did Jewel say to you?" she yelled, shaking the phone.

*   *   *

Clay hung up in a sweat. Nina happy was sometimes more high-energy than he could take. Nina when she wanted something—when you were telling her no—and what's with that crack, "my husband is a fraud investigator"? She'd mentioned her husband twice before, once to say he was working late, so could she come by for a quickie and, more recently, mentioning his conniption about what sex therapy cost.

In fact, that was only yesterday. Right before she sent up this obvious cop for an initial treatment.

Uh-oh.

Reluctantly, Clay realized it was time to visit his father.

For courage, he rubber-banded the latest batch of client checks together and sewed them into the left front pocket of his chinos. Then he walked ten blocks and a universe away from his suite at The Drake and up the front steps of Virgil's latest home: a marble-fronted landmark mansion on Marine Drive, facing Lincoln Park and Lake Michigan.

Griffy answered the door.

"Clay! Sweetie!" She had faded and she'd gained weight, but Griffy was still a showgirl down deep: lots of blue eyeshadow and great legs. "*Mwa!* You haven't seen the new house!"

He gave her a big, cuddly squeeze. She also had the nicest pair of breasts and warmest heart of any of his surrogate moms.

"Wow, Griffy. Marble floors, fancy pillars, chandelier in the foyer. You need a feather boa to live here."

"Virgil says feathers are low class," said the literal-minded Griffy.

"How is the mean old guy?"

"He's never mean to me." She smiled like sunrise. "He's in the collection room. Come on up."

"If he dumps you, call me and I'll keep you." Clay followed her swaying backside up—and up and up—the grand curving staircase. "How big is this joint?"

"Four floors plus full basement. Woof! Nothing but stairs," she groaned, puffing to a halt at a pair of carved double doors. She knocked. "Virgil, honey?"

Clay opened the door without waiting for an answer.

The author of his being stood at the old butcher-block workbench surrounded by his tools, looking like a dried herring in Harris Tweeds.

"Clay, good to see you! How's the job going? Griffy, how about some coffee and sandwiches up here?"

She clattered out in her showgirl high heels.

The top floor was big enough for all Virgil's antiques. Wooden Indians stood beside complex medical mechanisms, one-armed bandits, ghost-detecting equipment, and Kirlian cameras: cons and frauds, every one. This collection had been Clay's school.

"Job's going great. Griffy looks good."

"She's still with me," Virgil announced. "I think it's the real thing this time."

Clay had liked all Virgil's girlfriends. Considering they were stuck babysitting a con man's brat, they'd showed him more affection than his own father had.

"Say, you know that brass bed I borrowed from you?"

Virgil smiled insincerely. "Rented." He stuck a jeweler's loupe in his eye and bent back over the workbench.

"I'm scoring. I'm piling up the green." Clay hooked his thumb in his pocket and just touched the wad of uncashed checks. "It's paying off big-time. That is," he said, entering phase two of their time-honored routine, "when I say the bed's paying off, naturally, it's really all about my deathless charm. Couple of big-time repeaters, too."

"Careful with repeaters. They'll turn on you. That why you came by?"

"Can't hide anything from you, Dad."

"Pity, but no. What happened?"

"This one repeater? Her husband's getting cranky about the credit card charges."

Virgil looked up, frowning. "You take a credit card from a repeater? Didn't I teach you anything?" He fiddled with a length of bent metal on the table. "And she's married. Now tell me her husband owns a gun."

"She says he's a fraud investigator," Clay said and winced, waiting for a roar.

"Mm-hm. What else?"

"She thinks I'm slipping her drugs."

The old man brushed that off. "You're not that stupid. And?"

"She referred a friend to me last night. Obvious cop."

Virgil looked around and his eyebrows snapped together. "Did the cop charge you?"

"I'm better than that, Virgil. I got her out of my suite in one piece, emotionally speaking. But she accused me of having an accomplice."

As expected, Virgil lost it. "She what? What the heck are you doing? Don't tell me you're pimping now. My own son! With your training, everything else you could be doing! Why the—"

"Dad, Dad, Virgil, take it easy, I'm not pimping. There is no accomplice." The more he denied it, the creepier he felt. Jewel Heiss had seemed mighty convinced.

Virgil shook his head and went to a computer desk by the wall. "Are you making your nut? Let's check the account." He tapped keys.

Clay said to his back, "It works like this. I troll the bars for unhappy socialites. Wine 'em, dine 'em, listen to their troubles, sympathize. Then I pitch the con." In his head, Clay was going over every inch of his suite. He couldn't see any way somebody could get in without a key. "Three-hour treatment on an antique brass bed that was built in 1700-something to cure sexual dysfunction. Three hundred smackers."

It was three-fifty, but Virgil had taught him too well. Never tell anyone, not even your nearest and dearest, the truth about money.

"That's not Hamilton's Celestial Bed. I never did establish provenance. This bed can't be any earlier than 1805. The brasswork alone—"

"My clients don't know that. They think they're getting a nap on a piece of history."

"That's it? A nap?" Virgil cackled. "That's the silliest con I ever heard in my life."

Clay went to look at the computer screen. "There. You see? There's your rent, plus a percentage of the take."

Virgil grunted. "I hope to heaven you're holding out on me."

Clay felt the checks sewn into his pocket with his thumbtip. "Wouldn't dare."

Virgil couldn't hide how impressed he was. "They go for it?"

Clay grinned. "After I've convinced 'em there's no such thing as frigidity. Only men who are lousy lovers."

Virgil started to smile and stopped.

Zinged you, old man, Clay thought.

"And you're not servicing them yourself."

"Absolutely not." Damn, this felt good. The money in the account on Virgil's computer screen wasn't a third of the total.

"And they're paying you."

"You're looking at the balance. Every charge goes into it." Virgil didn't have to know about the checks or the cash. "You get your ten thou and twenty percent of the extra, as agreed."

Virgil looked Clay up and down. He said slowly, "I wouldn't have believed it. I'll check the balance daily, mind."

"Feel free," Clay said, feeling smug.

"So why'd you come by? Why's this repeater think you're working with somebody? You think she set you up with the cop?"

"I swear there's nobody in this but me. Nina's my best customer. She's in some marital kerfluffle right now—they all are—and sex therapy is her outlet. Only thing she wants from me is treatments. But now I'm afraid to have her over because of this friend of hers, this cop."

"Tell me about the cop."

"Now, that's funny," Clay said. "She's wound tighter than Sister Mary Joseph. I'm positive she's single."

Virgil snorted. "You would know. You're a softy, boy. Last time, you *gave the money back*. What kind of grifter do you call yourself?" Shaking his head, he went back to his workbench.

Clay's good feeling vanished. "It was the old lady's life savings. I didn't want her to hate me."

Virgil mocked him. " 'I didn't want her to hate me.' You're not a businessman, you're a gigolo. Your problem is, you believe your own malarkey. If you stuck to the lonelyhearts, I'd never have to worry about you. Marry a rich woman. Problem solved."

"You know that's not enough for me." Virgil didn't care if every woman in the world hated him. "I'm doing great business here." Clay's stomach had a knot in it. "C'mon, admit it. Your son's not such a failure."

"I still can't buy it they pay money just for sweet talk. If you have a partner—"

"Swear to God, Virgil, I have no partner."

"—You could wind up in jail and never know what hit you. They'll turn on you without warning. I never use help. I haven't worked with anyone since your mother left me."

You mean, since you left my mother. Clay had no memory of his mother, but he knew Virgil.

He admitted his real fear. "What if my repeater produces somebody who claims he helped me? Plants him in the room, and the cop finds him with her?" Nina was such a loose cannon. She could talk anybody into anything.

"If the plant testifies, you do time."

Clay felt a shiver. He'd never been in jail and he didn't want to be. "If she can't produce anyone?"

"You'll be okay. If you skip," Virgil said, sounding sure.

Clay's tight gut eased. "What about this cop? How do I stay on her right side?"

"Don't serve her again. Send her away. Tell her the bed broke or something."

"I can't." *I don't want to.* He lied, "I don't know why—I have a feeling there's a ton more money in this, if I can play her right."

That made Virgil look impatient. "You idiot. What did I teach you about holding on too long? When you start getting nervous, pull the plug."

"I'm not nervous."

"Malarkey. You believe your own malarkey. You're no son of mine. I don't pay pity visits to the big house, remember?" he said coldly. "You'll do your time on your own."

Clay set his jaw. "So I'm asking. Specifically. What can get me in trouble with the cop on this job?"

Virgil laid it out for him. "She needs material facts. That means you making claims to medical expertise, or promises that contradict the deliverables or probable deliverables, or leaning on the mark too hard, or if she can find evidence of fakery. For example, if there's wires that go nowhere. That's good for two to ten years right there. Or if there's an accomplice."

Rolling his eyes, Clay remembered hearing Jewel come screaming so loudly that he heard her through the wall.

"I already told you. There is no accomplice." He also remembered a deep-voiced echo to Jewel's scream. He tensed every muscle in his shoulders. "No fucking way," he muttered.

"Don't curse," Virgil said. "Nothing puts off a mark more."

The treatment room was a fortress. He knew it. He forced himself to relax.

"I promise their money back if the treatment doesn't cure their frigidity. And I tell 'em they're not frigid, it's their stupid husbands."

Virgil's eyes narrowed and the crease showed beside his mouth. "Son of a gun. You snaky devil," he said, as if the words were forced out of his gullet. Clay said nothing, savoring his father's awe. "So you're home free. But if you're smart, you'll refuse to do business with the crazy bitches."

My father, the sensitive new age guy. "Virgil, to you, they're all crazy bitches."

"Amen."

CHAPTER 8

On his way back to the Drake, Clay cashed his clients' checks for new fifties at a currency exchange. He felt a whole lot better. Handling the green stuff reminded him why he did this. Pay Virgil. Pay his credit card bill—he wasn't stupid enough to stiff them. Then do something cool with the rest.

Back in his treatment room, he rolled and banded the fifties, ten at a time, tipped the brass bed up against the wall, and stuffed the rolled bills up inside the hollow brass legs.

He'd never felt like he actually earned money before. Not conned, but earned. Virgil sneered, called it the lonelyhearts scam, but Clay was proud of himself. It was like getting cash proof that you were sexy. Plus, the customers were actually satisfied.

He shook his head, smiling.

Virgil was right about one thing. The whole operation was perilously close to honest work.

Then he remembered Virgil saying *two to ten years* and sobered. How could this cop-ette possibly plant an accomplice on him? On instinct, he'd asked for a suite whose second bedroom was without an exterior corridor door. That left what, the windows? He was eight floors up. The closet? Bathroom?

He circled the treatment room, tapping walls, lifting carpets, checking for loose tiles in the treatment-room potty. Nothing.

To be on the safe side, he sprinkled a little talcum powder on the carpet in front of the windows and in front of the closet and bathroom doors.

Whenever Jewel had too much on her mind she would walk from her apartment to The Little Corporal across the river and buy a bag of their homemade doughnuts.

Wednesday morning she still felt full of Gorgonzola ravioli and family discord, so she kept it to three powdered cinnamon cake doughnuts and one double-chocolate cake doughnut. She took the esplanade east along the river toward the lake, cut under the Drive where it joined Wacker, and crossed the river again, wolfing doughnuts and brushing the crumbs off her navy polyester.

She felt sick over the whole business. At least her last two families had died. This time the members were flying apart. Over something stupid. *I can't fix them. I don't know how.*

They might even split over this. No more noisy family holidays. No more girl talk with Nina. At work, Ed would go morose, or worse. What if he started wearing his shirt collar open and a gold medallion with his zodiac sign around his neck, peeping through grizzled chest hair? She would miss listening to them yell at each other.

She longed to phone Nina and do some yelling of her own.

Better go back to the Drake for a redo. Only this time, don't blow it.

Below her on the lower esplanade, a bum sprinkled

crumbs on the ground, trying to con a pigeon into dropping the lighted cigarette in its beak. That reminded her to check in her pockets for unshelled peanuts.

She detoured north to the Ogden Slip, a little canal that dead-ended near Dick's Last Resort, bordered with sorry little locust trees, green in their concrete holes, but so small and tame. She threw her elbows over the railing, bit into a cinnamon doughnut, and looked across the dead-fish-smelly water in the slip at a patch of undeveloped land on the opposite bank.

Wild cottonwood trees grew there, sheltering coyote dens and possum holes. Her heart gladdened at their defiance. Rising like weeds under the skyscrapers, the cottonwoods seemed like a secret between her and the slip.

The sun glinted on black wings. Across the slip, somebody yelled wordlessly.

She yelled back. Five crows tipped out of the cottonwoods. The first turned toward her, pumping its shoulders, crossing the slip straight to her, lifting her spirits. The others followed.

Thrilling. *Come to me. Come to me.*

The crows settled in trees and on lampposts on her side of the slip. They cocked their heads and turned on their perches like impatient parakeets. She laughed.

A crow yelled twice. She pitched her voice to match its tone and yelled back like an echo. Then she threw down a peanut.

One crow floated down feetfirst, its feathers gleaming with purple highlights. It snatched up the peanut and flew away.

"You are beautiful," she said, holding absolutely still.

The guard crow yelled again, four times. She yelled four times, then threw down more peanuts. The last three crows stayed on the sidewalk, cracking peanuts with their beaks.

She played copycat with the guard crow while the other crows ate—five yells, six yells, some long, some short, some quirking up in a fancy wrinkle to trick her. The guard crow skipped seven and eight, and gave nine yells. *Trying to fool me.* She laughed. She imagined it telling the other crows, *Doggone, Bob, I'd swear they're intelligent. This one can count.*

The guard crow got up to fourteen yells and she lost concentration. The crow jumped into the air as if disgusted with her.

"Game over. Gotta go, guys." She threw down more peanuts.

The guard crow watched her walk forty feet away before it, too, grabbed a peanut, and then flew to the top of a lamppost where it could see her and the other crows at the same time.

"I wouldn't trust me either," she murmured.

A bicyclist roared up the path, bell jingling, scattering crows, and screeched to a stop beside her. It was Buzz. He threw her a salute. "Hullo, officer lady. Feeding the vermin?"

She handed him a doughnut. "Yep. Here's yours."

He downed it in one bite. He was so scrawny, he didn't exist sideways. "Nice morning," he said thickly. "If it would only ftay like this."

"No people?" she said.

He looked at her funny. "Cool and green." He puffed out his skinny chest. "I'm a people person. I can tell about people. Like I can tell you're gonna be famous someday."

She smiled. "How do you figure?"

"Your personal space is big, like a movie star. Plus you're

hot." He wiggled his eyebrows and she laughed. "You wait. You'll be, like, gettin' the keys to the city someday."

"Enough of the soft soap already." She handed him the doughnut bag. "How's biz, Buzz?"

"I got a new pitch," he said thickly, wolfing doughnuts. "I'm making money hand over fist."

"What's in the backpack today?"

He grinned. "Are you ready for this?" Sunlight gleamed on his zits. "I got a genie in a bottle!"

Oh, shit. She covered her eyes with her hand. "Buzz! Do you have any idea of the trouble you've caused?"

"I'm granting people's wishes. Well, the genie does." He perched on his bike seat and twiddled the right pedal.

"Darnit, we're trying to keep this stuff under control! You could create a panic! Chicago is da city dat woik— that works," she said, quoting da mayor. "Hinky stuff upsets people."

Buzz squinted. "It's people like you that get all upset. You probably *make* panic by trying to outlaw magic."

"You can't outlaw something that doesn't exist."

He looked perplexed. "But it does."

"Don't talk like that!"

"No, here, I'll show you—" He fumbled in his backpack.

"No!" Cripes, he had it on him? "Uh, yeah, I mean, sure! Give it to me." She reached for the backpack, but there were no flies on Buzz. His personal space was larger than hers.

"Thanks for the doughnuts, gotta go." And he was off at top speed.

She didn't bother to chase him. She could probably find him at Buckingham Fountain, or the zoo.

She stopped by the office to run yesterday's paperwork, borrow her handcuffs back from Britney, and pick up a lab kit. Then she got in her car and headed back to the Drake. On the way she bought and drank two triple-shot lattes. This time she wouldn't fall asleep.

By nine, she was driving up North Michigan Avenue. The shopping district was a total clusterfuck. Suburban-ites packed the sidewalks. Every intersection was grid-locked. She craned her neck out the Tercel's window, checking the sky for pink haze.

Her cell rang. "Heiss."

"This one's hot," Ed said. "Get up to Clark and Lill Street. Guy called in a complaint on the genie two min-utes ago."

"He's complaining about the genie? Under what ordi-nance?"

"Service. Claims he asked to be in movies and he doesn't like the way he got it."

"How did he get it?"

Ed sighed. "Get up there. And be creative. The com-missioner is gonna have a big fat upset nervous hissy."

At the first opportunity she cut west off the Mag Mile and crawled zigzag until she could pick up Clark Street. That turned out to be such a mistake that she ditched the Tercel in front of a Starbucks, slapped the OFFICIAL BUSINESS tag on her dashboard, and hiked the next half mile north.

Two blocks south of Lill she began to get an inkling.

White sawhorses sealed off vehicular traffic on Clark Street in the middle of the block. A huge, white trailer was parked across the entrance to a new condo enclave. In front of the trailer was parked another white trailer, and another. Cables snaked out of each one and ran into the gutter, where they joined and lay bundled neatly to-gether with little plastic wraps. As if that would comfort the neighbors.

She called Ed. "Okay, I'm getting close. Did this guy give you contact information?" She stepped over the cables and crossed Clark, which teemed with curious citizens.

Ed read off a phone number. "And don't call me back until it's over."

"You're a tremendous help, boss."

She called the complainant and found him, as promised, right at the corner of Lill and Clark, trembling with indignation. "Look at that! I can't get my car out of the garage! And they won't even let me be an extra!" He wasn't bad looking in a whiny yuppie way.

"Maybe they want you to get your teeth re-whitened," she said. "When did this happen?"

"About an hour go," the citizen said.

The movie people seemed unflustered at having manifested less than an hour ago in a city that wasn't expecting them.

What does Ed want me to do? Wave a wand over all this? "I didn't hear about a shoot going in on the North Side."

"That's because it's my movie. I wished for it. I opened the bottle like he said, and the genie came out, and I asked to be in the movies, and wham, all these trailers and things were here! But then there's all these snotty people with clipboards! I've tried and tried to tell them it's my movie and they won't listen!"

She knew all about the power of clipboards.

She glimpsed bright lights. "Stay here, sir, until I phone you."

"Why?" whined the citizen. "I know my rights. This is *my* movie. *I* wished for it, it's *mine*!"

She cocked an eyebrow at him. "Then you'll take responsibility for all the ordinances they're violating?"

The yuppie drew back as if he'd been stung. "Nobody said anything about ordinances."

"Genies never do," she said. "Wait here."

Gripping her ticket pad, she followed the bundled lines of heavy, black electrical cable until they converged in front of a bar painted up like an old-fashioned Irish pub. Closer to ground zero, everyone seemed to be looking in the same direction. She stood with the crowd on the south side of Lill. Bright lights blazed against the pub's front door.

A guy came out of the pub and stood holding a cellphone to his ear, pinned like a bug under all the lights.

Somebody hollered, and everyone convulsed for three minutes.

The guy went back into the pub. He came out of the pub. He held his cellphone to his ear. Somebody hollered again.

She used her own cellphone to call Health and Sanitation.

"Yeah, I see a big buffet table out on the street, a roach coach, and coolers in front of every trailer. Hell, yes, beer. Lill and Clark, ASAP." She pressed the next speed dial. "Larry, Jewel. Never mind my ass, how's your wife? Say, you want to fill your July quota, get over to Clark and Lill. It's a bonanza. You name it. Tell me later, I gotta call Inspectional Services."

It took three tries to find somebody at Inspectional Services, but it was worth it. Then she flipped open her ticket pad. By the time a tanned, self-important, too-skinny blonde with a clipboard found her, she had a nice sheaf of citations started.

"You can't make calls here," Clipboard Blonde hissed, scandalized. "We're shooting."

"You can't shoot here. You have no permits. Get me your logistics supervisor."

"Permits have been arranged." Clipboard Blonde's eyes shifted.

"I think you'll find they haven't." Jewel held up her badge. "Logistics? Soon? Because the longer I stand here, the more tickets I can write."

Clipboard Blonde bustled away. Jewel stood still, counting the violations within view, and wondered if the whole thing would go poof in a little while. Maybe it would disappear, like the Kraft Building getting demolished in reverse.

Genie magic. Something new for Chicago.

But in her experience, when things went hinky, they stayed hinky. It was damned awkward. Your Shrink's advice might soothe you when you were trapped on the expressway hip-deep in the pink stuff, but da mayor had the only sensible Policy: Keep your head down and cope.

His father had said it over and over: *Chicago is da city dat woiks.* It was the difference between a thriving economic and cultural nexus and, say, Pittsburgh right now.

Larry Kyard showed up, looking extra burly in his cop suit with protective vest. He moseyed to her side, clearly delighted to be in the middle of a movie production. "No permits at all?" he said.

"Nope."

Kyard smacked his lips. "I can't wait."

"There's Wynette." They watched Wynette, on the far side of Lill and Clark, take two steps toward them and stop to write a citation, look around, take two more steps, scribble scribble.

Jewel chuckled.

"It's a beautiful day," Kyard said. "Wanna have sex?"

"I'd rather write tickets. And you're married now."

Officer Kyard grinned. "For once, *I'd* rather write tickets."

A pretty, skinny man with a clipboard and ridiculous hair bustled up. "Whatever can be keeping Logistics?" he fluted. "They have a checkbook."

Jewel looked at Kyard. "Did you hear him try to bribe me? I think I heard him try to bribe me."

"I think I did, too. I'm insulted."

"Wait 'til Inspectional Services gets here," she said with a smile. "They'll feel hurt they were left out. The fines for bribing Inspectional Services are wicked."

Silly-Hair Man looked pale and went away.

A woman with a checkbook finally showed up. Jewel and Kyard and Wynette kept telling her that she couldn't pay her fines directly to them, which made Checkbook Lady miserable. The fines could run over two hundred and twenty thousand dollars.

Checkbook Lady got snarky.

Then Inspectional Services arrived.

Between the four of them, they cited up to three hundred grand in fines by lunchtime. What a coup! Ed would have to give her a decent assignment now. Breathless with her own brilliance, Jewel even got the whiny yuppie introduced to somebody who promised to make him an extra on the shoot.

She called a messenger and sent her share of the citations to the office.

Then she phoned in.

"Did you get the goddam genie?" Ed growled.

"I scored ninety-thousand-dollars' worth of tickets."

"Why didn't you get the goddam genie?"

"Aren't you proud of me? And I fixed the genie complaint." Walking down Clark Street, she felt lighter than air.

"For chrissake, what am I paying you for? Get on the damn—"

"Quit cussing, it's bad for your blood pressure."

"Get the freakin' frankin' flukin' fun-lovin' genie!"

Gratitude. "I'd love to, but I've gotta go shut down your wife's con artist now."

Ed gobbled like a turkey. She laughed and hung up.

In a fit of cockiness she hit speed dial and caught Your Shrink at the end of her show. "This is Ruby again, Doc."

"I remember you, Ruby. You're worried about your boyfriend."

"The thing I didn't tell you, he's, well, I think he's a male prostitute."

Your Shrink paused. Jewel interpreted this to mean that, as usual, she had managed to top all previous records for kinkyness. "I thought you were concerned about his, um, powers."

"I am. Frankly, Doc, I'd feel better if he was a hooker. A ma-magic hooker is, like, too much." Departmental training ran deep. She couldn't say *magic* without stammering. "I think it's the way he disappears in bed. Plus the giant swa—"

"Ruby, I'm concerned about you. You're giving this man power over you by believing he exists."

"Doc, he was no hallucination!"

Your Shrink said firmly, "He is what you want him to be. If he's not what you want, then you know he's real."

"Your logic sucks, Doc."

"I call them like I see them, Ruby."

Jewel hung up, thinking scornfully, Bunch of woo-woo hooey. She fingered her ticket book, counting blank citations. She hoped she had enough for what she wanted to do to Clay Dawes.

Still feeling cocky, she retrieved the Tercel and drove downtown to the Drake.

CHAPTER 9

At the Drake, she didn't bother to phone upstairs first.

Clay Dawes answered the door of his suite with his dopey-surfer smile. "Well, well, what a surprise, officer," he drawled. "It's nice to see you."

"I'm not a cop."

"Okay." He looked her up and down. "Didja bring pajamas?"

She laughed lightly, thinking of her ticket book, and barged past him into the suite, her heart thumping.

Nina wasn't there. Her blood pressure sank a notch.

Clay smiled as if he'd been praying she would come by. *Stick to the script this time.* "I'd like to try your treatment again."

He smirked. "Let me see when I can fit you in."

She said too sharply, "I'll do it now, or I'll file a complaint with the city."

He opened his eyes at her. His pouty lips made an O. "I thought you weren't a cop."

"I'm not." She tried to loom over him, but the guy was too tall. A nice size, her treacherous libido noted. In the other universe, the one where Nina wasn't involved, she was probably hitting on him and taking sex therapy. "Now, if you please."

"If you're sure. The treatment is powerful mojo." Implying again that she couldn't handle it.

She snapped, "Is that a medical term?"

His hands came up in mock surrender. "No, just a colloquial observation about the effects. Which are somewhat subjective."

It was as if he knew exactly what material facts she was fishing for, and knew how to skirt making a claim that she could hold him to.

He said with sympathy, "I see what it is. You want your money back from last time."

"No, I—"

"It didn't work after all. Is that it? It can take awhile to get up your nerve to admit it," he said understandingly, and Jewel felt her composure slipping.

"I want," she said through her teeth, "to try it again."

"No problem. No problem." He hesitated, and she thought, *There's somebody in that room now and you're stalling, letting him get into hiding.* Clay said, "I hate to send you in there when you feel like this. Can I offer you a glass of wine first, maybe sit down, get you off your window ledge?"

"I'm fine! Although I will take that wine."

He turned away and the whole front of her body relaxed. She took a few deep breaths behind his back.

"Cabernet okay?" he said. She didn't try to catch him in the act of doping the wine. *Let him think he's too slick for me.*

"Yes." Another deep breath calmed her. When he handed her the glass, she was ready. "Thank you." She poured the wine into an evidence bottle and screwed it shut. "Now, the key, please?"

He looked amused. "Aren't you forgetting something?"

She dropped the evidence bottle into her purse. Didn't anything faze this guy? "I don't think so."

"Three-fifty? A check will be fine."

She flushed hotly, as if she'd been caught shoplifting. She counted out cash and slapped it in his hand.

"You small-time operators think you're so smooth," she hissed, grabbing for her dignity and missing. "I know crooks like you inside and out."

"You should," he drawled. "Cops and crooks are all in bed together." He leaned closer. "We need each other to make our lives interesting."

And kiss a turtle if she didn't feel slippery.

I need therapy.

"Is this what you call preparing a client for treatment?" she demanded, half furious and half stunned.

"It is for you, Ms. Straight Arrow." He fished the key out of his shirt pocket and led her to the treatment-room door. When he brushed against her, her body flamed up on that side.

She pretended not to notice.

In the treatment room she tested the bed for electrical current, tested the air coming out of the ducts for volatile chemicals, and tested the locks. She found no tricks.

In spite of all those triple lattes, within five minutes of stretching out stiffly on the coverlet, she fell asleep.

Clay went through her wallet at warp speed. "Credit card, library card, voter registration, gym card, what, no Sunday schoolteacher ID?" he muttered. "Bond card. What's this?"

The photo showed Jewel's uncompromising chin and vulnerable blue eyes, and a suit so ugly it looked like a nun's mug shot. He read the fine print carefully.

"Department of Consumer Services, Target Investigations Division. Holy Moses." He'd dipped a cop's purse.

It all made sense now. Nina, whose husband was a fraud investigator. Jewel, her friend. Clay felt his chest go tight.

"Let's take this slow." He pulled a chair up to the treatment-room door and sat down with the wallet in one hand, covering his mouth with the other to make himself breathe deeply.

His uppermost feeling was disappointment.

No, his uppermost feeling was a dumbbell horniness. On beyond the hard-on, this horniness was for something more, something he'd seen in her eyes on her first visit when he said the words "risk" and "hope" and "love." His father had trained him to watch for those tells and lean into them. Usually he let his mouth run during the introductory part of the con, watching to see the pupils of the eyes change, the blush, the little sensitive movements that signaled when he'd struck a nerve. That was why he talked slowly: to see which exact words hit pay dirt.

But while he was revving Jewel up, all he could think was, *She has my hang-ups. I could get into this girl.*

His radar told him that, under all her armor, she was lonely and unhappy in exactly the way he was. He'd found himself believing his own malarkey, throwing his heart into his patter until tears came to his eyes.

And now it turned out she was a cop.

What a turn-on.

Virgil was right. He was stupid.

He felt the congenital liar inside him turn the con back on himself.

I can always seduce her if she decides to bust me. She's me, only she's safe on her side of the law. And she hates it over there on the safe side. I could show her what it's like on this side. I could cure her sexuality, all right.

She spoke on the other side of the door and wrenched him out of his reverie. She wasn't moaning, a sound he often heard on this gig. No, she was conversing. He put his ear against the crack in the door.

Was she talking in her sleep?

"Who are you?" he thought he heard her say.

A man's voice answered her! Uh-oh.

She'd done it! She'd planted an accomplice on him!

He sprinted to the desk, yanked out a sheet of Drake Hotel stationery, thought a moment, and wrote. He lay the note under her wallet on the floor in front of the treatment-room door, where she would step on it when she came out.

As he straightened up, he heard more sounds he'd been dreading: a man's deep voice talking back to her, soothing and obsequious, her voice—accusing, suspicious, hysterical, and the man—who the heck was that, and what was he doing in Clay's con?

No sense hanging around.

Jewel dreamed she was walking around inside a house, a huge, dark, empty house. Dust covered the floors. She felt ashamed, a shame so deep that she needed dirt and darkness to breathe in. The windows hadn't been washed in forever, yet the faint daylight that came in made her want to hide in the shadows, in corners, behind doors.

Nobody must see me.

She flitted from room to room, climbing ever more stairs to get away from something she knew about in the basement.

As she thought this, the light outside the windows brightened, as if the sun had come out from behind a cloud. Golden light pierced the room where she cowered, making dust motes leap toward the window.

Not me. I'm not going out there to get caught.

She looked toward the doorway. If she ran . . .

But the sunbeam moved. *That's not right.* It moved like a searchlight, poking first one way, then another, up, down, lighting up the corners of the abandoned room while she thought, *No fair, no fair,* and tried to flatten herself against the wall with the window in it. If the light hit her, she'd be a sitting duck. She would become too stupid to run away.

And yet some dumb, secret part of her yearned toward that golden yellow sunbeam.

I could forget who I am. Seductive thought, terrifying.

It knew she was in here.

The sunbeam blazed across the room, trapping her in a corner.

Then, impossibly, it turned, the beam of light bending, questing in her direction.

Feeling as if she were destroying herself, she held still and let it find her.

Bliss sacked her like an ocean wave.

Let me go, she said, and knew she didn't mean it. Her last conscious thought was, *I am so messed up.*

When she returned to herself, she was dancing, resting her head on her partner's tux shoulder. Every movement felt like sweet sexual penetration. She saw her hand clasping his. They swung together into the bliss. Looking higher, she saw his face, his black eyes burning down on her. She felt his triumph, the roar of orgasm blasting through him, as if it were music coming through the wall of his body into hers.

You have made me so happy, he said. *How can I please you?*

He would give her anything she asked.

The wild horn of sex music quieted inside her.

She held her arms up, beseeching, childlike.

Find me?

He nodded. *We will look together.*

A sun burst inside of her, flooding her with joy.

That woke her up.

She became aware of her pounding heart and her skin cold in some places, scorching in others. She froze. She was nestled against a naked body.

I'm gonna kill that Clay.

His face nestled between her breasts, and he still penetrated her with a nice thick one.

Big naked body. Lots of shoulder. She pretended she was still asleep and let her hands move over his back, found his hand where it rested on her thigh.

Okay, then.

Reaching out, she found cold steel on the night table.

Her stealth fuck mumbled against her skin.

Three swift movements later, she had him handcuffed to the brass bars of the bed. She bounded away to stand naked on the carpet, blinking against sleep, trying to glare.

The man in the bed was not Clay Dawes.

CHAPTER

10

"Who the hell are you?"

He was big. His dark hair was too long. His lean face glowed with emotions inappropriate for a guy headed to prison for fraud, conspiracy, and date rape. He looked triumphant, delighted, even welcoming. His black eyes were huge with happiness.

"Who are you?" she said again.

He rattled the cuff against the bedstead and seemed tickled to death. "I am Randolph Llew Carstairs Athelbury Darner, th—" He gulped. "Third Earl Pontarsais. What's your name?"

"Jewel Heiss, Department of Consumer Services, Target Investigations. I'm about to bust your ass."

Actual tears shone in his eyes. "Jewel. Bright Jewel." His smile got trembly. "You may do anything you like to my ass."

Involuntarily she glanced at his naked body, which took some time. He was built like that all the way down.

"Think I'll get dressed," she muttered. "Don't go anywhere."

She snatched up her clothes, which were scattered not so far this time, and retreated to the bathroom.

If she planned to charge him with date rape, she certainly shouldn't shower.

But, hell, she had him cuffed naked in bed smelling like an orgy. Nina would back her up on the terms of the scam. Plus, she didn't feel like yelling "date rape." Jewel had had sex on trains, behind the velvet curtain of the opera house during a performance, and under tablecloths in restaurants, but opening her knees for a police nurse's speculum was just plain not sexy.

Her sleep-fuddled hindbrain was still trapped in the dream. The empty house. The sunbeam. The dance. She would rather wash away evidence than lose those feelings in the sordid humiliations of a rape investigation.

At the thought of the paperwork ahead of her, she felt an unpleasant rush of blood to the head. She sat down on the toilet lid to think.

She should write a couple of tickets. Misrepresentation of service. Dispensing medical advice and drugs without a license. Clay might wiggle out of those, but the wiggling would give her time to get more evidence. Operating an unregistered place of adult amusement. Conducting commercial business in a hotel room, no city business license, no hazmat inspection certificate on display, oh, a bale of goodies there.

She would submit to a blood test. Nothing short of narcotics could have put her to sleep so fast, when she was so on edge.

With her still-sweaty panties in her hand, she realized she would have to testify at a department hearing.

Full details. With Ed listening, and all of it on record for, oh, say, Digby to read later. She felt hot all over. Again, testimony in county court. She pictured Clay Dawes giving his evidence with that smirk on his face, and she prickled.

Uh-oh. She'd left Earl Whosis in that room where he could yell to Clay for help.

She dressed hurriedly and bolted past the naked guy still handcuffed to the bed, through the connecting door, into the suite parlor.

No Clay.

Her wallet sat perkily in the middle of the floor with a piece of paper under it.

She picked up the paper.

Thought I would give you a little extra privacy, it read.

She checked her wallet—everything still there—not that she'd bet a nickel against him using the credit card numbers—she clenched her fists, trying to keep her blood pressure down.

Thinking, she went slowly back into the "treatment room." "Okay, Randolph Lou Whoever—"

Her captive lolled comfortably, holding his handcuffed wrist over his head. "Call me Randy. Everyone does." He beamed at her.

"I bet." She eyed him. "Your buddy skipped. You're holding the bag. Want to spill it?"

He watched her and nodded his head as she threw the words at him. "Spill it. That means you want me to tell you things. I've watched a lot of television," he said proudly.

"Bully for you." Was he retarded? She really wanted a shower. She sat on the end of the bed. "Want to tell me?"

Her glance fell on his naked cock, standing like a jaunty public menace against those admirable abs, and she got up again and went to the parlor for a chair. She parked in the chair two feet away from the bed, covering her lap with a pen and notebook.

"How did you begin your association with Clay Dawes?"

"Aren't you supposed to read me my rights?" he said, not sounding mad, just curious. He had a faint accent, sort of like Hugh Jackman's, something in his emphasis, plus a touch of formality. Funny coming from a guy who was handcuffed naked to a bed.

"I'm not a cop. I'm a citizen who found herself getting date-raped. I can cheat. Clay Dawes?"

Randy sat up. "Did you dislike it?" His eyes were serious.

"Shut up." She blushed hot again. "Clay Dawes?"

"You couldn't have disliked it. Else I would not be free." Randy smiled at her as if he didn't know he was smiling. "Yes, Clay. He brings me women. One by one. Now I am free."

Spooky. *Now I am free.* Was Clay keeping him prisoner? "Where do you live?"

"I live here, in this bed."

"Uh-huh." Not retarded maybe, but definitely nuts. "Does Clay feed you?"

"I don't eat."

"Do you at least have clothes?" she said tartly. She'd feel better with him dressed.

He shook his head. "I'm an incubus."

"An incubus."

"Yes." He met her look.

She raised her eyebrows. "A box with a tooled leather lid."

"No."

"An aftermarket attachment for my carburetor."

"No."

"A long-winded lame explanation? I suck at twenty questions."

"No. An incubus is a sex demon."

Her breath hitched. "Bull." *Wow*, her body said.

He squirmed until he sat cross-legged, then looked at her. "May I tell you how I come to be here?" he said eagerly.

She nodded.

He looked serious. She imagined she could see him getting his story ready. "Well." Slowly he rubbed his free hand from his knees to his ankles and stared, looking fascinated and delighted, at his bare toes. He had beautiful knees. Her nipples crinkled. She folded her arms across her sex-stinky polyester blouse.

"Once upon a time, I was Randolph Llew Carstairs Athelbury Darner, third Earl Pontarsais. I had a mistress. I had a number of mistresses, but this one counts because she was a magician." He flushed and glanced down at his amazing schlong. "It seems I was an inconsiderate lover." He looked embarrassed. "She complained. I was boorish. I said ill-judged things about a woman's sexual needs and she lost her temper. And she did this."

Jewel put a hand over her mouth. A giggle was forming deep in her belly. "If all this is true, why are you admitting it to me?"

"I want you to know how deep a hole I dug for myself."

She stopped herself from smiling. "So you're a sex demon."

He nodded. "Like the chap in *The Witches of Eastwick*."

Her nape prickled. "He was the devil."

"Technically, merely an elemental. A creature with one job and one job only. Harmless on weekdays. Take away his lawful work and he makes trouble." Randy didn't look a bit harmless.

"Is that a threat? Because that's a criminal charge—"

"Dear lady," he said, sounding more cheerful and more like Hugh Jackman every minute. "I am in no position to threaten. You've broken the curse. I'm yours. Thanks to you, I have my body back!" He split a grin, then threw back his head and laughed.

Some of those scenes from *The Witches of Eastwick* came back to her. She edged her knees an inch farther away from him. "What if I don't want you?"

His grin vanished. "I won't make a mess with raw fruit. I can't conjure snakes. I'm good only for one thing."

She remembered giggling at the sensation of his felt-tip marker as it wrote RANDY WAS HERE up the inside of her thigh. Up—and up—all the way up.

"If you're not human—" She swallowed hard. "Disappear."

He looked at her. And from the toes up he disappeared slowly, like the cat in the kid's story. Only his eyes were left. He looked soulful even without a face. Except for the fact that her hair was standing on end all over her body, she felt sorry for him.

His eyes closed and he was gone.

With a trembling hand, she reached out and prodded the air where he had been. Her hand connected with warm flesh.

"Aaaack!"

"I'm invisible," his voice said.

"I can see that!" she snapped. "Don't do that!"

He faded back into view. This time his whole body appeared, rippling faintly like a reflection on water, then darkening and solidifying. He seemed not to have moved a muscle.

Sex demon. It could be true. "That is freakin' scary. Don't do that."

His lips pressed together.

"How come you disappear one way and come back another way?"

"Variety. I've watched a lot of television." He shrugged. "You seem remarkably levelheaded."

Here comes the butter. "I'm an officer of the law."

"Of course," he said, but he looked as if this was big news. "You have me where you want me." He gave her a doe-eyed stare that didn't fool her for a minute.

Another con artist.

What did you think, Jewel? He's some innocent retard who happens to be able to turn invisible and make love like the Temptation of St. Teresa?

"I thought you were, like, the slave of the bed."

"You've freed me. And now I belong to you." His words gonged through her and made parts of her vibrate and swell.

She said, "You know, you don't seem to me like a sensitive new age guy. You seem like one of those buff bastards who always gets everything he wants and walks all over people."

"Oh, I was. That got me into this mess."

"And now you're all reformed."

"For the most part. Except during sex." His eyes glinted. "Can the Ethiopian change his skin, or the leopard his spots?" His teeth showed. "I am more sensitive now, but I get what I want. Fortunately most of the women in this bed prefer—" He examined her from head to foot and she thought of Wilcox County Fair judges scoring her 4–H heifer. "Prefer an assertive partner."

She licked her lips nervously. "Let's back up." If he could turn invisible, he must be laughing himself sick at that handcuff. Still, she didn't unlock it. "Tell me again about the incubus thing, only with footnotes." *I'm turned on because I'm scared. Or am I scared because I'm turned on?* "Your mistress was a witch?"

"No. A magician uses principles of science to cause

action at a distance. A witch is a cottage shaman, kisses trees, has little furry friends in every hedgerow."

She swallowed. "Go on."

"So. She bespelled me and then she put a curse on me."

"Wait, wait," Jewel said. "What's the difference between a spell and a curse?"

Randy put out his free hand. "A curse is an act of vengeance. It makes you miserable, and carries a condition that you must do one supremely unpleasant thing in order to avoid eons of other unpleasant things. A bit like God expecting mankind to repent and reform their lives in order to avoid Hell after death. Unlike God, mankind must use magic to make a curse work."

"You seem pretty cheerful about it."

"I've had time to come to terms." He tipped his hand over. "A spell is the mechanism by which a curse is carried out. You can say to your lover, 'You cur, may your cock never crow again so long as you live.' That's a curse. But it takes a magic spell to keep him limp."

She glanced into his lap. This particular curse didn't seem to involve keeping Randy's dong down.

"So, what was the curse?"

"The curse is simply this. I may not leave this bed nor resume normal human existence until I satisfy one hundred women."

"But it's been how long? Five-hundred years?"

"Oh, please, if I were five-hundred years old you couldn't understand a word I said. No, I was born in 1785. I was twenty-glorious-six when Lady Juliana threw her magic dust over me in the year 1811."

"What happened then?"

"I had no choice, had I? I got to work." He eyed her as if wondering whether she was buying it. "My new job is satisfying women." He bared his teeth. "I'm good at it."

She found herself nodding. "No kidding. So how does Clay Dawes work into this fairy tale?"

"He brings me women."

"He knows about this curse?"

"He doesn't know I exist. You mustn't think I don't appreciate his efforts. Before he put the bed to this use, I had satisfied only sixty-odd women."

"In two hundred years?" she said in disbelief. "Boy, there are some truck-sized holes in your story."

"Tell me something," he said softly. "Imagine that you are married to an unpleasant man. The sex is dreadful. In your century, divorce is unheard-of. Or perhaps you are old and widowed. You discover that there is an incubus in your bed, a lover with extraordinary powers who can never escape, who can never say no, who cannot even climax unless you do first. Do you summon a priest and have the bed exorcised? Do you sell the bed? Throw the bed on the ash heap?"

"I guess not," she admitted. "So you've only had a hundred orgasms in two centuries?" She grinned. "That's gotta suck."

"I kept count for a long time—feel behind my head here." He reached up, but the handcuff wouldn't let him touch the top rail.

She got up and ran her fingers along the brass bar behind his head. On the back, invisible from the front, there were scratches in the brass. She peeked. Four hashmarks and a slash, the convict's marker of days, a long row of them. "How many?"

"Only the women can be sure. I lost count in the 1980s."

Trapped for two centuries. To her surprise, she was moved.

"So Clay doesn't know you're in this thing?"

Randy looked haughty. "Decidedly not. The poor fellow fancies himself the sole origin of all his customers' delight."

A smile spread her lips as she thought of Clay's smugness, his insufferable pity for all the sex-starved women in Chicago.

Randy's story shot some holes in her case. In fact, she was so far off script that her best move now would be damage control, regroup, figure out what crime had been committed here, and what use Randy's testimony might be. Certain crimes were out of her jurisdiction, plain and simple—kidnapping, unlawful restraint, whatever Clay had done to this poor doofus. Randy might have something useful to contribute eventually. If she could get him to stop spinning fantasies about his supernatural mojo. She could discount the whole sex-demon thing if he hadn't actually disappeared on command. Woof.

She'd better keep him where she could find him for the time being.

"I'm going to let you loose. But you'd better not try to run away."

He heaved a huge, smiling sigh. "I won't."

She unlocked the handcuffs. "Let's find you something to wear." She let him use the shower and rummage in Clay's things.

Meanwhile she summoned the head of hotel security.

The security guy showed up with the day manager. She showed them her badge.

"Where's all the furniture that was in here?" the security guy said.

The manager was appalled. "I'll fire the maids. They must have been bribed."

"How much has Mr. Dawes spent here, if I may ask?" she said.

The manager got on the phone. When he hung up, he looked thoughtful. "Eighteen thousand dollars so far." He bit his lip and said in a new tone, "Mr. Dawes is a valued customer."

She regretted asking about the money. *Give this guy a chance and he'll have the manager kicking me out.* "You been paid any of that?"

"Oh, yes. We debit his account daily, until his credit card maxes out."

"I'd like to ask for your help, as much to ensure that you get paid everything you're owed as to hold on to the evidence."

"Of course."

"Can you stick this bed away in storage somewhere? Put it in a room nobody goes into much. Not the regular bellman's lockup."

"Certainly."

"And don't tell anybody where it is. This man Dawes is a professional con artist. He can talk an eight-dollar-an-hour employee into anything."

"You won't arrest Mr. Dawes without telling us first?" the manager said, and Jewel and the security guy turned identical looks on him. The manager wheedled, "As a courtesy to a valued customer."

Randy came out of the bathroom looking tacky, squeezed into Clay's expensive silk Hawaiian shirt, slacks, and loafers.

"Is this man a male prostitute?" the security guy said.

She held up a hand. "I'll take him out of here shortly."

"To the police station, I trust," the manager said, properly horrified, since Randy wasn't a paying guest.

"We're not ready to bring charges," she said. Understatement of the year.

The security guy didn't ask her who the hell Randy was, but she could see the question quivering on his lips.

Since she didn't know what else to say, she said, "We appreciate your cooperation."

While they walked toward the parking ramp, her cellphone beeped. She'd missed a call during her "sex-therapy treatment," a number she didn't recognize. She pressed the CALLBACK button.

A woman's voice answered. "Hello?"

She did a double take. "Did you call me?"

"Ruby?" Who the hell was this?

"Uh," Jewel said. "Maybe."

"This is Your Shrink, Ruby. We're not on the air now. This is my private line. You hung up too quickly last time, and I called to let you know, I'll have to report our conversation to the authorities—"

"What?"

"Because you called about—"

"The hinky stuff." For one little moment she'd forgotten da mayor's Policy.

"Ruby, you did say the word"—Your Shrink lowered her voice—"magic. You know we don't use that word on the air."

Now she'd done it. "Do you have to give them my cell number?" There was no room on her dance card for more trouble.

"I usually tell them I didn't get it."

Jewel breathed easier, though her chest thumped. "You're a pal, Doc."

"No problem. I want you to feel free to call me anytime. Only, please, remember—"

"I know, I know, don't say ma—the M-word."

Jewel hung up, feeling tired. She still smelled like sex, and she couldn't help eyeballing Randy's muscular butt.

She asked him, "Are you wearing underwear?"

"There wasn't any."

She didn't know what bothered her more, Randy commando beside her or the thought that Clay had been smirking at her with no undies on. She felt off balance, overwhelmed by emotional and physical vulnerability mixed with sheer sexual triumph. It was an extreme version of how Chad the Choker and Nathan the Napkinfucker had made her feel: fooled and used, unsettled by her extreme response to something that was probably wrong, yet helpless not to be turned on.

Somebody's ass will be busted. She clung to that thought.

CHAPTER

11

Nina knew Ed would be coming home because he'd left the lunch she made him in the fridge. Lately he'd been in the habit of stopping by the house at noon. Checking on her.

This time he had the Visa bill in his fist.

He stomped into the laundry room where she was pressing sheets and napkins.

"For the love of Christ, Nina, what you been doing?" He brandished the Visa bill. "There's no excuse for this spending."

He'd sent Jewel after her *before* he confronted her about Clay's credit card charges. That meant he was screwing around again. The realization depressed her.

"You don't trust me."

"What's to trust? Three hundred fifty bucks a pop!"

She unballed a damp shirt and spritzed it angrily with starch. "You sicced my best friend to spy on me." That hurt.

"She's my employee. Chasing bunco is her job. You're up to your neck in it."

She didn't cry, because he didn't like to see her eyes red.

I am such a fool.

"Why couldn't you have sent somebody else?" she said. It was hard not to blame Jewel. In Nina's experience, crappy jobs were the same everywhere. You didn't betray your friends. "You have no right to try to wreck my friendship with Jewel out of stupid jealousy! We won't let you!"

His eyes narrowed. "Is she in on it now, too? You and your strays. I never shoulda introduced you."

"Oh, shut up," Nina said. "This is not about Jewel, this is about you and me. You're never home. And when you're home, you don't talk to me." She slammed the iron down. "I have to keep myself occupied somehow."

"Who with, Nelson Rockefeller?" he exploded. "What happened to charity work?"

She faced him, letting her eyes flash. "I'm sick of charity work. I'm sick of committees and golf and the country club and shopping. I'm sick of waiting for you to take time off. We were going to Mexico and you bailed. Jewel came with me! Last year you said we'd go to St. Thomas, and I'm still waiting."

He looked hunted. "Go to Elizabeth Arden. Costs half what you're spending. A tenth!"

"I don't want a goddam spa! I want my husband!" A couple of tears leaked out at that. She dashed them away angrily.

"So you spend three-fifty a pop on a cabana boy!"

She squared off across the ironing board. "He is not a cabana boy! He's a sex therapist!"

"Oh, bull. Jesus, Nina, most I ever spent on a whore was a hundred bucks. And that was a twofer!"

She gasped. They'd been married since high school. His hundred-dollar whore must have been since then.

"You might as well say it right out, I'm not enough woman for you!" Wounded to the heart, she cried, "If I'm frigid it's because you made me that way!"

"Oh shit. I never said you were frigid." She waited for him to confess to his affair so she could ask for a divorce. To her relief and misery, he didn't. No, it was all, *Clay's a gigolo and you're not frigid.* "Not totally anyway," Ed said in a thin voice. "Maybe you're bored."

She screamed, *"That's what I'm telling you!"*

His face fell. "Well." He glared at her. "Fine." She felt the awfulness between them open up like a hungry grave. "Guess I'll get back to work." He stomped up the basement stairs and flung out of the house.

She put half an hour into a good long cry. When she raised her head from the pillow, she thought, *I have to have that bed. I deserve it. Because fuck Ed anyway.*

Since she couldn't arrest him yet, Jewel had nowhere to put Randy Lord Whosis, so she drove him to the office.

"Okay, these are the rules. When we get there you are not to talk to anybody. Stay close to me. Don't tell anybody where we met. Don't answer any questions. If he figures out who you are, my boss will want to ask you about his wi—about Clay's clients and I need my ducks in a row before he meets you."

She couldn't imagine why Randy would do as he was told unless he was retarded or insane. These were strong possibilities. He gawked out the car window.

"But I may talk to you?"

"You haven't stopped talking."

"I'm sorry." He seemed cowed, which she didn't buy.

She still hadn't had a shower. She felt yukky all over, in kind of a yummy way. The sun beat down on Lake Shore Drive. She opened her window. The surface of the lake wavered in the hot July haze.

Randy's window was open, too. She eyed him, but he

seemed content to sit jammed into the front passenger seat of the Tercel. His shoulders were a mile wide.

"Don't have me arrested. I beg of you," he said humbly.

The car in front of them surged forward a whole ten feet and stopped dead. She thumped the steering wheel. "Why not? Besides, what should you be arrested for?" Maybe he was dumb enough to tell her.

"I must remain near you." He said it with such intensity that her crotch got hot.

She squirmed. "We'll see. I still don't get why." She stared at him until the cars behind them honked. "How can you be sure I'm the hundredth woman, anyway? Those marks scratched on your bed?"

"No one can be certain if a woman has achieved climax," he said, looking glum. "Sometimes not even she knows. But my mistress made it clear. Only when I have satisfied one hundred women may I live as a man again. Clay had another customer between your visits. She did not free me. You did. But for how long?"

Jewel felt an urge to ask him if he could still do it like a swan in the air, now that he was free, but she couldn't think of a tactful way to say it.

"What if my hours of freedom elapse? What if I return to that bed? If you are not near, you won't know I'm gone. No one will know. And I will never be free," he said mournfully.

Sucking smog into her lungs, she said, "Let me get this straight. You promise you'll stick around so I can have sex with you whenever you get in a jam?" She shook her head. "I've heard lame lines before."

He raised pleading hands. "So I can give you an orgasm."

"This is the weirdest conversation."

* * *

The office was a mob scene. Every investigator on shift seemed to be there, typing reports, logging citations, talking, slurping coffee, getting yelled at by Ed.

"Terrific, he's mad already."

"That is the man you work for?" Lord Randy murmured, as Ed turned purple and slammed into his office. She felt every eye in the office focused on them. "A deplorably underbred person."

"Shut up," Jewel muttered back. She led him to a corner. "Here's what you do. Sit here and don't move. Don't talk. Don't make eye contact. Wait for me."

She parked Randy as far away from the coffeepot as possible and approached Ed's office. Tookhah and Lolly both warned her, "He's pitching hissies today." When she looked back, Britney was offering Randy cleavage with his cup of coffee, while Digby watched them with smoldering bedroom eyes from behind his workstation monitor. Oh, well. She slipped into Ed's office.

He was on the phone. "Yes, Commissioner. I understand. We're doing the best we can." She sat mousy-quiet. Ed kissed butt awhile longer and hung up. "Christ, he's on a rampage today. Heiss. What you got on this genie-bottle guy?"

"Uh, I think I'm getting a handle on his MO."

"Fine, great. Shut him down this week and you get a bonus."

She looked at him with surprise. "You feeling okay, boss?"

Ed wiped his balding head with a tissue. "What a year. Couple more empty cars on the Edens this afternoon, center lane. Saw 'em myself. Pink stuff so thick I couldn't

see my hood ornament. Some nuts are out there picket-
ing the Daley Center, blah blah fuckin' End Times, hell,
it's as bad as New Year's two thousand turn of the millennium twenty-first friggin' century."

"And the commissioner's an idiot," she said sympa-
thetically.

"And the commissioner's an idiot," he repeated and
twitched. "Don't tell anybody I said that."

"You didn't say it, I said it."

He sent her a grateful look. "You're a good girl, Jewel.
I don't mean that. Woman. Friend. Employee. Fuck,
what a day." Ed wiped his neck this time. "You know
what I mean."

"What you mean is, the election's coming up, da
mayor wants everything squeaky clean before the Tuesday, the commissioner is fussing, and we face staff cuts if
we don't show some flash."

"You need a partner," he said sorrowfully. "But yeah.
You sure you couldn't take Digby—?"

"Positive." She licked her lips. "I talked to Nina this
afternoon."

"So did I," he rushed out. "So that's taken care of.
What do you know about this gigolo?"

"He's a therapist of some kind," she said carefully.
"Skipped on his hotel bill, far as I can tell. They're holding his property hostage. Security promised to get back
to me if he turns up. And I got something today that I
need sent to the lab." She produced the sample bottle
containing the cabernet Clay had poured for her. "Check
for hallucinogens and aphrodisiacs."

Ed didn't blink at the word "aphrodisiacs." "Good.
Good. I don't suppose you found any records, any, I
dunno—"

"Boxes of cash or credit card receipts with your name on them? Nope." She was screwing the guy who had screwed her best friend and boss's wife. Ick. If she looked at it that way, she and Nina were both cheating on Ed. Double ick. "I want a real case, boss, like this identity-theft ring."

"What, so you can quit my team and go to work for the state's attorney?"

"So you could reward my loyalty to the department," she said pointedly.

"Look, you done good on that thing with the haunted skybox and the scalper. Plus that day-care clown scaring those kids. Hell, it scared Sayers into a three-week psychological. I couldn't send some dipshit like Sayers. He screams like a little girl over a rat."

She snarled, "You have other investigators." *I don't know what's worse, Ed sticking it to me or Ed apologizing.*

"Wusses. Conventional thinkers. Plus, they would ask too many questions." Ed lowered his voice. "Like about my wife and this sex therapist."

Uh-oh. Sounds like they talked. Distract him. "You can't call Tookhah a wuss, Ed. And Sayers and Lolly are total freewheelers."

He rocked back and forth. "The thing is, you're so solid."

She opened her eyes in outrage. "Is that a remark about my weight? You just called me fat!"

"No, of course not!" Ed danced in an agony of political incorrectness phobia.

"I'll have you know, I am big-boned. This is muscle, boss. I work out constantly." She mourned, "I'm sorry if I'm an embarrassment to the department."

"Fuck, I didn't mean that! You're smart and—and sensible and incorruptible. Unflappable. Discreet. Down-to-earth."

"Fat." She nodded. "I'll try Jenny Craig again."

"I didn't say that!"

"So how about that transfer? That identity-theft ring case sounds good."

"I need you in Hinky Corners," Ed said with finality. *Britney was right, his mind's made up.* "I'll get you a partner as soon as I can. 'Til then I'm counting on you. The chief attorney is a good guy, he'll back us up if you get anything solid with meat on the bone like material facts the prosecutor can work with, but not if it's fluff. Get this genie guy." He lowered his voice again. "Find out what you can about the other thing. Don't fuck up."

"I won't."

"Who the hell is that?" he snarled in surprise.

She looked with Ed through his office window to see Randy getting a Britney-style hand job. "Uh, he's my cabbie. He, uh, asked for some help with his medallion."

Ed looked black. "He's getting too fucking much help."

Britney simpered at Randy.

So that's who Ed's snogging with.

Jewel barrelled out of his office. If she learned any more about Ed's family life, she'd start being grateful that her blood relations were underground.

"You have an amazing lifeline," Britney was saying as she stroked Randy's palm.

"In fact it has been curiously monotonous." Randy looked anything but bored. The tomcat. Jazus, wasn't two hundred years of horizontality enough for him? "I spent most of it in bed."

Britney's eyes got bigger. "Is that a come-on? Because I just love your accent."

" 'Scuse us." Jewel took the hand and towed Randy out of the Britney zone, past a scowling Digby, while Ed turned the blinds shut on his office window. "C'mon, sport, let's get you straightened out."

CHAPTER
12

In the end she took Randy home with her. She couldn't send him back to Clay, who had clearly brainwashed him. Ed shouldn't talk to him yet. For sure not Nina.

That bothered Jewel. It bugged her more than the hinky stuff. She'd half-decided that Randy had hypnotized her. She only *thought* he'd disappeared and made her fly and turned into a swan and boinked her in midair.

Her libido wanted to believe it all. Especially the part about him saying he was her sex slave.

But she couldn't kid herself about one thing. He'd done it with Nina a couple dozen times. Ew.

She wasn't pissed at Nina for messing up her marriage. She was jealous. Her dumb body wanted to keep Randy. Not a fun thing to discover about yourself.

Randy looked cheerful, as if Britney's attentions had perked him up. He was quiet all the way to her condo in the Corncob Building. She took time with him over the Thai delivery menu, which seemed to baffle him.

"So tell me, what kind of a lord are you?" she said after she had phoned in their order.

He watched her set the kitchen table. "What you might call nouveau riche. My great-great-grandfather prospered in coal. My grandfather and father elevated our name, first to a baronetcy, then an earldom. I spent money with both hands and did little else. I've no idea if there is still an earl-dom Pontarsais. The property was probably sold up the year I disappeared." He stopped short. "You are a kind listener."

"Do you know who the current lord guy is?"

"No." He looked thoughtful. "There is one, I suppose. Descended from cousins of my father perhaps."

She was already walking into the living room. At the computer she said, "How do you spell this Pont-arse thingy?"

He spelled it.

Google turned up 2,230 hits. "Not much here."

"So this is how a computer works? You can ask it anything?" He bent over her shoulder.

"I'm scrolling. We got a florist. We got a village in Wales."

"Ours."

"Yours? You owned a village? Hang on, still scrolling. Here's a pottery, cool-looking stuff. Judo. Massage therapy. Computer company. Pontarsais is a famous fly-fishing spot, did you know that? Mining reports."

"I told you, the family money is—was—in coal."

"Pony and Cob Society. A mill. Karaoke sites, is nothing sacred? Gajillion guest cottages and B&Bs. Singles dating service, civilization comes to Wales, huh. Things to do in Carmarthenshire, holy crap, would you look at the spellings of these names. Apparently nothing's hot but the pottery now."

"Look for an estate called Llew's Howe." He spelled it.

"Your house has a name? Okay." She beat the keys. "What about this?" She found a picture of a nice bit of woods and a big, ugly house. Beyond the house was nothing but glittering water. "You didn't mention it's on the ocean."

"It's not." He squinted over her shoulder. "Lake Michigan?"

She scrolled down. "Sorry, wrong house. That's the family estate of a Milwaukee beer magnate."

He put his hand on hers. "No. It's my house."

"Not on Lake Michigan. 'Strom and Wilitha Katzele, founders of the Katz Beer Company'—it's okay beer—'house purchased in Wales and moved to the United States in 1924,' well, what do you know?" He wasn't lying. Or else he was a consistent liar.

He knelt at her side. His face was slack with amazement. She wondered if she was a fool to feel sorry for him.

"How could they do that? Move a house?" His hand touched the screen.

"People did it a lot in the twenties."

He sat on his haunches and stared at the house. "Can you discover why the original owner sold it?"

She poked around on the website but found nothing. "We could try the library. Or the Pontarsais Chamber of Commerce or the county courthouse in Carmarmaladeshire."

He swallowed. "No. Look me up."

She eyed him. If Randy and Clay had done their homework, she would find this guy online. "Okay. Let's google Burke's Peerage."

And by golly, there was a Pontarsais title. "'Earldom created in 1715 for services rendered to the Crown. First Earl'—"

"Find the third earl."

"Third Earl, Randolph Llew Carstairs Athelbury

Darner." Son of a gun. "Here's a picture. Maybe I can make it bigger."

Beside her, Randy's eyes blazed with excitement.

It sure looked like him. Haughty. He had apparently been attacked by a rabid dinner napkin. She skimmed down the page. "Disappeared in 1811 while living at his London residence."

A sigh escaped her companion. He seemed to deflate.

"Want to find the next earl? Or the latest one?"

Shakily he got up and went to the kitchen. She killed the browser and followed. She found him sitting in a chair, staring around the kitchen with those big, dark eyes.

"Coffee?"

He looked at her as if she were speaking Chinese. At length he said, "Yes." When she had put coffee in front of them, he said, "I'm here."

"No kidding."

"Marooned." He stared at the coffee cup, or his hand, then around the kitchen again. "It never seemed quite real, you know. The television in the bedroom."

"Television isn't real," she said.

"It was always on. There was a whole world inside it, but I didn't quite believe."

"Thank God for that. What bedroom was this? Clay's?"

"The one before someone before him." Randy's hand made a circle. "She was an old woman with terrible arthritis. She owned the bed for forty years."

The doorbell rang. She paid for the Thai food and served it. Randy examined everything before he put it in his mouth.

"I thought incubuses don't eat."

"Incubi don't. I am apparently human," he said bemusedly. Looking at the stove he said, "I shall teach you to make Yorkshire pudding."

So he thought he'd be sticking around? "How come you're all frank and forthcoming about all this? I would think you'd be dying to get away. If your spell-curse-thingy is broken."

"Do you remember the first time you came for me?"

She bridled. Then she realized he referred to Clay's hotel room. "You were there. Like, poof."

"Momentarily. The merest breath. Then—er, poof—I was trapped again."

"You disappeared."

He held up a finger. "Then you returned. And again I am free."

"So? I thought you had to satisfy a hundred women."

"So it seemed. There was another woman between your visits." His eyes narrowed. "I suspect a sting in the tail of the curse."

This would be the pitch, the get-Randy-out-of-jail-free card. "And I care because?"

"One climax for you freed me for a few moments. The second has freed me for—" He glanced at the kitchen clock. "Six hours now."

"You think you're going to poof again?"

"I fear it. Once in bed—inside it, you understand—I am trapped. Until my hundredth woman frees me again." He raised his eyebrows and turned up a palm. "It would suit my magician-lover's sense of humor that I must please you and continue to please you for, oh, some fitting number of climaxes. One hundred, perhaps? A thousand?"

She let her chopsticks fall into her *pad thai*. "You're nuts."

"Probably. After two centuries in that bed I would defy anyone to remain in control of his faculties."

She didn't buy it. "I take my eye off you, you'll run away."

He said with decision, "Impossible, dear lady. I am, as the television says, your new best friend."

Her tingly bits were doing a conga dance. How long would it take him to give her a hundred orgasms?

Start thinking like a cop and not like a slut, fool. "Tomorrow morning you take me to Clay Dawes. Then we'll talk about the future."

He shook his head. "Clay was useful before you freed me. Now? He would be another slave driver, earning money while I languished in the bed awaiting your return."

"That wasn't a social invitation," she said sharply. "You're Clay's accomplice in an illegal scam."

He looked stiff, more like the guy in the 1811 portrait. "In what way is Clay's business fraudulent?"

She opened her mouth. "Because—he—because—"

"He promised a service and I rendered it."

"He claimed he had no accomplice!"

"He didn't know I was there. If anything, he has cause to complain of your destroying the source of his income."

"Now, wait a minute."

"You must be reasonable, Jewel. You freed me from the curse, liberated me from the bed, and now you have impounded it. You have cast doubt upon his honesty with the management of the hotel."

"This is the guy who could 'enslave' you! How come you're sticking up for him?"

"Merely, I point out that you may have no grounds on which to charge him."

She swallowed spicy shrimp. "Now, look. Regardless how hunky-dory and lovely this business you were engaged in—"

"I was not engaged in business. I was fulfilling my obligation to the curse."

"—You are coming with me to the police tomorrow. I will file a complaint against Clay for putting you in bed with me—or putting me in bed with you—and not telling me about you—"

"How could he have told you? He didn't know I was there."

"He's still responsible. He solicited payment for services rendered. He must have known there was something fishy going on. And if he didn't, he should have."

"Ask him."

"I intend to ask him. Even if you won't lead me to him."

"I don't know where he is."

"Then you'll sit it out in chokey until he turns up to exonerate you," she said implacably.

"No."

She stood up, put her knuckles on the table, and went nose to nose with him. "Yes."

"I d-don't want to be separated from you," he stammered.

She flushed. He so obviously didn't want to admit that to her. In the past hour his humble-slave-of-the-bed routine had faded and the buff bastard had started to show. But the more she talked about the cops, the more nervous he seemed. She felt weird, meeting his anxious eyes.

"Don't leave me," he whispered.

It was really, really hard to say, "I have to."

And then he vanished. His coffeecup tipped over,

spilling. His clothes—Clay Dawes's Hawaiian shirt and slacks—wilted slowly over the kitchen chair opposite her.

She put her hands over her mouth.

When she started breathing again, she said, "How the hell does he do that?"

She searched her apartment thoroughly. No Randy. She cleaned up the empty Thai food cartons.

"Typical male." She jammed dirty chopsticks into the takeout bag. "Claims he can't leave me and then he ups and leaves."

She went out on the balcony to watch traffic twinkle up at the night sky. Had he jumped off? From the twenty-third floor, he might have hit the river. She peered down, grossed out and feeling guilty. No ambulances swarmed below.

"Well," she said, "it's not many guys who can say they've dumped me before I dumped them." She stared down at the river, feeling hollow-hearted.

For a moment she regretted leaving Homonowoc, Wisconsin. All her kinks had started coming out when she moved to Chicago. How had she got stuck in this damned city anyway? A hundred miles away from the nearest farm boy with a clue.

A seagull screamed in the night. She stared up into the haze, colored pink and yellow by city lights. He could be up there somewhere, on a balcony above her.

She went in, slid the balcony door shut, and locked it. As an afterthought she put on the pole lock. He would have to smash the glass door to get in that way. She checked the locks on all the doors and windows.

It had been loads of fun doing him as a swan.

For two bits she would leave the balcony door unlocked.

She realized she was standing in the darkened apartment staring at the curtained balcony door and shook herself.

Four hours later she half woke from a dream of frenzied sex to find her own fingers buried inside her.

Whoa. That explained some things. "I've heard of sleepwalking," she said aloud, feeling her legs tremble. "And I've heard of sleeptalking." Gingerly she slid her hand free. Her wrist ached, and her whole body zinged with orgasmic aftershock. Her voice shook. "Gonna give myself carpal tunnel."

She breathed deeply, backing away from the intensity of her arousal.

The sound of her own voice reassured her. With a sigh, she rolled over, into the arms of her naked hunk.

"You're not awake," he whispered. "You only think you are."

"Mmmm." He was smooth all over, and his buns were marvelously made for grabbing. She grabbed. "Nice ass."

"Sleeptalking," he murmured with a smile in his voice.

She gasped. For some reason that smiling tone jerked her completely awake. In one bound she leaped backward out of bed, groping for the light switch on the wall.

And there he was again. Big as life and twice as naked.

She opened her mouth to scream.

He hung his head. There was no reason on earth why she shouldn't scream the building down, but he looked so resigned. So *this again*. He didn't move.

"Randy?"

The room seemed to get smaller when he turned his hot, black gaze on her. "Would it comfort you," he said in a sad voice, "to know that I am as frightened as you are?"

She shook her head wildly.

"No one but you knows who I am. No one but you knows I exist." Now he was scaring her for real. *Here come the threats.* "I'm alone, without a past, in a world I don't understand."

Her heart hammered so loudly she could barely hear him. "I don't want you following me around."

"What do you think will happen to me if you abandon me?"

What if she opened the door and told him to scram? She thought of homeless shelters. She thought of him trying to beg from strangers with his sucky fake humility. She thought of county lockup. She tried to imagine him flipping burgers and how-may-I-help-you-ing and couldn't. She thought of the lines at the Social Security office. Oh, right, he couldn't get relief, he didn't have a number. Good grief, he'd probably be jailed as an illegal immigrant, if they didn't decide he was a terrorist and ship him to Turkey for torture.

As she thought, he smiled with a light of hope in his eyes. She shivered. He folded his arms more securely around his knees, as if to say, *See, I'm not moving.* He looked happier and happier, and she was darned if she could tell why.

"Let's talk about sex," she said. Sex talk didn't bother her and it might push him off balance. "How did you get good at it?"

The tip of his tongue came out and touched his lips. "The first thing my mistress did? She sold the bed to a brothel."

Jewel raised her eyebrows. "Giving you a head start. She must not have hated you all that much."

"Think about it."

He watched her with that county fair judge look again. She considered. *How many prostitutes enjoy the sex they have?* According to the movies, prostitutes either love their jobs wildly, or they get forced into drug addiction and beaten to death by their customers or their pimps. Targets of casual violence. Unprotected by the law. Smile, honey, the johns like that. A brothel was probably full of satisfied men. But satisfied women?

Not so much of a head start after all. Huh. She felt a fresh respect for the vengeful mistress-magician.

"You had a bad time in the brothel."

He tested her silently with his eyes.

"How many?" she said softly.

"How many women did I satisfy in that house of hell?" he said, his voice finally seeming to slip away from his control. "From the brothel, none. Not one." He said slowly, "You may well imagine—perhaps you see that most women like to experience me as the embodiment of a fantasy. I've spent two hundred years learning to please my, how do you put it, my target market."

She let out a bark of laughter. "Why tell me about the brothel?"

"The perfect woman for what I am is alone. She is a widow who did not particularly enjoy her husband. Or she is an older spinster. And she'd best be middle class. My grandfather cursed the middle class and my great-great-grandfather was middle class and my whole education was built upon a pretense that I am of noble blood. But rich women don't need me. They can buy fantasies in the flesh. Poor women don't trust me. They still believe in the devil and, besides, they can't afford a brass bed."

This practical summation left her speechless.

"I whisper to them in their sleep, as I whisper to you. I see their dreams, their desires. The way a woman reacts about the brothel helps to guide me toward what she wants. If she is titillated, we embark on her fantasies about whoredom. If she is disgusted, I skip to stories about women of better class. If she doesn't notice—" he made a face, and Jewel knew that he had been judging her after all.

"What would you have thought if I hadn't caught that? The part about how you flopped in the brothel." He watched her with caution. "I'm way off the script, aren't I?" She laughed shakily. She wanted to get away from this guy and think.

As if he had heard the thought, he reached for her hand. She let him take it. His hand was warm and gentle and strong.

"I need you, Jewel. I need you more than you need me. You can't make a mistake. Only I can."

Something in her chest turned over. "Is this another test?"

"It's the truth." His gaze wavered a little. He wasn't quite telling the truth.

"And also a test?"

He said with care, "I'm learning how you will define the boundaries of our contact. Whether I lie, or bluster, or sneak, or throw myself at your feet with my belly exposed, you hold all the cards. The sooner I know the rules, your rules, the sooner I can satisfy you." The truth of his words flew out and punched her across the heart. "Stay here tonight," he begged. "In this bed. I shan't touch you. If I can't convince you that I can be trusted, I fail."

In his lean face, his great black eyes were stark with desperation.

Against her better judgment she said, "All right."

Jewel didn't sleep much. She lay on her side curled up against the head of the bed, staring into the dark at Randy's pale shape at the foot. She'd asked him not to disappear. When you have a magical guest in your bed, it's nice to know exactly where he is.

He wouldn't talk. "Sleep. You need your rest, working girl."

God, he had a fascinating voice. She could have listened to him talk all night, if she hadn't been dead beat plus frantic not to jump his bones. *Do I want him?* She was slippery and swollen with *yes*. But good grief, a sex demon? *I must be crazy. I should buy a gun. I'll be lucky to survive the night. The super will break down the door in two months and find my rotting corpse.*

No. He wanted something from her too badly.

He wants to satisfy me.

Well, bully, I want him to satisfy me, too. I want to do fun things with him all night long. Her eyes drifted shut in spite of themselves. Gradually the dim, fuzzy image of Randy sitting naked at the foot of her bed became the dim, smoky image of Randy in an old-fashioned tux saying, *Please take off your clothes. You are so beautiful naked.* His eyes were big and black and beseeching. She was already naked.

But she reached up to her bare shoulders and slid off a little strap of skin, all studded with pearls, and he seemed to melt into a puddle of gratitude. She felt the melting. She felt him reach out to her and she let the strap of her skin fall. Underneath her skin she was a blaze of diamonds or scintillating yellow sunlight or the cold blast of moonbeams on water, God what a relief to be free of her skin, and the light flickered and played over his face and the pristine white and black of his old-fashioned tux, and his hand reached for her, and he touched her with one finger right on her naked heart.

She woke up. Her heart was hammering in her chest. Her pulse made hissing noises in her ears. She blinked and sat up, backing up until she felt the headboard against her spine.

His dim, pale form sat crosslegged against the foot of the bed, his eyes closed. While she watched, pinching herself to wake up, his eyes opened.

He didn't say anything.

You did that! she would have accused, if she could speak.

Her heart heated up her whole chest, like a furnace door, opened and flaming hot inside. She wanted to say, *Don't do that.* But his face grew sad, so she didn't.

She lay down and curled her body around a pillow at the head of the bed again. She pulled the coverlet over her ears, leaving only her eyes exposed. He watched her for a long minute, then closed his eyes again.

He's still watching me. Just, he's watching me in my dreams.

On that disturbing and impossible thought, she shut her own eyes, gritting her teeth against the dream.

At dawn she looked for him and saw him still sitting there, his head thrown back against the footboard of her bed, his mouth open, snoring.

She slid to the edge of the bed, feeling stiff all over from her cramped sleeping position, and backed away.

As she got farther from the bed, he tipped over in his sleep and curled up on his side. And, as she watched, he faded from view.

"I am totally losing my marbles." Gingerly she tugged at the coverlet. It slipped lightly off the bed. She made the bed as if she were setting a bear trap.

He stayed gone.

She put on her swimsuit and shorts with the minimum of noise. It was tempting to go back and prod the empty air over the bed. See if she could feel him this time. She didn't try it. Last night was enough freak-out.

On a last compassionate thought, she brought a cup of hot coffee with cream and sugar into the bedroom and put a plate over the top to keep it warm. Nobody in there. The coverlet was wrinkle-free. Feeling crazy, she slipped out of the apartment and headed for the lake.

Jewel's hands were cold. She swam steadily along the Olive Park Beach, pacing herself, listening for the chug of a motorboat or the squeal of a Jet Ski. Her legs churned water and her shoulders pulled deep and clean. Long, slow swells of cold water rolled her gently forward, heartbeat slow. She felt as if she were paddling on the bosom of the world.

It felt good to work her hips as hard as she wanted, dig deep with her arms, swivel her whole body at every stroke. Most of the day she had to act smaller than she was, to keep people comfortable. In the water she could let herself be big.

Her skin talked back to the cold, cold lake. She hadn't felt this good in months.

If I were stupid, I'd come out here at night and skinny-dip. Imagine how dark and quiet. Through her goggles she stared down into the depths, wishing they were blacker.

Layers of smells lay on the water. Every time she breathed, her stroking arm pulled smells down to her: dead fish, live fish, bus exhaust, dark chocolate from cacao beans roasting at the Blommer's plant a mile west, and the sweet exhalation of the lake itself washing back and forth, playing tag with an offshore breeze.

A great vibrating honk crossed the water to her. *Tour boat coming up the lakefront. Time to quit.* She turned over on her back, took a bearing on the shore, and lazed, looking at the sky.

Here came the Darth Vader tower, poking into her field of vision to her right, across the street from her office. On the left, the Gotham condos. West, south, north, there was no edge to humanity, only a fractal diminishing of skyscrapers, housing developments, and strip malls, crawling like cancer into the cornfields.

Right here, at the lake, the works of man came to a stop.

Her dipping hand touched sand, and she rolled over on all fours, shook herself like a dog, and stood up, grateful for the warm air. She took a long last look at the endless nothing of the great cold sweet-water lake, then picked up her towel.

Olive Park Beach's Thursday lifeguard was coming on duty as she shoved into her shorts and sneakers and unlocked her bike.

"Hey, Brad. Was The Little Corporal open?"

He waved a white paper bag. She pedaled over to him and handed him three bucks.

"What do you think?" he said, looking out at the water.

"Sixty-six degrees." She shoved half a cinnamon cake doughnut, still sizzling hot from the fryer, into her mouth. Bliss.

"That's not what the weather service says." He dipped into his own paper bag.

"Weather service is an ass," she said around the doughnut.

"Yup."

He turned away and she mounted her bike. Brad knew exactly when and how he wanted to deal with people. If he were straight, she would have dated him by now.

She scoped his butt from behind and pursed her lips to whistle, then caught herself in shock.

What was that about? She'd always been a horndog, but she'd never bothered making passes at gay men before.

Shaking her head, she pedaled slowly south along the lake path to the river mouth, crossed Lake Shore Drive, shouldered her bike, and climbed the long flights of steps to the pedestrian way.

While she moved west toward home, the whole city moved east. Traffic picked up on Wacker Drive. Inches above the opaque green river, a pair of Canada geese flew toward the lake, occasionally slapping the surface with a big, rubbery, black foot, or raising rings with a wingtip. A tour boat chugged after them, full of fools wearing inadequate sunscreen who waved madly to her from their rooftop seats. She waved back.

She was letting another bite of cinnamon doughnut melt on her tongue when her cell rang.

"Heiss."

Ed barked, "What's this expense report you turned in? Seven hundred dollars? Three hundred fifty dollars per day? You're not on taxis to fucking Argentina!"

"Ed, I had to—"

"And I don't see nothin' about the genie-in-the-bottle guy. You turn in one deli—"

"Ed."

"—You flop on the genie-bottle guy—"

"I know where to fi—"

"And now you expect the department to pay for—"

"Ed, you know darned well those charges are for Nina's sex therapist. I had to go undercover."

"Jesus Mary and Joseph. You undercover. I got gray hairs from your last undercover job. Don't bother coming in this morning. Find this genie guy."

"All right, all right." She hauled the bike up the stairs to McClurg and headed for home, the phone glued to her ear.

"And what about this sex therapist?" he said, swerving back to his obsession.

You could have asked me that yesterday. "He's hiding. I've put a cork in his operation. We'll see if that flushes him."

"I'd like to put a cork in his—" He grunted. "Keep an eye on my wife."

"Don't have to, Ed. I told you, the guy's out of business."

"He can still fuck her!"

"He never fucked her. At least," Jewel said scrupulously, "I highly doubt he did. He's too cagey. And she told me no. She doesn't lie to me."

"The hell she doesn't." But Ed fell silent.

"She wants the best for both of you," Jewel said. "If you'd only talk. Openly," she added, thinking of Ed and Britney. She remembered the extra-bright look in Nina's eyes in the Coq d'Or. "She's hurting."

He uttered a weak expletive and hung up.

She felt totally icked out. She was getting deeper into the mire of their marriage. But family wasn't all lasagna on Sundays. A certain amount of ick came with the territory.

She tried Clay Dawes, both at the Drake and on his cellphone. When that flopped, she stood on one pedal at the Sheraton's esplanade, listening to the gulls yiping over the river, and bit her lip.

"Call me stupid," she said aloud and punched the speed dial on her cell. "Nina?"

Nina opened on the attack. "There you are! What happened with you and that bed of Clay's? I'm not your friend anymore? You don't tell me stuff anymore? You hate me now."

"I don't hate you. Let's talk about Ed."

"You hate me because I'm an adulteress."

"I don't think you're an adulteress."

"You were in that bed."

"I'm not going to talk about the bed."

"Okay, I'm not going to talk about Ed."

Jewel paused for breath. It would be smart to stop here. But she could hear pain in Nina's brash, aggressive voice. She felt the quicksand sucking at her heels. She crossed Michigan, took the stairs down to Lower Mich past the Billy Goat, walked her bike around hunky truck drivers unloading liquor boxes and copier paper, and doglegged to Rush and Kinzie, smiling at a construction worker sweating over his jackhammer while Upper Mich roared overhead and pigeon shit crunched under her tires.

Nina broke the standoff. "I need you to help me get this bed away from Clay."

"Whaaat?"

"I deserve something for twenty-two years of bullshit. You won't begrudge that to me."

"I can't steal this guy's property."

"So bust him. Confiscate it."

"If I confiscate it, it's evidence. Property of the city."

"Which you can get at if you want. So it falls off the back of the truck on the way to the impound."

Jewel sputtered. "You are—you want me to—"

"I'd hate to get you fired over this. Fourth of July's

coming up. Basil polenta. Cannoli. That bread pudding you love."

She rolled her eyes. This was so Nina. "No."

"Ty's kids will be there. They love their Auntie Jewel."

Quicksand to the knees. "You won't get me fired."

She wrestled her bike up the steps and into the Corncob Building from the Hubbard Street side.

"You are gonna help me get that bed. I need it. I deserve it," Nina pleaded, and Jewel couldn't argue. "Unless," her tone turned sinister with suspicion, "you want to keep it yourself."

Jewel's mouth opened to deny the charge and the breath stopped in her lungs. *Is that true?*

Nina pounced. "I knew it. I should never have sent you up there."

"No, please, wait. Have you talked to that guy?"

"The guy in the bed? Uh, we don't talk, actually. Did he look like Russell Crowe for you? Half the time I thought he looked like Russell Crowe, and the other times he was all over the place."

Jewel felt the last of her self-control slip away. "More Hugh Jackman-ish."

Nina said avidly, "How was the sex, by the way? You never said."

Jewel lowered her voice in the echoey lobby. "Oh God," she admitted.

"He's something, isn't he?"

"Amazing." She felt a flood of lust and an overwhelming urge for girl-talk. "I have never, ever, *ever*. Oh God."

"Better than Chad and Nathan?"

Jewel lowered her voice. "Miles better. Light years."
Plus, he says I own him. He wants to give me a hundred orgasms. She didn't want to think about how this made her feel, all runny and fierce and guilty.

"So you see why I need him," Nina said in a too-breezy tone.

"You can't take him."

"Why not? Clay has no clue what that bed is. You're not gonna fight me for him, are you? That's not fair. You're twenty-five, you're gorgeous, you got all these men after you. I'm an old bag."

"Nina—"

"What do I have to look forward to? Thirty more years of Ed's infidelities. I'm not dead yet. I got needs."

"What about his needs?" she burst out. "Why should this guy be stuck in this bed for another thirty years," she hissed, rolling the bike into a corner, "because you want a sex slave?" Just saying those words made her zing all over.

"Admit it, you want him, too."

Jewel bit her lip. "No—"

"I knew it. You'd love to have a sex slave."

"I'm not proud of that feeling. I won't act on it."

"Well, I can't afford your scruples," Nina said. "We both want him. I saw him first, and my need is greater because I'm married and Ed doesn't want me anymore."

"Oh, Nina." *If you told Nina about the curse and the hundred women, that would trump her claim*, whispered her evil, slutty, covetous soul. "I don't think it's that bad."

"Huh. If it gets any better I may kill myself. Don't tell the kids I said that," Nina said quickly. "I'm letting off steam. It's been two days since I had a treatment and Ed was such a bastard this morning and Clay won't schedule me."

"He won't?" Finally, something was going right.

"I'm going crazy, I tell you."

"Well, don't—don't do anything drastic, okay? I know you're fed up, and in your shoes I guess I would be, too—"

"Why? What do you know?" Nina was way too sharp. "You work with Ed. Who's he screwing?"

"Oh, for Pete's sake," Jewel said uneasily. Quicksand over the ankles.

"He's lucky I don't do a Lorena Bobbitt on him."

"Nothing drastic," she repeated. "You hear me?"

Nobody was in the lobby. She wheeled her bike onto the elevator and punched TWENTY-THREE.

"Make you a deal," Nina said, filling her with dread. "You stop Ed from screwing around, I'll let you have the bed. You still have to get it away from Clay, mind."

Jewel lied. "I can't do that."

"You mean you won't." A sound came through the phone like Nina sighing or dragging on a cigarette and whooshing out smoke. "All right. I don't want you getting fired. I'll deal with this myself."

Jewel shut her eyes. "Thank you."

"See you for Sunday dinner?"

Jewel sighed. *Still family.* "I'll bring the wine."

Alone with the bitter certainty that Ed was doing some slut at the office, Nina tried Clay's cellphone again. No answer. "He's avoiding me," she said aloud. Tears filled her eyes. This wouldn't have happened if she hadn't introduced Clay to Jewel. At least Jewel still loved her.

Hm. Ed could stonewall her, but Jewel was the weak link. If she could put more pressure on Clay from that end.

After some thought, Nina drove to the pay phone at the convenience store down the street.

A receptionist answered, "Department of Consumer Services, Chief Attorney's office."

"Yes, I'd like to make an anonymous citizen's complaint."

As Jewel unlocked her apartment door she wondered if she'd made it all up.

No. No way. The hotel manager had seen him. Britney and Digby and Ed had seen him.

And now she saw Randy, big as life, wrapped in her kimono, sitting at her computer.

"What are you doing?"

He looked up with a joyful face. "You came back!" In that moment she knew he'd been honest with her.

She went hot with lust and embarrassment.

Nina's right. I own him and I love it. Yesterday I was scared shitless, thinking he would never leave me alone.

"Duh, I live here. You disappeared this morning, what's with that?"

"Mm?" He stared at the screen, clicking away. "I seem to have retained some of my, er, demonic characteristics."

"Hey, are you buying stuff on Amazon?" She looked closer at the computer screen. "Using my account?"

"I don't have an account with them," he said mildly. "Look, they have a history of Welsh titles. I was able to find a chapter mentioning my disappearance! The computational device tells me I can receive the book in two days with expedited delivery."

She hit the power button. "Expedite this, dude. You do not spend other people's money. In any century." She grabbed him by the ear and towed him to the bedroom. "Come on, get your clothes on. Obviously I can't let you out of my sight."

With a big sigh, he said, "I have been saying so."

He threw off the kimono and she felt every nerve in her body jump a foot forward. Wow.

"Uh, I'll go make some coffee for the road."

Gloriously naked, he turned toward her with a wistful look. His cock stuck out at her like a flagpole. She swallowed.

"Get dressed." She shut the door on her way out.

Her cell rang. Ed again. "Get the hell up here. Taylor wants to see us. We got a meeting in twenty minutes."

"What about the genie guy?"

"Later. Meet me in my office and we'll go up to the chief's office together."

She decided she couldn't bring Randy into the office again. As she drove she tried to explain the basics about twenty-first-century property law, personal credit, and identity.

"I need some of that," he said. "Identity."

"We'll get to that. Today I just hope to get you dressed."

She found parking under the viaduct where Lake Shore passed over Illinois Street. She told him to wait for her there.

"Don't get out of the car. Don't talk to anyone. Don't mess with the car."

He smiled at her.

"Here, educate yourself." She got a pile of newspapers out of the back seat and dropped them on the driver's seat. "I won't be long."

As she walked across Lower Lake Shore and Illinois,

she tried Clay Dawes's cellphone. No luck. Then she tried the Drake. The operator made her wait, then told her Clay wasn't in, which was clearly a lie. She left a message calculated to terrify him and marched into the Kraft Building.

In the office, Ed was in a swivet. They took the elevator to meet with the chief attorney.

"Don't say nothing about anything relating to something that might pertain to nobody. I'll do the talking. Not a word about—you know," Ed said, looking gray.

"I wasn't going to." He looked more frazzled than usual. "You okay, boss?" she said as they trooped into the chief attorney's office.

"Ed. Ms. Heiss." Sampson Taylor made it short and sweet. "Somebody called in an anonymous complaint today about a con artist running the lonely hearts scam out of The Drake Hotel. The informant says he's using magic to, ah, meet her needs. She says he has eighteen or twenty regular customers. Shouldn't be hard to prove, if he's getting that amount of traffic in and out."

She swallowed.

"Does she say he screws her?" Ed blurted. After a silence he added, "Does he give her drugs?"

"She denies it. No drugs either. She says it's magic." The chief attorney looked sour. "The mayor will not be happy. He's worried about this genie. The commissioner—"

He left the commissioner's remarks to be inferred. Pretty much the entire department shared an understanding of the commissioner, who dwelt with the mayor and the rest of the city's upper management on the fifth floor at City Hall, rather than down in the hinky trenches of the Kraft Building.

"How come you got the call?" she said and Ed glared at her.

"She phoned my office. My assistant took the complaint."

So Nina's playing hardball.

Ed cleared his throat. "Di—did you talk to her?"

"She wouldn't talk to me. Wanted to confide in a woman." Taylor set the file aside. "Then there's this genie salesman."

"I almost got him the other day, sir," she said. "He, uh, promised a guy he could get him into the movies." She would have to tap dance a bit to keep from identifying Buzz.

Taylor rolled his eyes. "I need material facts, Ms. Heiss," he said, and she shut up. He looked at Ed. "Hinky Corners is your division. Whatever I may think of Policy, we're stuck with it. Shut 'em down if you can get material facts. If you can't—or if the facts play too tabloid—" His lips pressed together. Taylor was the straightest arrow in the department. She knew it killed him to say things like *hush it up*. "Do your best." He spoke to Ed, but his eyes went to her.

"Yes, sir," Ed said.

"Yes, sir," she said.

Taylor nodded. He handed the file to Ed.

They left.

In the elevator, Ed handed Jewel the file. "This is your fault," he grumbled. "If you'da kept my wife out of trouble, she wouldn't of called this in over my head."

"Ed, I can't be in the middle on this anymore."

He grunted. "Who you working for? Her or me?"

She met his eyes. "Who has us both by the balls?"

He stomped out of the elevator. Reluctantly she followed him into his office.

"It's like this," she said as she closed the door. "I think she means well. She loves you a lot. She—"

"She's spendin' all my money on a sex therapist," he spat.

"I shut him down. That's over," Jewel said, hoping it was true. "But it would help if you met her halfway, know what I'm saying?" She wouldn't say Britney's name aloud, but jeez.

He chewed. "No."

"C'mon. You hit on me my first week in the office," she said, hoping Nina hadn't made that part up. "I wasn't the first or the last." She watched the boss's face swell up and turn red. *Nina's right again. Hell.* "Be a pro, boss."

"I'll tell you professionalism, missy," he said, jamming a forefinger into the desk. "Professionalism is stayin' out of your supervisor's private personal confidential off-limits none-a-your-beeswax business!"

"So I don't have to follow your wife around or keep her from getting back at you for the Britneys?"

He slapped his hand down on the desk. "Ow! Ow, ow."

"What you're trying to tell me is," she said, having made her point, "you want me to keep this story out of the papers and keep Nina's name out of my reports."

"Fucking stapler. Ow. And get my money back!"

She thought she had a pretty good chance of connecting with Clay Dawes again, since she'd impounded his "treatment" bed. "I'll give it a shot, boss. But without material facts—"

"So get some!"

"Talk to her, will you?"

"You talk to her. Talk sense to her. Tell her if I get fired over this, it's no more meal ticket, *capisce*?"

She backed to the door, nodding. "Yeah, yeah."

"Christ, she phoned in a complaint over my fucking head!"

She put her finger to her lips. "Catch you tomorrow."

Ed glared her out the door.

She slunk out of the office, past flapping ears and grins from the other investigators.

It didn't look good. Nina had gone too far. Of Ed's fifty-seven unfavorite things, getting reamed by the chief attorney was high on the list, right under a ream job from the commissioner. Maybe worse, since Taylor was not a political appointee and therefore actually gave a hoot about the work.

I'm making things worse, she mourned. *What if they get a divorce? What if he fires me?*

Of the two, she thought she'd prefer to be fired. Even if Ed kicked her out of her job, Nina would still have her over to Sunday dinner.

When Clay walked into the treatment room on Thursday and found it empty, he knew. Jewel Heiss was holding the brass bed hostage. Plus the front desk had handed him a dozen irate messages from her.

So when his cell rang he answered without thinking.

"I want that bed," Nina Neccio said without so much as *hello*.

"I don't have it anymore," he blurted.

He heard Nina gasp. "That scheming bitch!"

So much for keeping that cat in the bag. "I should never have left it alone with her," he said.

"Why not?" Nina said, turning on a dime to attack him. "She's an honest person. Unlike some people I could name. Where do you suppose she put it?"

"God knows. How did she get it out of the room is what I want to know." He heard a sound and turned to see a piece of paper slide under the door. With a sense of doom he opened it. His hotel bill. His credit card must be close to maxing out. Five figures, ouch. "I think I know what happened to it."

"What? Where is it? I'll help you get it back!"

"I'm sure you would." He crossed to the window and looked down. Yep, Nina stood there on the sidewalk below, looking up at him. He waved. "But I'm busy this afternoon. Hang in there another day or so, okay? Talk to you soon." He hung up.

She gestured up at him in Italian. He waved again.

"Don't hate me, Nina," he murmured.

After five minutes talking to the hotel manager, he banged the house phone down in a rare state of rage.

They had his bed. Worse, they had his money. Now he couldn't pay his credit card bill.

The house phone rang. "Mr. Dawes, another call from Jewel Heiss," the operator said.

"Thank you, no, keep holding my calls."

He ground his teeth.

Jewel crossed Peshtigo Street with her phone in her hand and murder in her heart. "He can run," she promised herself, "but he can't hide. I've got what he wants."

She had left Randy in the car under the northbound Lake Shore viaduct, but as she came around the corner, she spotted him leaning up against the viaduct outside the tiny lot, reading the paper.

I told him to stay in the car!

He looked hot in Clay's beach-bum clothes. As she thought this, he looked up, and she felt a bolt of heat-lightning zing her through the ying-yang. She walked toward him in a dream.

What happened next came nightmare-slowly.

Every vehicle in sight started honking its horn.

She turned her head.

A taxi screeched the wrong way, southbound, down the northbound ramp to Lake Shore, and cornered squealing onto Illinois, again going the wrong way.

She was crossing Lower Lake Shore smack in its path.

Stunned, moving automatically, she noticed there wasn't anybody in the car.

Randy ran forward, grabbed a big metal wastebasket off the curb, and threw it in front of the taxi.

She heard herself scream in slow motion. "Noooo!"

The basket jammed under the front bumper of the taxi. The taxi slowed, though its engine screamed as though the pedal were to the metal. The wastebasket threw sparks.

The taxi hit Randy and tossed him into the middle of the street. He landed horridly limp and rolled to her feet.

The taxi hit the viaduct pillar. With a sucking *whump*, it burst into flames.

She came out of her dream.

Cars screeched to a stop in front of Randy's body.

She knelt beside him. Her heart pounded in her throat. "Are you okay? Randy?" *Oh God, he's only been outside a couple of days!* "Randy!"

He groaned. When he took her hand to pull himself upright, he hissed.

"That hurt!" he said, sounding betrayed.

"Duh. You maniac," she said. Her voice was shaky with relief. "Can you walk?" She helped him to the car. "We'll go to the hospital and get you x-rayed. Right now."

He complained, "When they do it on TV they don't get hurt."

Her legs were weak with too-late panic. "Welcome to life outside the tube." He was scuffed up and filthy and there was blood on each knee and each elbow and more blood on his left cheekbone, but he was moving. "Any bones broken?"

"I don't believe so." He frowned as if he hurt.

Ohmigod, ohmigod. "Are you sure?"

He pulled himself upright and leaned against the car.

She took a moment to lean against the car, too, feeling nauseous. "That was horrible. Don't ever do that again." Her heart hammered harder, as if it had finally caught up with the action. "Ugh, I think I'm gonna fwow up." She was ice cold. She shut her eyes and breathed deeply.

Warmth wrapped around her. She opened her eyes to find Randy pulling her off the Tercel's fender, into his arms. "Shh," he murmured against her hair. "Don't fwow up."

She heard sirens in the distance. His warmth penetrated her arms, her back, everywhere he touched her. The urge to vomit receded. She tried a few more deep breaths. "Are you okay?"

"Did it work?" a familiar voice said gleefully behind Randy.

She opened her eyes to see Buzz beaming at her.

Randy turned his head, looking annoyed. "Yes, well done. You may go now." He waved a lordly hand.

"That was so excellent!" Buzz said, apparently thrilled to see her in Randy's arms. "Like I promised. Wishes granted!"

Buzz. Genie.

She pushed Randy away. "What. The. Hell." She looked into her car and saw an open liquor bottle sitting on the passenger seat with shreds of gold foil sticking to its neck. She looked at Randy. "What did you do?"

He raised his eyebrows. "This fellow happened by while I waited for you. He offered to sell me a magic bottle containing a wish-granting djinn."

"And you bought it? With what? You don't have any money!"

"There was money in a little metal pocket in the car."

She plunged through the passenger window and pulled open the dashboard ashtray. "My meter money!" She stood up again to glare at him. "What did you ask for?"

Randy looked sheepish.

"He said you don't appreciate him," Buzz said reprovingly. "He said you question his devotion to you. He asked the genie for a chance to prove how important you are to him." Buzz fawned on Randy. "That was soooo romantic."

The taxi blazed merrily in the street behind Randy and Buzz. Tourists stopped in the Navy Pier crosswalk to rubberneck. A badly shaven guy in bedroom slippers came flapping around the corner of the Darth Vader tower. He stopped when he saw the fire, sat down on the pavement, and wailed like a baby.

Buzz sniffled. "It's never worked so good before."

Jewel stabbed an arm in the direction of the blaze. "Dammit, Buzz! You made a huge mess! You scared the crap out of me! Both of you!" She rounded on Randy. "I'll deal with you later." To Buzz she said, "What the heck is this?" She reached into the car. "Alcohol? Buzz, you're underage."

"It's Drambuie. This is so cool," Buzz enthused, his zits glowing in the light of the burning taxi. "I copied the sultan's seal off the bottle, and then I took it to Swiftyprint and made up a couple of sheets in gold foil. I sell the bottle—customer opens it—out comes the genie—grants the customer his wish—I open a fresh bottle—back the genie comes like a boomerang—wham, I cork the fresh bottle and slap a new seal on it—ready to sell again! I knew you would be proud of me."

"Proud of you." She was speechless.

A fire truck sirened up Illinois through the intersection, swerved north, and blocked Lower Lake Shore. Hoses deployed. Cop cars converged. She got that old familiar get-me-out-of-here feeling. *I love the city. It's people I can't stand.*

"Well, hello, handsome," a female voice said behind them. "What happened to your poor face?"

Jewel swivelled her head so fast she got whiplash. Britney. She'd better get Buzz out of here before Britney connected him with the genie.

"A disagreement with yon flaming chariot," Randy said like a caveman shrugging off the woolly mammoth on the end of his spear.

Britney cooed, "Oooooh. Did you ever get your medallion straightened out?"

Buzz sidled up to Jewel and wiggled his sandy eyebrows. "You saw how good it works."

Jewel grabbed his shoulder. "It does not work 'good.' It works 'bad-ly.' As in cat-a-stro-phi-cally. You destroyed this guy's cab. You held up traffic, nearly killed poor Randy here—"

To her annoyance, poor Randy was chuckling at Britney.

"I'm supporting myself," Buzz said. "I thought you'd be proud of me."

Digby strode up to them, lifting his chin jealously at Randy. "Who is this guy, anyway?"

"Now beat it before I have to tell some cop about your you-know-what," she told Buzz. She turned to the next disaster. "Britney, what are you doing out of the office?"

Britney stuck her tits out proudly. Randy smiled. Digby scowled. "I'm an investigator now," she said.

"You're what?" Jewel said. "I mean, congratulations, when did that happen?"

"Well—" Britney brushed past Randy with a thirty-eight-double-D apology and went tête-à-tête with Jewel. "I've been angling for this forever. You know I hate office work."

"Yeah."

"So Ed finally made it official. I'm riding along with

Digby for a week, then I get to start training." Britney gurgled, "Isn't it great?"

Jewel shot a look at the men.

"Yo, turkey," Digby said, jinking his shoulder and jerking a thumb. "Back off." Boy, hanging with Britney was sure making Digby more assertive.

"I fail to take your meaning," Randy said in a snotty voice.

Jewel whispered to Britney, "Did you screw Ed for a promotion?"

Britney said haughtily, "So you're better than me?" At Jewel's scowl, she added, "We assumed you did Ed, but you were too discreet to say so."

Jewel's eyes bulged. "What? Who's 'we'?"

"Us girls." Britney tossed her big hair. "Well, of course we all know you're the real office slut, the slut-de-la-sluts, I mean nobody else actually does all that stuff. And I thought, Here's Digby with no partner, and Ed seemed loose at the moment, so why not make the play?"

"Digby's on target investigations." The identity theft case!

"I know. Cool, huh?"

Jewel tried to think of some way to say it tastefully. "Britney, Ed's married."

Britney waggled like an affronted duck. "He was married when you came along."

"I did not—" Jewel lowered her voice. "I did not screw Ed. He's married. He's my boss." She hadn't even noticed him making a pass, sheesh. *I was young and lonely and so dumb that when he said, "Come to dinner with me," I thought he meant come over to his house and meet his family.*

"You know what?" Britney was mad now. "There's a

word for people like you. It's hypocrite." She narrowed her eyes. "Maybe you need therapy."

Jewel drew back, shocked. "I didn't mean—"

"So don't be mean. I'm trying to advance myself. You're jealous 'cuz you're in Hinky Corners. Admit it," Britney choked. "Admit it, so we can still be friends."

Jewel simmered down. *I can't afford to lose a friend. Not even a fluffy bunny like Britney.* "I admit it. I'm sorry."

"Well, okay then." With a sniff, Britney said, "Come on, Digby. Let's bust some real criminals."

Jewel worked her jaw. "Let's get out of here," she said to Randy.

Naturally it wasn't that easy. Randy got into the car carefully. Cracked ribs, she guessed, but she was so mad at him she decided she wouldn't ask him until he broke down and confessed he was in pain. The fire went out, the cops let the gridlocked cars trickle on, a tow truck came for the wreck, and the luckless cabby was put into a squad car, weeping. She killed time by trying to phone Clay Dawes at the Drake and telling Randy what she thought of his efforts to roam twenty-first-century Chicago without a leash.

Her cellphone rang at the moment when the cops let her slip onto the southbound Lake Shore ramp and out of the nutso zone.

"Yeah, hey, good to reach you," Clay said, sounding over-relaxed as usual. "You stole my bed, you vixen you."

She felt her blood pressure rise with an eardrum-popping thump at the sound of his voice. "It's impounded. I warned you I would."

"Really?" Clay said, sounding only mildly curious. "On what legal grounds?"

She hunkered down over the phone. "Because you're running a scam? Because you're either selling sex or you're offering sex-slash-psychiatric services without a license?" Her voice rose. "Because it's a *fake* and you have an *accomplice* and I have him here in my car *right this minute*?"

"Really?" Clay said again in exactly the same disinterested tone, as if he was only flirting, as if he could listen to her voice all day no matter what nonsense she spouted.

Her skin tingled on a rush of rage. "Yes, really. Someone," she said with relish, "lodged an anonymous complaint against you with the Department of Consumer Services."

Clay clicked his tongue. "That Nina. She didn't believe me when I told her I can't offer her a treatment right now."

Jewel swallowed. *That Nina. Think I'll kill her.* "It doesn't matter who complained, buddy. You're under official scrutiny now." One thing was true, unfortunately. If Nina wouldn't come forward, Jewel had no case.

As if he heard that thought, Clay drawled, "If your anonymous complainer shows up, I'll refund her payment. Money-back guarantee, like I told you. Or was it you who complained?" His tone turned sympathetic and she decided to kill Clay first. "The treatment can't work for everybody. Frigidity is a terrible thing, can come from many caus—"

"I am *not frigid*, you *son of a bitch*!" she screamed into the phone, and the tourists in the next lane rolled up their window.

She had been working her way north and west toward the Drake, but now she turned south on Michigan.

Breathing hard, she said, "Meet me at Field's in half an hour. The least you can do is buy your poor accomplice some clothes of his own."

Silence from the phone. "I still don't understand this stuff about an accomplice," Clay said, and for once he didn't sound smug. He sounded tense. "I don't get it."

"You will. Men's haberdashery, first floor of Marshall Field's on Wabash, half an hour. Be there or kiss your bed goodbye." She punched the OFF button with vicious satisfaction.

They drove in silence into the Loop. When she felt cooler, she turned to Randy. "Will you testify against him?"

"Do you think my testimony will weigh with lordship?"

"Huh?"

"In a court of law. Who am I?" Randy said, sounding bleak. "In legal terms?"

She opened her mouth. *You're a nutcase*, she thought. That would go over big at a hearing. She couldn't reveal where she'd found him. Her orders were clear. Suppress the hinky stuff. And she'd have to be darned careful introducing Randy to Clay. If she told the truth, Clay would only sneer. *I suck at undercover.*

Feeling trembly inside her chest, she screeched the car up a parking ramp next to Field's.

"Who am I, Jewel?" Randy said again. When she glanced over at him she imagined she saw his soul in his eyes, and she nearly creamed the fender against the curving ramp wall.

"You're a guy with no clean pants. Let's go shopping."

CHAPTER

17

Again with the accomplice, Clay fumed, putting his phone in his pocket. She was making him crazy. Plus she'd done something with the bed, with his profits stuffed up its legs.

He debated calling the old man. That would necessitate explaining how he'd got the bed impounded, how the repeater had gone bad on him, how he'd lost his money and might not be able to pay his credit card bill—let's see, how many of Virgil's wise words had he ignored so far?

He took a breath so deep it made him light-headed.

Instead of calling Virgil, he took the bus to State Street.

Jewel the cop-ette was waiting for him near ties and wallets on the first floor of Field's. Clay hung back, scoping for more cops. So far so good. She seemed to be checking out the rear end of a big, scruffy-looking guy in a pair of tan chinos and a ragged Hawaiian shirt. Hey.

"Hey, isn't that my shirt?"

The guy turned and saw Clay. He pointed. Jewel turned.

Clay sauntered toward them feeling perplexed and annoyed. "Ms. Heiss. More beautiful than ever, I see."

"Mr. Dawes." She nodded. "Meet your accomplice, Randy."

The big guy looked down a long nose at Clay. "Randolph Llew Carstairs Athelbury Darner."

Clay looked him up and down. "Gesundheit. Aren't those my clothes you're wearing? What did you do, wrestle gators in 'em?"

"He has no clothes," she said tartly. "As you should know."

"Gosh, you're hot in polyester, babe. Dude, what's this line you're handing my girl about you and me?" he said to the big guy. "I've never seen you in my life."

"Nevertheless, we have been partners." The tall guy looked smug, yet jealous whenever Clay spoke to Jewel. Hm.

"I am not your girl," she stated.

"Negative, dude," Clay drawled. "I work alone." Jewel seemed to be eating up the guy's malarkey. Clay threw his charm into high gear. "Ms. Heiss—can I call you Jewel? It makes your eyes flash, I love that—where did you meet this guy, anyway?"

"I met Randy in your treatment bed," she said triumphantly.

She seemed awfully sure.

Clay looked at Randy. Randy lifted his eyebrows. Clay looked at Jewel. "This is a setup, isn't it? I mean, nothing personal, we all have to work. You have quotas to meet."

She looked evasive. "I am not setting you up! All I'm asking is that you get your accomplice something to wear. He has nothing but the clothes he stands up in."

"My clothes."

"So where are his clothes? I don't suppose he was naked when you hired him."

Clay grabbed her by the hand and held it. She faced him. "Look at me," he said slowly. "I'm not lying. I don't know this guy."

Her chest rose and fell in that ghastly polyester suit. She glanced from Clay to the Randy guy and back. Clay could see her eyes shifting. Setup, all right. But she couldn't pull it off.

"How about this," he suggested. "Let's start over. You tell me what happened. Throw no punches. Tell me."

She turned crimson. She hesitated, then choked out, "I was in that bed alone. And then—I wasn't."

"Did he come in through the door to the parlor?"

"I—didn't see him do that."

"Did he come out from under the bed? Through the window?"

Her shoulders slumped. She said, "I think it's magic."

"Can I halp anyone fend something pliz?" said a salesclerk.

"Yes, please," Jewel said.

Magic? "We're busy right now," Clay said. *Boy, entrapment is getting more complicated every year.*

"Breeches, boots, hose, a few shirts," the Randy guy said in his fake English accent, man, this guy had a nerve.

"Jins are upstairs," said the salesclerk, eyeing Randy. "May name is Hervé. Ee will take you dare." He swept away.

Randy stalked off after the salesclerk. Jewel looked indignant. Clay offered her his arm and, after a moment, she put her hand on his elbow. It was a bit too much like a cop's come-along grip, but he'd take what he could get, contact-wise. A hot spot in each of her blue eyes told him he was getting through.

" 'Ave you seen the new Fild's? So allegant," Hervé said to Randy. He gestured upward. "The Tiffany chandelier."

Randy looked up. "Do you have any beds?"

Hervé batted his eyelashes. "Flars eat and nane. But *jew* need dose jins *immediemant*, I am chure."

"'Ave you seen the new lawn-jare?" Clay murmured to Jewel. "He's not wearing underpants. I wonder if Hervé will let him try jeans on naked."

"How do you know he doesn't have underpants?" she hissed, looking suspicious.

"Because if he stole all his clothes from me, he didn't get any in my room." Clay felt more in control already.

She flushed. "For somebody who doesn't screw his clients, you talk an awful lot about sex."

"I'm a sex therapist. It's an occupational hazard." When he saw her color rise higher, he took his chance. "So I'm dying to know, Officer Jewel, exactly what you're charging me with? Didn't you come?"

He heard her gasp, but she didn't look at him. They got on the escalator. He leaned backward and murmured over his shoulder, "Okay, you came. Maybe it was a substandard orgasm. You get a refund for cheap crummy orgasms, too, you know."

Something hard and sharp jabbed him in the ribs.

"Hey." He turned around.

She held up a knuckle near her eye. "Watch it."

"Just getting up to speed here." He moved down onto her step. Her eyes were level with his. "Boy, you're tall."

Up the escalator a few steps, the Randy dude was glaring over his shoulder at them. Maybe he could drive a wedge in there, get somebody to admit something he could use.

In an undervoice Clay said, "Okay, okay, I guess it was a good orgasm. So what other charges can you point at me? You admit you don't remember seeing this guy come into the room. What if he's a random psycho?"

Her pupils changed at that.

"I don't blame you," Clay murmured, "if you're afraid of him. He seems to have a bug up his butt for sure."

At that Jewel laughed.

The Randy dude glared back down at them and nearly fell over on his face as the escalator dumped him off at the next floor. Jewel laughed again. As she came off the escalator and pulled Randy to his feet, he groaned.

"You are hurt. Cracked some ribs, didn't you?" she said.

Randy was holding his side with one hand. "Perhaps."

She clicked her tongue. "That's it. You're going to the hospital."

"No!"

Clay lounged against the escalator wall. "Hervé, what's in style this year, jeans-wise?" he said to draw off the salesclerk.

Hervé seemed fascinated by Randy. "We haf the Lauren collection of cars," he said in an inattentive voice.

Randy seemed furious. "I tell you, I won't see any doctors!"

"We could go to the police station instead," Jewel suggested, smiling maliciously at Clay.

Clay made an "uh-oh" mouth and met her eyes.

Jewel scowled.

Randy shot Clay a nasty look and hustled Jewel onto the next up escalator. "The police cannot hold me," Clay heard him say.

"C'mon, Hervé, let's give them their space," Clay said. He and the salesclerk mounted the escalator and flapped their ears shamelessly from ten steps below.

Jewel seemed to have things under control. She had her cop face on.

Randy became increasingly agitated. His arms sawed. "No hospital!" He slapped the escalator rail, his color darkening. *Our phony lord has a temper.* When he grabbed her by the arm again, Clay stepped up one step higher.

Noticing, Randy let go of her.

She got up in his face for thirty tense seconds, arguing in a low voice Clay couldn't distinguish.

Then Randy shouted, "Very well, try to put me in hospital! Try to arrest me! I'll be in a bed for eternity, and you'll never set eyes on me again!"

Clay rolled his eyes and turned back to Hervé. "I wish."

Jewel gave a shriek and Clay looked back at her quickly, ready to defend his would-be arresting officer from her plant.

But the Randy dude was gone.

Clay leaped up the last steps.

Hervé was right behind him.

Everybody arrived at the top of the escalator at once.

Jewel looked aghast. The clothes Randy had been wearing lay in a crumpled heap at her feet.

It was the fastest strip job Clay had ever almost-seen.

"You! Hey! What the fuck you doin'!?" Hervé yelled, sounding a lot less exotic. He grabbed up the clothes and hurried away, presumably in the direction of the presumably now-buck-naked Randy.

"Those are mine, you know," Clay called after him.

Jewel seemed overcome.

"Your first streaker?" Clay put his hand on her shoulder experimentally. She didn't sock him.

"He's gone," she choked out. She swayed. "Oh, God, where can he have gone this time?" Her cop personality seemed to have run away with the bare-assed Randy. She turned a stricken face toward Clay. "I have to find him. If I don't find him—oh no!" she gasped, slapping a hand over her eyes as if at a thought too horrible to contemplate.

"Always tough when your state's-evidence witness

goes bonkers," he muttered with as much sympathy as he could manage.

"He's not bonkers," she said in a bleak voice. "Oh, Hervé? Where—" She gulped. "Where did you say the beds are?"

"Eat and nane," Hervé said, reappearing along with his accent. "He iss not on this flar. You think perhaps in hame fairnishings?"

She turned her eyes upward into the escalator atrium, cringing as if she expected to see dragons hanging over their heads. "That'll be it."

"Ee will call securitay."

"Um, I'll, we'll find him, thank you." She looked at Clay with such begging eyes that he knew that his legal worries, as far as this woman was concerned, were over. "Help me," she mouthed silently.

"Ee will call securitay," Hervé repeated firmly.

Clay put his arm around her and led her to the escalator. "You can count on me, officer," he murmured.

"Did you totally miss that? He, like, vanished! Disappeared!" She shuddered. "I only hope I can find him." This was a whole new Jewel Heiss.

"Sorry. I was talking to our native guide."

But she raced up the escalator ahead of him.

CHAPTER
18

Jewel walked into home furnishings in a daze. She knew she was in trouble when she saw how many beds Field's carried. Couches. Hide-A-beds. Or, Randy might have taken a fancy to a big pouffy armchair or a leather La-Z-Boy.

Tentatively she lay a hand on the nearest headboard. "Randy?" she whispered. *Randy?* Would he hear her thinking? Would he answer if he did hear her?

Oh, he must. He would have to. He didn't want to stay here any more than she wanted him to. Hadn't he threatened to vanish? *And you'll never set eyes on me again.*

She moved from bed to bed to sofa to La-Z-Boy to bed. *Randy?*

"Randy?" she hissed. "Somebody's gonna buy that bed you're in and then your goose is cooked!"

She wasn't getting a tingle anywhere. It would take all afternoon to check every bed and sofa in the joint.

Then she realized that even if she found the right bed, or whatever furnishing he'd ended up in, she would have to lie down there and let him, well, give her an orgasm.

She glanced around furtively.

No way.

The place was mobbed. Every yuppie on the Gold Coast seemed to be shopping for beds.

"No way."

"No way what, officer?" Clay said smoothly behind her. He took her hand.

"Quit calling me that!" she cried, pulling away. First she screwed up interrogating him and now this. "He's in terrible trouble. I'm in terrible trouble."

Clay looked as if she'd given him an early birthday present. "Trouble is my middle name, officer. How can I help?" He took her hand again and this time she felt too beaten to fight.

"You can't. Only I can."

It had finally happened. She'd officially lost her marbles. She'd bought into Randy's story. If she was lucky, none of these yuppies would take home the bed he was hiding in. For that matter, how in Hades could she afford to buy it herself? Everything on this floor was over a thousand dollars.

"Oh, Lord." She plumped down on the nearest couch and let tears come.

"Hey, hey." Clay sat next to her and cuddled her. He didn't ask her to explain, thank goodness. It was dawning on Jewel that Clay Dawes might be as innocent as Randy had claimed. While still being a bunco artist.

Exactly what she needed. She had to have sex with an incubus in a crowded department store and her only help was a criminal.

Actually, that might be a plus.

She eyed him. "Huh."

He drew back at the expression on her face. "You make me nervous when you think, officer."

She pulled in a deep breath. "Can you get me in here at night? After hours? So nobody knows about it?"

He went still. "Break in?"

"Sneak in," she amended. "I want to spend a couple of hours in this department—alone. In fact, I'll need you to be lookout so nobody comes near. Especially not you," she added fiercely.

He made one of those poochy-lips faces, like he was trying not to smile at her. "This is a new side to our relationship," he said, but his eyes glowed. "You've been pretty high-horse so far. You can't incite me to commit burglary out of one side of your mouth and then try to prosecute me over totally innocent, fully consensual sex therapy out of the other."

She swallowed. "I know."

He held both her hands in both of his. His were warm. She felt like one solid block of ice. Except for a little tingly bit somewhere down below.

"You don't have any material facts, do you?"

She lifted her chin at him. "Nothing but Randy."

"Whom you want me to help you find by burgling a major department store after hours."

"You are not to steal anything!" Oh, God, could she trust him to behave himself while she was, uh, indisposed?

Who was she kidding? The worst part of it all was that the longer he sat next to her, touching her, making kissy-faces at her and cooing in that Mr. Relaxed voice, rubbing her nose in her helplessness, the hornier she got.

Maybe it's this couch we're sitting on. Randy could be in there right now, yelling for me.

She stood up.

"Why not let security search the building?" Clay suggested. "He's probably hiding in a broom closet in his birthday suit."

"He's not," she hissed. "He's in a bed somewhere on this

floor. I have to find him and, and sleep on the bed." She shouldn't have let all that out. Saying it made her hotter.

"So he's in one of these beds?"

"Yes."

"The way you say he was in my bed?"

"Yes."

His eyes crinkled and she knew it was payback time.

"Okay, let me get this straight. You want me to break the law to help you recover your only evidence—which is imaginary—that I've broken the law—which I haven't? What if he gets out of the store—sorry, the bed, on his own? We get caught and you blame it all on me and I go up the river." He smiled. "Nuh-uh."

"That's not why I have to find him. He can't get out of here on his own." She squeezed his hands. "He'll be trapped for another two hundred years! If a Barcalounger lasts that long." She ground out a word. "Please."

Clay's smile grew. "No prosecution. Charges dropped. My spotless name cleared. I keep Nina's money. And I get my brass bed back." She frowned. He said, "What if Field's sells the bed while you're making up your mind? I suppose then you'll ask me to hack into their computer to find out who bought it, and then—how are you going to get to sleep on it? Do I have to burgle somebody's house, too?"

She bit her lip. "No. I mean, yes, we'll do it tonight. No charges, no prosecution." She thought of Ed, furious about the money, and Nina's broken heart driving her to do crazy things. "I'll talk to Nina about the money. No promises," she added, because it would be insane to promise anything about Nina. The only promises Nina herself made were to cook like an angel, and to stay married to Ed. Well, at least cook.

He said, "I can't afford to give her money back at this point. I have expenses."

She thought of his five-figure hotel bill and was forced to agree. "I'll do what I can."

He whipped out his cellphone and began talking into it. She hadn't heard it ring. "Uh-huh. Yes, officer. Thanks for calling. We'll be right down." She gaped at him.

"Ve haf not found your frand," the polyglot Hervé said in her ear. She jumped a foot. A security guard frowned beside him.

"It's okay," Clay said, putting his phone back in his pocket. "He sneaked downstairs and CTA security stopped him. If we could have his clothes?"

Hervé scowled. "I cannot eemagine how I mees him skowlking through the stowr in the altogather." She thought Hervé seemed more disappointed than disapproving.

"He's always doing that," Clay said. "It's impossible to keep the guy dressed. One time at the Art Institute he got from Seventeenth-Century Religious Paintings all the way into Masters of Postmodernism, wearing nothing but a pair of socks. Nobody ever saw him."

Hervé looked dreamy-eyed. "What a peety."

"So if we could have his clothes?" Clay repeated. "He'll need them when we spring him from the transit lockup."

"This must never happen again," the security guard said. "We'd appreciate it if you wouldn't bring him back here to shop."

"No problem," she said shakily. "I'll, uh, see to it that he takes his meds."

They all trooped down the escalator. Her legs were rubber. Clay patted her on the back. "Nice backup work," he murmured.

For a moment, she glowed.

But it wasn't that easy to get away.

Hervé couldn't find Randy's clothes.

Clay of all people pitched a hissy. "That shirt was six hundred dollars!"

He wouldn't shut up until he had talked Hervé into giving him a replacement shirt worth five hundred and fifty and a pair of two-hundred-dollar chinos. When Hervé drew the line at replacing the loafers, and she hissed in his ear, "You are a dead man," Clay graciously agreed to call it a bargain.

The security guard walked them all the way to the basement exit by the subway station. Clay chatted nonchalantly with him. Jewel slunk ahead, fretting. At the subway entrance, the guard offered to come to the CTA lockup with them. "In case you need help with your naked guy," the guard said.

"You've been great, thanks for all your patience," Clay said warmly. "But I think we can take it from here." He shook the guard's hand a little longer than necessary.

The guard stuck his hand in his pocket, thanked Clay profusely, and went back into the store.

"Did you tip him?" she said, handing a quarter to a bum as they escaped down the subway stairs at top speed.

"Never overlook the little guy. Oftentimes he's your ace in the hole. Look at this shirt. Suede-weight silk! We should bring your pal Randy to Neiman Marcus next time."

She punched him solidly on the arm. "No!"

They went through the tunnel and up the subway stairs to the other end of the Field's block, where a bunch of guys were playing congas, cricket sticks, cowbells, dumbeks, djembes, bongos, and rattles. The noise lightened her spirits. She tossed them a dollar.

Clay said, "We should go back inside."

"No way."

"They know we want to shop," he said.

"That security guard could be anywhere in the building."

"Wabash side only," he said. "They don't cross the alley."

She raised her eyebrows. "And how would you know this?"

"I tipped him fifty."

"I'm astounded you make anything on the grift, the way you throw money around."

He grinned. "Worth it, having you beg me for help. Compromise is hard for you, Ms. Straight Arrow. Don't you ever have to compromise in your job? Not even for a bare-naked friend?"

"No."

"I thought Chicago invented compromise."

"Not my Chicago."

The drums got into her blood. Her feet woke up and said, *Buy us some shoes!* It was hard to stay mad at Clay. She'd felt wobbly-hipped ever since she realized what had happened to Randy. Because only one person in the world, according to her stealth fuck, could get him out of a bed. Neither Nina, who had certainly tried, nor any of Clay's other lucky, lucky customers had managed the miracle.

Nope. Just me.

And she could only do it if she let him give her an orgasm.

Boo hoo.

The fact that she had to do it after hours, with a con man playing lookout, in the middle of a storeful of beds and mirrors and night watchmen, oh, and let's not forget security cams—*please, God, let it be too dark for security cams*—she shivered. *I am so in trouble.* And, *I can't wait.*

Clay eyed her with his lids half shut. "I think the safest place in the store would be home furnishings."

"Spend hours and hours around all those beds?" she squeaked.

"Maybe we'll spot him. I've got clothes for him right here." Clay flourished the Field's bag. "We might get him out without breaking the law."

She leaned forward and lowered her voice. "I told you. He is not *under* a bed, he is *in* a bed. He's magical." She hissed, "We will not hang around Field's all day."

"What if there's an emergency and they close the store early?"

The hot July street was filling up with bus exhaust, lunchtime shoppers, and tourists. Jewel flinched whenever someone bumped into her. Every time Field's revolving door turned, cool air puffed out invitingly.

"Ooooh, all right. But I need shoes."

She put in a couple of hours on the third floor and finally found some nice red pumps. She asked for them in a twelve.

Clay was propped against a pillar. "So you give beggars money? I had you figured for a 'get-a-job' gal." He hadn't complained once during thirty-five pairs of *Do these make my ankles look fat?*

"I'm not heartless. It's like a prayer that I don't end up like them someday."

Behind her, he chuckled. "Officer, you would be last on my list to end up homeless."

"I could have been homeless," she blurted.

"You intrigue me, Officer. Thanks, I'll take it from here," he said to the clerk. Mystified, Jewel watched him pull stuffing out of the pumps and slide them on her feet. "So what happened?"

"My parents died in a car accident when I was seven. My grandparents came out of retirement to work the farm and take care of me."

"Hard-luck story," he said coolly, raising his eyebrows. "Stand up and look at them."

She glared. "My grandparents died ten years later, two months apart. Cancer got Gramps, and pneumonia and overwork got Gram. I couldn't keep the farm going, so the lawyers fussed over the estate until I was old enough to be on my own."

He smiled politely as if he didn't believe her. He shook his head. "I'd say you were never in any danger of being homeless. Walk around in those."

She couldn't believe she'd told him all that. The past rose up in her throat, choking her. She stood and went to the mirror so she could put her back to him, feeling stripped naked, and not in a good way.

He'd squeezed her until her sob story had popped out and then he snubbed her! If he didn't want to hear it, why did he keep pushing?

She put a hand up, found a tear on her face, and angrily flicked it away.

"See, you could have done that better," he said, coming up behind her and looking over her shoulder into the mirror. "Wait 'til I tell you my story." His hands touched her waist lightly, sending flinches up and down her torso. "I'll do it funnier, but I'll get the gimme."

She met his eyes in the mirror. "You're punishing me because I won't screw you." Her breath caught in her chest. *Mistake. He's never actually hit on me.* Except by breathing.

"Oddly, no. Sooner or later you'll screw me." In the

mirror his eyes looked colorless. "It's screw or be screwed in my line of work."

He pushed her down onto a bench, took the pumps off, and started massaging her feet.

She nearly slid off the bench. "Ohhhh. God, my feet hurt."

"Did you ever have a dog?" he murmured. He pulled each one of her toes and twisted gently.

"Lots. That's wonderful. More. Ooh, don't stop that. Why do you ask?" she added with belated mistrust.

He spoke slowly to her foot. His hands were warm. "When you discipline a dog," he said, squeezing each of her toes until she moaned, "whatever you do has to make the dog more miserable than it makes you. If he has a great time and you get sore feet," he said, smiling up at her while he squeezed her instep, "it's a total failure, discipline-wise."

She was stunned. "You like shoe shopping." Fabulous feelings raced up her legs. She moaned again. "Please don't stop that."

"You have great ankles. Let's shop for bikinis."

She could have kicked him over on his back with one foot, but that would have stopped the massage. "I don't believe this. You like shoe shopping?"

He switched feet. His too-long blond bangs swung over his forehead as he pinched her Achilles tendon. Her eyelids fluttered with pleasure.

"My father had many girlfriends over the years. All beautiful. All real nice women. He worked a lot and he had a short attention span. I got a new mom every two, three years."

She must have made another noise, because he glanced up. She would have offered sympathy, but he'd set the rules when she told him she was an orphan.

"Just a poor little rich boy surrounded by gorgeous, lonely women. I like women." He glanced up a second time. "See? Little tug on the heartstrings. Little laugh." He slid his hand up inside her polyester pant leg and patted her on the calf. "Learn from the master." He put the red pumps on her feet and cocked his head at them. "Better, don't you think? Kickier. But still very responsible-public-servant."

She put her foot against his chest and pushed him clean off his stool.

He looked up from the floor at the clerk. "I guess we won't take these."

On the eighth floor of The Drake Hotel, Nina skulked next to the vending machines and smoked. She folded a twenty-dollar bill into her palm and approached the maid who was opening Suite 807.

"Ma'am, there's no smoking on this floor."

"Oh, gee, I'm sorry." She scrubbed the butt against her shoe sole and dropped it in the maid's waste can, eyeing her badge. "Trudy, is it? Listen, hon, can you do me a huge favor?"

Jewel remembered how easily Clay had lifted her wallet in his suite. She towed him down the street to a bank and went to the lobby ATM to check her balances and make sure he hadn't used her credit card number.

One minute later, four bank security guards bustled past her and ran out the door into the street.

With a sigh, she followed.

Out on the sidewalk, Clay stood with his mouth open and an open Drambuie bottle dangling in his hand, staring up.

Oh, shit.

Big canvas bags were piled around his feet. She looked where he was staring at the wall of the bank.

A genie came through the bank's wall with canvas bags slung over both shoulders. Big, bare-chested type with a silky little beard, a turban, too much jewelry, gauzy pants, and a stream of iridescent smoke where legs should be. The genie dumped the bags in front of Clay. Then it oozed back through the brick wall.

The security guards had their guns out, pointed at Clay, but they were staring at the brick wall, too.

Traffic clogged the intersection. The sidewalks and street were crammed with gawkers bumping into her, stepping on her feet, yelling in her ears. She bumped into somebody. "Oh, sorry."

It was Buzz. "Hello," he said with a sickly grin. He made as if to slip away, but she grabbed him by the backpack strap. Bottles clanked in the backpack.

Over the noise of the crowd she shouted into his ear, "I warned you! I hope now you see how serious this is." She lowered her voice. "You could go to the penitentiary."

"No! Please!" He jerked against her grip.

"I'm not kidding. This is huge. Technically you're not old enough, but crimes like bank robbery—and the feds are very down on anybody messing with banks—it's definitely jail."

Buzz looked frantic. "I don't wanna go to jail!"

"Make it stop. I'll do what I can for you," she said. She was livid. People looked out of office windows in the surrounding buildings. *I hope nobody has to bring an ambulance through here.* "Make it stop now!"

Buzz pulled a sheet of gold foil labels and another Drambuie bottle out of his backpack. He opened the bottle.

Immediately the genie stuck its head out through the bank wall. It sniffed the air with a huge pug nose.

The security guards turned their guns on it. She didn't

blame them. The damned thing was nine feet tall and it floated.

"Hide behind me," she said, but Buzz had already slipped into the crowd. The genie surged overhead, scattering shrieking onlookers and leaving a contrail of iridescent smoke that was soon sucked away out of sight.

She took the opportunity to step into the circle of clear space around Clay, the moneybags, and the guards with guns.

The guards finally turned back to Clay. "Hands up!"

He raised one wrist, showing them his watch. "You guys so totally suck!" he said loudly. "You have the worst time of any bank from here to the East Coast! The team in *Boston* did better than you! I could have had your depositors' money into a cab and outta here while you watched the show." And then, to her complete lack of astonishment, he produced a leather folder from his back pocket and flipped it open. He barked, "Now get these bags back inside before somebody else thinks of it!"

The guards blundered into each other, rushing to pick up the bags. She smiled bitterly.

Clay stopped the last man. "You. I need names and shield numbers for your whole team."

She barged forward and flashed her Consumer Services badge. "Heiss, Target Investigations. Are you responsible for this outrage?" she said to Clay. "For a security test?" She didn't have to fake her fury. *In my city.* "This is unconscionable!"

Clay obligingly showed her the folder he'd shown the guards. The security-company name was generic, but the badge and ID were high quality. As she looked them over, she set her jaw.

"That's all very well, Agent Lybster, but you've made a royal mess on this street. You've stopped traffic, created a public nuisance, oh, and, by the way, endangered the security of the bank's funds. What if this mob had grabbed the money? These men are scared and they're pointing guns."

The longer the list, the madder she got, the more she trembled.

With a swagger Clay swung toward her. "*I've* endangered bank funds? Did you see how long it took their team to respond?" He pointed at his watch. "Worse than Boston. Worse than *Boston*!"

"May I be of assistance," stated a freezing voice.

A banker in a thousand-dollar suit stood beside her, hot pink with executive displeasure.

Jewel took a deep breath. Her choices were to play along with Clay or set the cops on Buzz's trail. "Sir, I'll have to ask you to terminate this exercise." She showed the banker her badge.

He did a double take. His eyes got big. "You never returned my calls," he said with reproach.

She opened her mouth and shut it. Oh shit.

He did look familiar.

He leaned closer. "That was the most amazing night of my life," he muttered.

Dimly she remembered a Rush Street bar, a smooth-looking, pompous guy in a fancy suit, margaritas, chocolate-flavored condoms, a cab ride to an X-rated club on Elston Avenue—had that been her idea?

"You seem different," he said, looking at her clothes. *Because I don't wear spandex to work, thank God.* "You wouldn't give me your number, so I went back, searching for you." The banker moved closer to her and she fought the urge to push him away. "Every weekend."

There was only one thing to say.

"Do I know you?" she said weakly.

The banker went from pink to red.

Oh, hell. Another kicked puppy for St. Peter to chalk up on her record. It wasn't even as if he turned her off.

What is the matter with me?

She tried to look remorseless and unapologetic. "I'm sorry, I don't think we've met," she said, and watched his face fall. She raised her voice over the babbling crowd. "Sir, I understand surprise bank inspections must be made, but this disturbance must cease now."

The banker blinked rapidly. He stuttered, switching gears back to vice president. "We d-didn't know he was coming."

"Nobody ever does," Clay said sinisterly.

"Regardless," she said, "it's not worth the risk to infrastructure and public safety." She turned to Clay. "Agent Lybster, if you've finished disrupting traffic, perhaps we can adjourn and discuss your company's lack of regard for public—"

"What's up, Jewel?" said another voice. She turned to find the beat cop at her elbow and her heart sank.

"Officer Dobbs." She shook hands with him. "I hope to God we're done here."

At least she remembered dating him.

They all stopped and watched the security guards return, grab up the last of the moneybags, and hustle away, the backs of their necks sweaty in the presence of an irate vice president. As the money went home, the crowd began to loosen and disperse.

"What happened?" Dobbs said.

"Simulation exercise," Clay said crisply, giving Jewel a heart attack by waving his fake ID. God help them both if Dobbsy asked for a closer look. "*Nine* bags full of bank funds got all the way to *this spot*," Clay said, jabbing his finger at the sidewalk dramatically, "before anybody showed up."

"Sir, I'd like to talk to your supervisor," the banker said.

Clay got up in his face. "Sir, you flunk. And you will be speaking to my supervisor's supervisor in short order."

Jewel tapped him on the shoulder. "Before you get medieval on the bank, you have to talk to me." She pulled out her ticket book, glancing at the banker. "If you would be patient, sir." *Don't tell Dobbsy you slept with me.* She'd been refusing Dobbsy a third date for a year. "Agent Lybster can meet with you when we've finished. Unless— Dobbsy? You want a piece?" Remembering the date thing, she stammered, "Y-your badge trumps my badge."

He backed away, waving and grinning. "No, thanks. If nothing's missing and nobody's hurt, you can have the paperwork." He knew the unwritten Policy. For once, her reputation as the department's Hinky Corners specialist worked for her. Dobbsy would leave her the unenviable pile of reports.

She breathed easier.

The banker glared Clay up and down, as if Clay's casual Friday look hurt him. "You have a lot of explaining to do."

"Trust me." Clay sniffed. "I'll spend the afternoon in your office, writing my report. You will explain to my supervisor. And he will talk to your board of directors."

She took his elbow in a come-along grip. "After I write these tickets. If you gentlemen will excuse us?"

She frog-marched Clay through the dispersing crowd, around the corner and up the street into a coffee shop, through the kitchen into the alley, and from the alley out onto State Street.

"No compromise in Ms. Straight Arrow's Chicago, huh?"

"Oh, shut up."

When they were a quarter mile away from the bank, power walking up State Street, Jewel slowed. "Jesus H., Clay, I leave you alone for two minutes. I need ice cream."

They found a Ben & Jerry's. Clay bought. She had four scoops of everything chocolate in a dish, and Clay had one chaste scoop of vanilla on a plain cone.

"That went well, I thought," he said, licking delicately while he watched her eat. "You were made for undercover work."

She gave him a look across a spoonful of Chunky Monkey. "Bull. I suck at undercover. I'm known for it."

"Guess I know you in a different way. You were calm, you played your role perfectly, and you didn't talk too much. You got the mark off balance right away, too. Remind me to ask you how he knows you. Plus you squared the cop with the right kind of vig and you got us out of there at the right moment. You were," he said, and she felt a hot spark in her chest, "wonderful." He looked deep into her eyes.

"Really?" The slide of the ice cream melting on her tongue seemed to run all over her body.

He wiped her chin with his thumb. "Really."

She pulled in air, trying to shake off great feelings. "You make me feel fat. One scoop?"

"Moderation in all things."

She chomped a big bite of Chubby Hubby and scowled. Her heart still raced. All that banker had to do was ask Dobbs for her name and she was in the doodoo. She felt wonderful. "At least I got the lid on. Did you notice any cameras?"

"Who needs cameras? Everybody's got a phone."

"Oh, hell." She took a bite so big she got an ice-cream headache.

"So it hits the Internet, big so what?"

She winced. "Don't say that. I'm paid to keep stuff under wraps. Ow." She shut one aching eye and put her hand over it.

"What?" He laughed. "Genies out of bottles?"

"Yes. Ow, ow." Her forehead felt like it was splitting.

"Convenient, your running into an old, uh, friend."

She squinted at him. "My boss has yelled at me twice today for not catching that genie. I assume you bought the bottle off of—you bought the bottle?"

He shrugged. "It seemed like the thing to do at the time. I wanted my money back. Still do, by the way. This kid came by with a good patter, very talented I thought, so why not? Surprised heck out of me when I saw that thing come fizzing out."

"What happened then?"

"It bowed, and I said something like, 'I want money.' I dunno exactly what I said. It went right through the wall. You saw."

"God, I hope nobody got a picture."

He reached across the rickety, sticky table and put his hand on hers. "Enjoy the moment, officer. It's all we ever have."

Her phone rang. It was Ed. Her heart sank.

Ed wasn't yelling. In a leaden voice he said, "Heiss, da mayor saw your genie on the news."

"Wha—*my* genie?"

"You were standin' right there. Taylor recognized you. You're suspended."

Her insides twisted. "What—I'm—but—" Suspended.

After her coup on Clark Street yesterday! "But what about all the tickets we wrote?"

"The commissioner killed 'em." Ed grunted.

"All of them?" That hurt.

"Policy is, we wanna keep the movie people's business."

"What good is their business to us if they get it for free?" she said, her voice rising. "What about the rules? We throw out all the regulations and say, 'Come to Chicago, because if you're rich, we have no rules'?"

Ed made whuffling noises over the phone. "Shaddap," he said. "You're suspended until you figure that one out. This don't mean you can slack off on this sex therapy scammer. Find him. Bust him. And if you want your job back, maybe you'll get around to shutting down the genie thing."

The phone went dead. Limply, she stuck it in her purse. "You," she said with loathing. "You got me suspended."

"Correction, your pimply little friend with the Drambuie bottle got you suspended. Too bad you won't compromise to protect a buddy."

CHAPTER
20

They entered Field's on the State Street side and took the elevator to the eighth floor. Jewel's role was to sneer, which was harder than it sounded. She swanned through home furnishings, towing Clay, looking down her nose at couches.

"Honey," he whined, "I like the Lauren mission couch."

She saw a salesman two feet behind them. "It's leather," she said stupidly. She was running out of sneer.

"You know how you love leather," he wheedled. He was the perfect pussy-whipped husband. "Leather never wears out."

"How much is it?" she snapped. *I cannot, can NOT snarl at a pretend wimp all afternoon!* "I'm sick of this," she muttered to Clay through stiff, smiling lips as the salesman woffled.

"Thirteen-two in cordovan," the salesman said.

Jewel gasped.

"Could we have a moment alone?" Clay said to the salesman, man-to-man. The salesman skipped away.

Jewel and Clay sat on the thirteen-thousand-dollar couch.

"I will. Kill. You. I can't sneer at furniture all day. Especially if you try to make me beat you up the whole time."

His blue eyes crinkled. "We could take turns."

"Find us a hideout. Now. I can't take any more of this."

He biffed her gently on the chin with a fist. "Hang tough, champ." Looking over his shoulder, he pressed down on her neck. "Under the couch. I'll join you in less than two minutes."

Heart thumping wildly, she dropped to the floor and rolled under the couch.

His legs stayed within view. She counted under her breath. One minute later, he walked away.

"Oh, hi, did you see where my wife went?" she heard him say.

"Sorry, I didn't," the salesman said, not sounding sorry.

"Oh, well, I'm sure she'll be back." Clay laughed a charming little laugh. "She never walks away from a fight. If you see her, tell her I'll be waiting right here."

"Certainly, sir."

A moment later Clay rolled in next to her. They lay face-to-face without room for a dust bunny between them. She felt her personal space compressing. The old crowd-o-phobia squeezed her chest.

He chuckled. "He won't come back to this area again."

"He thinks I'm a shrew."

"And therefore he won't remember what you look like. Selective memory. Clerks hate crabs and they have to deal with them all day, so they put you out of their mind as soon as they can." His breath smelled like vanilla ice cream. In the dark, his voice was smiling. "This is tight, isn't it?"

I hate it and you know that and you're enjoying it. "Do they remember wimps?" she said savagely.

"Nope. I'll turn up in his memory as short and blond. Wimps are all short in hindsight."

She lay squished up against him and inhaled fluff. Too close! Fighting panic, she said, "Why did you bug me about giving money to beggars?"

"Because you're such a straight arrow. There's probably an ordinance against it."

"You think I'm too tight to give away spare change?"

"Well—too tight."

He was too close. She never got this close to anybody unless they were having sex. She made a noise in her throat. "You think I have no compassion."

"You gave a quarter to the bum in the subway and a buck to the drummers."

That really gets to him. She remembered the heartbeat thump of the conga and her hips moved, hip to hip with a con artist under a couch. "They gave me something back." She breathed in a dust bunny and started to cough.

He pulled her against his shoulder and muffled her mouth on his neck.

Panic struck. She went rigid. Coughs shook her. She spasmed in his arms, and he wouldn't let go, dammit, she couldn't breathe, he was too close and she couldn't move. She struggled. He squeezed tighter. She got her hands between them and pushed, coughing too much to push, pushing too hard to stop coughing.

When the coughing stopped, he let her push away from him. "You okay?"

She breathed carefully, opening and shutting her eyes in the dimness under the couch, praying for light, trembling from head to foot like a spooked horse. "Panic attack. I—I need a lot of personal space."

His tone changed. "Oh. *Oh*. Sorry." He sounded sincere.

"Then what the *hmhmff*?" she tried to say as he pulled her close again. The panic came back. "*Mmf!*"

She tried to punch his arm but his arm tightened and smooshed her face against his neck. "Quiet," he breathed.

She heard voices and froze.

"—A nice mission couch in cordovan," said a saleslady voice.

Jewel's blood turned to ice. Clay nudged. She squeezed farther under the couch, which was, she realized, up against a fake wall. He tapped her shoulder and moved her hand to a bar over their heads.

"Hold tight," he breathed.

The saleslady said, "I can get the tracking number off the back." The couch moved. "Give it a pull."

Jewel grabbed with all her strength and held on. Her face was smooshed against Clay's throat. She felt his muscles strain.

"Seems to be stuck," said the saleslady, sounding flustered. "They're solidly built."

"Uh, that's okay," said a man's voice. "Thirteen is a bit steep."

The voices went away.

Jewel relaxed her death grip on the bar.

Her body was hot and sweaty, and the universe smelled like dust bunnies and Clay. In a few hours she would lie on every bedlike object on two floors until she could locate a sex demon who would then provide her with an earth-shattering and probably bizarre orgasm.

Down below her waistband, a single, isolated muscle trembled.

"We should have picked a bed to hide under," Clay murmured.

That gave her an uncomfortable thought. What if Randy was in this very couch?

Would Randy notice she was under his couch?

Would Randy even notice they weren't alone?

She made a noise in her throat. As motionlessly as she could, she squirmed.

Clay breathed ice cream into her face. "Hang in there, girlfriend." Then he kissed her on the end of her nose and snuggled back against her, throat, shoulder, every inch of his torso touching her torso, her hip, thigh, calf, ankle.

The evidence was unmistakable. He was enjoying this.

So was she. She concentrated on self-control.

Time passed.

After an eternity, the lights went out. She pulled away.

He yanked her close again. "Wait. If security walks this floor, they'll come by in the next hour."

"Another hour?" she squeaked. She remembered another worry. "What about cameras?" She realized how late in the game it was to bring this up. *Oh God, please let there not be cameras.*

"Not here. It's hard to shoplift a thirteen-thousand-dollar couch."

She collapsed with relief. They waited approximately forever, she feeling heat build in her bones because Randy was nearby—*Randy in a bed, waiting for me*—and Clay pressing against her with the banana in his pocket.

"Ms. Straight Arrow?"

"What."

"You're not tight at all when you go undercover."

The oceans dried. Mountains crumbled to dust. Volcanoes rose and made new mountains, an ice age swept over the face of the planet—although not under the couch, which remained a cozy hundred-and-ten degrees with rising humidity—and the moon fell.

Eventually he said, "Home free." He rolled away from her, leaving cold spots all over her polyester-covered flesh. She lay like a boned fish, waiting for death.

Fresh air wafted over her face, and she noticed that he had tipped the couch up off of her. "Need a hand?" his voice said in the dark.

"I'm fine."

"What's the move now?"

She sucked in a fluff-garnished lungful of air and scrambled to her feet. "Now you go to the other side of the department, out of sight, and watch for security. I will—I will proceed."

It was too dark for her to read his expression.

"Shouldn't we both look for him?"

She sighed tiredly. "I told you, only I can find him."

"No problem," he said, sounding huffy. "I'll go make myself useful, shall I?"

"Do. Away from here. Far away from all the beds."

CHAPTER 21

Clay tried to think of himself as an easygoing guy, a source of comfort to one and all, a Buddha in chinos who knew how to finesse those little moments when everything looks black, but his feelings were hurt.

This woman didn't give a darn. All she cared about was some dork who couldn't stay dressed.

Didn't she see how their kinks matched?

She's so trapped by being tough, she's got no wiggle room. Of course she'd had a tragedy, and of course she'd told him. *That's why they call us confidence men.*

The way her face fell when he snubbed her—ouch.

Instinctively he'd chosen a response that would let her stay tough. She might forgive him someday for rebuffing her story, but she would never forgive him for letting her break down her own defenses.

She wants other people to do that for her.

Now he knew why it was so easy to find her trigger words, why he felt like he knew her. Why he was being an idiot about her. *Separated at birth.*

He'd thought they were getting somewhere.

Thinking logically, things had been fine until Mr. No Pants showed up. Then she went all cop-ette on him. No Pants vanished, and she became a different woman, more approachable, a human being with needs and appealing vulnerabilities. He smiled.

Of course, if and when she located this guy hiding in a bureau drawer in his birthday suit, she might turn evil again.

So what a fellow needed in a spot like this was insurance.

He had a whole store to play with.

He gnawed his lip.

"Randy?"

She moved methodically, starting in one corner of the furniture department. The place looked weird, empty. Only the exit signs glowed. She was a thousand times grateful for the darkness. Every time she'd been in bed with Randy, her clothes wound up scattered all over.

Should she take her clothes off now, so she could find them later? Would she scream this time?

"Randy?"

She put both hands on a bed with a curving headboard and footboard. "Are you in there?" she hissed. She moved to a mission twin bed, then a canopy double.

After seven or eight beds, it occurred to her to sit down on the beds, and then she had to go back to the beginning and start over. Then, she remembered to lie down, and groaned aloud, realizing she'd have to start over yet again.

As she rolled upright on a platform futon, a little tingle shot up her palms and tickled her ying-yang.

"Randy?"

She lay back down.

Nothing happened.

She thought about the consequences if she couldn't talk him into it right here, right now. "I can't come back again, Randy. Clay's made us unwelcome with the staff. Plus I—I can't have sex with you with people all around, the lights on, hoo boy, that security guard. So this is your shot. Better take it."

Not a sound in the close, hot darkness of the un-air-conditioned home furnishings department. Somewhere out there in the dark, Clay was keeping lookout for the night watchman and, probably, listening for indiscreet sounds.

"Please don't make me scream." Boy, what a few nights with a sex demon did to a normally adventurous girl.

She yawned. "It'll wreck your rep if you put me to sleep instead of, you know."

Threats produced the same unresponsive silence.

She yawned again. Maybe this was the only way he could get to her. She turned on her side and burrowed her cheek against the faintly dusty coverlet.

"Because," she found herself saying vehemently, "you're a stuck-up pig of an aristo who thinks his shit doesn't stink." She stabbed a finger into the buff six-pack of her sex demon.

"Aristo, eh? Does that make you a Parisian *citoyenne*? I can do that one," Randy said.

"Don't wriggle, dammit! I've been chasing you all night! It's like trying to babysit a ferret! What is your problem?"

"Merely awaiting my cue," he murmured, and then she found herself riding a tall, dark horse in the middle of a woods, and the horse was cantering after something light-colored on the path ahead. There he was. She legged her horse. Wet leaves lashed her in the face. She hunkered down over her horse's neck and kicked it into a gallop, barrel-racing around tight corners, doubling back as her prey dodged, then dodged again.

"Criminal! Thief!" she yelled, and her whip came down to block his escape: a naked man, sprinting, his sides heaving and his pale back streaked with rain and splashes of mud. He ducked behind a tree and she brought her mount skidding to a halt.

In the sudden silence, she heard the rain stop. The wind passed on to the north. Droplets fell from the trees onto her bare head. To keep warm, she slapped her whip against her leg.

"Let me go," he called from the dark.

"You can't stay here."

"I'm too much trouble," he called from a closer spot.

"Forget it. I'm not leaving you here."

"Let me serve you then." His voice was nearer, though she'd heard no rustling, no footstep.

She set the horse sidling. "Where are you?" The shadows were black on gray. "You know I can't leave without you."

"Let me serve you," he said at her knee, and she lashed down with the whip in surprise.

"Why?" No answer. She raised her voice. "Why should you serve me?"

The horse stumbled, then righted itself, and a weight settled behind her on its back. Strong arms wrapped around hers, pinning her close. His voice came in her ear. "Because you are she whom I have awaited."

A shiver raced down her side, paralyzing her with shock at his nearness. The horse lunged forward and she clutched his arms to keep her balance, and with amazement and tremendous relief she felt the thong of her whip slip around her wrists. She hadn't had a clue what to do with him if she caught him. And now she wouldn't have to decide.

"You ride well," he said in her ear. They cantered into

open ground and bolted up a slope through tall grass shivering silver in the moonlight. "Can you ride on the withers?"

With that he pushed her forward. She clutched the horse's mane and drove her weight far down in the stirrups, feeling her bottom rise, feeling exposed, feeling the wind on her bare thighs as he pushed her skirt up to her waist. Then he entered, a lightning rod earthing in her pussy. As the horse loped strongly up the incline, he drove into her with its movement, forcing her to twist the bristly mane in her fists and bend her knees and balance on her stirrups, her every sense focused on rising and falling with its lunging canter.

"Wait, too fast," she cried, "you go too fast!"

"Sorry," he muttered, and the wind stopped whipping her ears and the horse's motion slowed like the last twelve seconds of an instant replay of a photo finish, every stride exquisitely long and powerful and unstoppable, and Randy crammed her, rammed her, and withdrew in perfect time with the horse's thundering hooves and it was as if they fucked the earth with the speed of the wind, ba-da-bup, ba-da-bup, and she knew she would never resist him. Her body began to release. She remembered not to scream, she had no breath left for screaming, it was too hard to balance herself and match the horse's stride and yet give in, let the perfection of this moment flip her high in the air and bring her thumping down on the soft, springing ground on her hands and knees as a sex demon penetrated her from behind with single-minded force. Her knees turned to water, the tendons in her groin gave way, and she slid slowly to lie flat on her face.

Every nerve in her body zinged.

When she opened her eyes she lay on her face on the

coverlet. She hadn't a stitch on. Randy didn't so much pull out as evaporate, rising effortlessly off her.

She snapped one hand out behind her and grabbed at random.

Randy yelped.

"Gotcha."

Thirty feet away, hiding behind the fake wall of a fake French Provincial bedroom, Clay heard her say, "Gotcha," in a thick, satisfied voice.

He turned away in annoyance. While her faithful guide was playing lookout for her, she'd been doing this guy!

After all that shoe shopping!

She'd been ready under the couch. Clay had smelled it.

He wanted to grab the guy by his phonus-balonus English testicles and say, *I saw her first.*

Clay thought of his insurance and smiled. One thing he had that the other guy didn't have, he had a plan.

She found all her clothes eventually, but Randy, of course, remained starkers. They were debating whether to wrap him in one of the coverlets when Clay turned up, clearing his throat behind them so loudly that she nearly jumped out of her skin.

"There you are," she said. "Now we need to dress Randy and find an exit that won't set off an alarm."

"Plenty of clothes downstairs."

"What's the matter with the clothes you bought today? Oh, pardon me, the clothes you *conned* the clerk out of. Hey." She noticed something as Randy passed under the red light of an EXIT sign. "You're not banged up anymore."

"Bang?" He looked down at himself. "No?"

"How's the ribs?"

"I feel perfectly well," he said, sounding astonished. He picked Jewel up in his arms. "See?" He was still naked.

She smiled in spite of herself. "Boy, you're strong."

"Let's make it snappy," Clay said. "I did not con them out of those clothes. They're mine, to replace my clothes that you stole and gave to this guy, and then Hervé went and lost them. If you give them to your buddy, he'll only lose them. And I'll still be out an expensive pair of pants and a shirt."

Randy led them down the motionless escalators and into menswear. It was eerie how his pale body wove in and out of the shadowy racks of clothes ahead of her, exactly the way he'd dodged her in her dream.

Clay grumbled the whole way.

"How was I supposed to know you didn't know he was in the bed?" she hissed.

"I still think you dreamed that up. Here, what's-your-name, these ought to fit you." Clay tossed a pair of pants in Randy's direction. "Besides," he hissed, "I still don't get this 'in the bed' thing. Is there, like, a trapdoor in the bed? I searched it pretty carefully and I didn't find one. That room is sealed."

She snorted in disgust. "Didn't you see him disappear?"

"Missed it," Clay said, pulling a shirt off the rack. "Wait, you." He yanked the tags off Randy's pants. "Rule number one for shoplifters, don't you know anything?"

Oh God, they were shoplifting, too! "We'll have to leave some money if we're taking things."

Clay took her by the shoulders. In the red light of the EXIT signs he looked a lot less wholesome. "How about no?"

"I need shoes," Randy announced, as if he had only to snap his fingers. She believed more and more that he was a lord. That let-me-serve-you stuff apparently only worked lying down.

"I can't believe we haven't been caught," she said, looking over her shoulder.

At that moment a door opened with a squeak and a light flashed over their heads. All three of them ducked.

Clay pulled her under a round rack of suits. "Don't breathe." She couldn't.

Once again he was pushing her personal space envelope. She would have elbowed him in the gizzard, but her horrified heart had stopped. *This is it. My career is finished. I'm going to jail. I'll have to appear in court with these two bozos.*

The beam of the flashlight came closer.

Where the hell was Randy?

She could see the guard's shoes. The flashlight beam was so bright, it weakened the light from the EXIT signs and plunged the whole floor into blackness. She held still, frozen with dread. Clay's arms were relaxed, wrapped around her from behind. *I am not panicking*, she lied. She made her mind a blank.

Another dreadful thought popped up.

Is Randy zapping himself into another bed?

The guard shuffled away.

She was blind in the dark again. She couldn't hear Randy.

He was gone. She'd have to go back to the eighth floor and start over. Oh, fuck! Her mouth was dry with fear.

Clay let go of her and she poked her head out from under the suits. The shapes of things came back with faint red outlines.

"Jewel?" Randy's voice said. Clay went *tsk*.

After a couple of false starts, she breathed again.

They bickered their way to the shoe department. Randy picked out loafers and a pair of silk socks. She hovered, frantic, trying to keep him away from the windows, and Clay was useless until it came time to choose an exit.

"Alley." Clay led them through dark service corridors. "We'll go out the employee entrance."

"Wouldn't it be quicker to use the crash doors onto the street?" she said. "We could be up the stairs and on the El platform in thirty seconds."

"Negative on that," Clay said, holding up one hand. "Okay, you two pretend you don't speak English. I just figured out where Hervé put Randy's clothes."

She turned, astonished, as he vanished into the darkness.

A bright light flashed in her eyes. "Stop right there."

CHAPTER 22

Jewel gasped. Her heart actually felt like it was in her mouth. *You hear people say that*, she thought dreamily while her pulse tried to punch holes in her eardrums, *but it sounds silly until it happens to you.* "Buh—"

"*Si tu me cherches des crosses, tu vas les avoir!*" Randy said in his most arrogant tone.

She turned to him, her eyes bugging out.

"Put your hands in the air. What's all this stuff?"

While the night watchman had the flashlight on Randy, she could see dimly, around the spots in her eyes, piles of black boxes. She swallowed.

"*Entschuldigen Sie mir, bitte,*" she said in a tiny voice. "*Ich habe kleine Anglische.*"

The watchman pointed a gun like a cannon at her and she raised her hands higher.

Randy looked down his nose at the watchman. By flashlight she saw that Clay had chosen black jeans and one of those black shirts with no collar that look so affected on high-priced hairdressers. Randy narrowed his eyes and put one hand on his hip, a gesture that would have looked swishy on anybody else.

"Tell your buddy to put his hands up." The watchman's gun wobbled. Not good.

"*Mange merde,*" Randy said. She could translate that one.

"*Aber ich hab' nicht so viel Franzoser auch,*" she said, trying to lower her voice and sound in control. "*In meine Arbeitbeschreibung keine dichte gegen*"—she opened her mouth and shut it, scrambling for German words—"*Die Revolveren oder scheissbeschmierenden Verraterssss, er, ist.*" Where the hell did you put the verb, anyway?

She licked her lips. This wasn't working. In a minute she would have to unleash Randy and his two-hundred-year-old excuse for martial arts on a man with a loaded cannon. The watchman's radio crackled. *Oh, merde,* she thought.

"*There* you are!" a Waspish voice exclaimed. "For *heaven's* sake, haven't you put this stuff in the van yet?"

All three of them turned. The watchman aimed his flashlight up the corridor.

"*Darnit!*" Clay struggled toward them with two huge armloads of poles, shoulder bags, cables, boxes, flat things, clanky things, and big shiny bowl things. When he saw the three of them staring at him, he dropped everything with a gesture of despair. "People, what are we waiting for? I just took thirty-two *hundred* digitals of pillowcases. I am *not* in the mood."

Her mouth fell open. Gone were the surfer boy, the boy next door, the cocky seducer. Clay threw both palms down in extravagant exasperation. "Isn't *anybody* going to help me?"

He wasn't lisping. Not quite. He was also wearing different clothes.

Both Randy and Jewel turned toward him. Randy spouted a river of French. She sputtered, "*Ich, ich, ich,*" because in the shock of watching Clay transform once again, she'd forgotten every other word of German besides the swearwords.

Clay shouldered them aside.

"You'll have to excuse them," he said to the night watchman in a far-from-excusing tone. "We've been shooting this ad for sixteen hours. They're tired. And quite worthless. Oh, Gudrun, take this and shut up, will you? *Vite, bitte.*" He handed the cable, the poles, and a flat thing to Jewel. She stood there holding them, feeling stupid.

"Excuse me, sir, but nobody told me to expect you." The guard still had his gun out but it was pointed at the floor. "I'll have to inspect your bags."

"Fine!" Clay threw up his hands. "Fine. Go ahead. We were supposed to be out of here *seven* hours ago, which I'm sure is why they never bothered to tell you we were in the *building*. Can Jean-Claude get the van now? I'm ready to *drop*." He turned to Randy. "*La caisse*, Jean-Claude. If you *don't* mind?"

Randy opened his mouth, looked at Jewel, and then said, surprisingly meekly, "*La caisse est foutu, espèce de sauciflard.*"

"*What*?" Clay shrieked. "Broken *down*? When did that happen? Why didn't you *warn* me?"

Randy responded in French. Clay gobbled like a fey turkey.

She watched the guard open all the cases and boxes. They were full of camera equipment.

"Don't forget the shoulder bag," Clay snapped. "It's got my twelve-thousand-dollar Hasselblad in it. If you kick it around a little I'm sure management will pay me back."

The guard had his hands deep in the shoulder bag, but at these words, he yanked them out, and Jewel had to lunge to catch the bag before it hit the floor. Glaring at him, she clasped the shoulder bag to her bosom. *Like a real assistant*, she thought with pride through her panic.

Clay found a folding chair and slumped artistically in it as "Jean-Claude" apparently exculpated himself in French about the nonworking van. He flapped his hands.

"Oh, very well, very well, fine, *vite, schnell*, go get us *un taxi*! Criminy," he added as Randy slithered out the door, looking hangdog. "Next time I'm bringing the Belgians. *They* understand machinery."

"It's all here," the guard said, the dumbbell. He stepped away from the pile of equipment, looking sweaty. She made a mental note to talk to Field's management about the quality of their rent-a-cops.

She was astonished to realize she was having a ball. This was the first time ever she'd done undercover with someone who didn't make her feel stupid. On a deep level it stunned her how completely she had bought into Clay's bumbling sweetheart act, and how swiftly he had turned into someone else. She felt fooled, scared, and somehow soothed, because she knew the truth.

Careful, girl. Nobody knows the truth about this guy.

Yet her gut assured her that her first idea of him was the real Clay—the cuddly boy next door.

Fool. The mark fools herself. That's how he gets away with it, she thought, as the guard helped Randy and Clay load the taxi.

And when Clay had convinced the guard that he wouldn't get in trouble for holding them up because Clay would keep quiet about it, when she was sitting in the taxi between the two men, when they were making their getaway with God-knew-how-many thousands of dollars of hot camera equipment, she realized something else.

She was totally turned on.

The taxi took them to a crappy motel out on Lincoln Avenue. Clay sent Randy in with a credit card to register, and when he came back with the key, the men unloaded the taxi and took the swag into the room.

"A nice haul," Clay said complacently, flopping on the nearest bed. "Great work, Jewel. I don't know why you say you're no good at undercover. That was amazing."

She went hot to her undies at his praise. *I'm going to hell.*

"I'm hungry," Randy announced, sitting and folding his arms as if this, like every one of his other creature comforts, was somebody else's problem.

"There's a Popeyes down the street," Clay said. "Anybody know if they deliver?"

"No, but the Thai place does," she heard herself saying.

Clay's eyes lit up. "And they'll take a credit card. Brilliant."

She held up her hand. "I'll pay. I don't believe in stiffing overworked immigrants."

With his lazy smile, he drawled, "Only banks."

She noted that he'd reverted to the Clay she knew. She forced herself to remember he was not that likeable idiot.

"You didn't stand lookout at all, did you? You spent the whole time stealing camera equipment." He started peeling off a big, baggy, expensive-looking sweater. Under the sweater he wore three Hawaiian shirts. "And more clothes! You're a thief!"

"And you helped me."

Mortified, she said, "If you think I'll sit here idly and watch you fence all this stuff—"

"Officer, as your B&E expert I advise you not to think too closely about all this stuff. Your department is keeping this compulsive streaker out of trouble. My department is getting you in and out with no fuss."

"I do not steal."

"That reminds me, where's your purse?" He swept it

off the bed and opened it. "Not much of a haul for a whole day's shopping." He pulled out the red pumps. "I'll teach you better next time."

She was speechless. In one day he'd got her suspended, robbed a bank using Buzz as an accomplice, and destroyed her professional integrity.

"By the way, you shouldn't keep condoms in your purse without a carrying case. They get ratty in there."

He folded his stolen shirts neatly and stuffed them into the shoulder bag with the sweater, leaving on only a silky little white tank top. She couldn't help noticing he was surfer all the way down, including nice abs and a sturdy pair of shoulders.

"I like Thai food," Randy announced.

"Good. You order," Clay said, tossing over his credit card.

She snatched the card out of Randy's hand and returned it to Clay. "Never, ever give this guy a credit card," she said.

Clay looked at Randy with more approval than he'd shown so far. "No kidding?"

Randy's ears were red. He picked up the phone and looked at the receiver carefully. "I've seen this on television so often."

"This is the important part," Clay said, handing him the bottom half of the phone.

"Never mind him." She remembered another grievance. "You left me alone in bedding! I could have been caught!"

"You told me to give you plenty of space. I wanted to have a cover ready," he said. "You must admit it came in handy."

"For you. Mr. Opportunist."

She folded her arms over her polyester and slumped

onto the other bed. It felt pretty good to be sitting down. In fact, if she weren't still so horny she'd be lying down. In a room with two of the sexiest men she'd ever—no, don't go there. She listened with half an ear to Clay supervising Randy ordering Thai food and smiled to herself. She'd gone undercover and she hadn't sucked!

She took Randy home after they'd eaten.

He was jubilant at having ordered supper himself. "Over the telephone! Without a menu!" he exulted in the taxi.

"Yeah, yeah." Consorting with Clay Dawes was so good for both their egos.

She knew darned well that Clay knew that *she* knew that she'd had to leave ASAP after the Thai food was gone because he was about to phone whatever fence he had lined up for the photography equipment he stole—*they* stole—she ground her teeth.

In fact, it wouldn't surprise her if he had phoned the fence from Field's. Probably from an employee phone.

The guy was an adrenaline junkie. There was no other explanation for the risks he took.

Takes one to know one.

"I remembered your favorite dishes," Randy said.

Poor Randy. He'd had a hell of a day and here she was ignoring him. "So you did," she said warmly. "I was impressed."

He pokered up. "You need not patronize me."

"Dude," she said, sighing. "I've dated men for months who couldn't remember if I smoke or not."

It was like babysitting a teenager. Call it babysitting and he was insulted. But you didn't dare leave him alone.

He was silent a moment. "Thank you for coming to find me."

"You're welcome." *Man, do you owe me.*

"I have no claim on you."

She was touched. "No big. I couldn't leave you there."

He faced her in the dim taxi. "I have been racking my brain for a reason why you should tolerate me and my—my needs."

Put that way, it did make her nervous. "I think you're suffering from Stockholm syndrome."

He blinked. "What?"

"You don't need me. You only think you do because I'm the first woman you've talked to outside of that bed in forever."

"I do need you. I know I am an inconvenience to you. Who knows how many orgasms I must give you before the curse is completely broken?"

"Shh!" She glanced up front, but the cabbie seemed to be in another zone.

"It could take years," Randy confessed.

A shiver ran up her insides.

"Randy." She took his hand. "I've been an orphan since I was seven. I put up with Nina because she took me in and she has this huge heart and otherwise I'd never taste home cooking again as long as I live. The idea," she said, and paused because her throat had tightened on a hot lump, "that this hot guy lives to give me the best sex I've ever had in my life." She had to pause again. She squeezed his hand to tell him there was more coming. "And he *can't leave me*—"

He sat quietly beside her, holding her hand.

That night, Jewel had an old nightmare. She was seven, standing barefoot on the front porch of their house on the farm, and it was cold, winter. Snow was piled up in the corners of the porch. The snow lay like gray sleep on Mom's garden, snow on the lawn, heavy snow on the spruces along the driveway down to the road, snow on the silent fields beyond, rolling forever toward darkness. The bottoms of her feet went cold on the porch boards.

She saw a flash of pink light. It poured across the snow like juice, then vanished. Then it came again, coloring a bigger patch of snow, glowing bright. Then the light disappeared, as if the snow had drunk it up. Fascinated, she watched the light get bigger, spilling pink over more and more snow. Pink light swirled around and around. It winked at her, as if it knew she was watching. It kept coming closer, right up to where she stood shivering on the front porch. *This is special*, she thought. *I'm glad I came out here to see it.* Her sides shuddered with cold.

Someone stood beside her. She looked up. He stretched up tall on the porch, a grown-up in dark clothes wearing show-jumping boots half as tall as she was, and he had a big fluffy bandage on his neck. *That's not right*, she thought, *I don't remember him*. He pointed at the pink swirling light. "What is it?" he said. And for the first time in years, she spoke in the dream. "It's an ambulance."

"Please, Jewel, stop!" She woke to the sound of Randy's pleading voice. "Don't cry. Stop it."

He was holding her from behind. She shook him off and sat up. "What time is it?" She felt ice cold, so cold her lungs rattled against her rib cage. "God, I hate that dream." She reached for the clock. Two-forty-five AM. "What are you doing here?"

He drew back as she said this, and then she remembered. *A hundred orgasms. Your new best friend.* He took up a lot of space in her bed. "What am I going to do with you?"

"You were crying in your sleep." His eyes were so big and dark they looked like spook holes in his face.

She turned on the bedside lamp so he wouldn't look so scary. "You were in my dream." She wrapped her arms around herself, willing her sides to stop trembling.

"You're still crying." Carefully he touched her face, then showed her his wet fingers.

"Oh. Yeah." Breathing deeply, she closed her eyes. Her face was the only hot part of her, and her eyes burned hotter. With her eyes shut she said, "Quit looking at me." The tears kept leaking out. She kept her eyes shut.

After a moment he said, "I've stopped looking."

With difficulty she recalled letting him get into this bed. *We had great sex, it was lovely, now can you leave?*

No, he can't. She'd thought that was a good thing, three hours ago.

He cleared his throat.

Don't. Don't say anything.

"Do you miss your parents?"

"I don't remember them," she said curtly.

If she could think, she could think of a way to get rid of him. Send him out to sleep on the couch. Something. Her brain seemed frozen, still trapped on the porch watching the ambulance move ever-so-slowly and silently up the snowy driveway.

Her foot began to warm up. She realized he had laid his hand over it.

She sniffled deeply, held her breath, grabbed a tissue, blew, and opened her eyes to see his ear. He really wasn't looking.

Didn't matter. *He's in my bed, and I can't send him away, and I can't get alone, and I'm freaking out, and I can't stand it.* To take control back she said, "What are you thinking about?"

His hand felt warm on her foot. She wanted to pull it away, but she didn't dare. He would know how freaked she was.

He said, "I remember something. I remember when I was six. I had broken a vase, and I was afraid to be beaten. So I ran back to the nursery and hid myself under the sheets in my bed."

"Did that work?" she said in a tight voice.

In a surprised tone he said, "Yes. Yes, it did."

She breathed deeper. Her heartbeat slowed. She pulled her foot out of his grasp and curled up under the covers on her own side of her bed.

"Are you going to cry again?"

"No."

After an excruciating pause, after she had dared to hope he'd gone to sleep, he said, "You are more comfortable being alone."

Her insides squeezed painfully. She curled up, hugging her knees. The air squeezed out of her lungs and her eyes squeezed shut and she bit her tongue until it bled.

Every muscle taut, she willed herself into unconsciousness.

Jewel spent all day Friday hunting Buzz. As she hung on a bus strap she became aware of an odd feeling. She felt great. Well, she felt sweaty and cranky and claustrophobic on the overcrowded bus, and her feet still hurt from yesterday, but down under the little stuff, she was aware of a big happy feeling, like her body was saying *finally!* With a start, she realized she had gotten laid, well and truly fucked by an expert for three days in a row, the first sex of any kind she'd had in—was it really six months?

Good grief, Nina was right. Was that all it took?

Jewel had carefully not kept track of how many men she used to sleep with, before Chad and Nathan woke her up to the stupidity of her lifestyle. What was the point? The city was full of men. If she didn't like one, there'd be another along in ten minutes. She hadn't really wanted to know.

Like Gramps, huh, never knowing how much whisky there should be in the house, even though he bought it because Gram refused. *Gramps was a drunk. Hopelessly addicted.* She stared out the bus window, feeling happiness like a balloon carrying her over self-knowledge and shame.

Sex addict.

Even Britney hadn't called her that.

Somebody stumbled against her and she automatically gripped her purse tighter. Her blood pressure shot up.

I hate crowds.

She followed her would-be pickpocket off the bus.

She walked to Oak Street Beach, followed the breakwater south to Navy Pier, and battled horrendous crowds at the Pan American Festival in Olive Park. No Buzz. South past the yacht club into Grant Park. A nerve-racking plunge through the Taste of Chicago festival's heavenly smells, while people stepped on her feet, bumped against her breasts, pinched her butt, spilled beer on her, and, on one occasion, pressed a lighted cigarette to her elbow.

She thought longingly of plague, meteor strikes, and neutron bombs.

Buzz was apparently avoiding the Taste.

She talked herself out of going near the old Petrillo Band Shell, since Buzz couldn't make himself heard over the Blues Fest. Instead she trolled the rose gardens and Buckingham Fountain, then plodded down to the Field Museum of Natural History. Buzz used to like the museum's front steps.

Not today, apparently.

The sun burned down on her navy polyester. Her feet were killing her.

She bought a frozen lemon full of gelato and a bottle of water from a pushcart, winked at the dinosaur on top of the Field, and dragged her aching feet around the Shedd Aquarium. No Buzz. The causeway out to the Adler Planetarium looked a mile long. Would Buzz go that far? Naw.

Late in the afternoon Ed called with a telephone tongue-lashing. "Where are you?"

"Millennium Park, under the Bean."

"Did you get my money back yet?"

"I'm suspended, remember?"

Inside a huge plastic tent, workmen sweltered as they welded, sanded, buffed, and polished the chrome Bean sculpture. Through the plastic she winked at a hunky guy in a welding suit and he winked back.

"Why don't you put Britney and Digby on it?" she said bitterly. "I can't believe you put her on the identity theft ring and not me."

"You wouldn't work with Digby and she would."

I wouldn't sleep with you and she would. "Did the lab report come back on that evidence I brought in?"

"Yeah, here it is. Nothing but cabernay saw-va-yong."

"Damn. That was the cornerstone of my material evidence." She heard him make a noise in his throat. "What's happened?"

"That radio psychologist called. Somebody's been calling her about a magic boyfriend."

Jewel felt a lump of ice in her stomach. "Oh."

"I'm scared shitless it's Nina," he moaned. "Sounds like her. Magic boyfriend! Christ. I'm gettin' white hairs." Dread rang in his voice. "She's outta control. I think she's gone."

Jewel burned with prickly humiliation. "It's not Nina."

"What? You sure?"

"Ed, it's me. I'm sorry. I don't know what got into me. Nina's been weird and I needed somebody to talk to."

"That, and not gettin' laid in six months," Ed blurted. "Never mind, forget I said that. What more do you have on the genie guy?"

Jesus, even Ed thought she was a sex addict.

Deep breath. "It seems the genie's a lush. If I can lay

hands on some Drambuie, I bet I can lure it away from Buzz and put it on a shelf somewhere."

"Buzz? *Buzz?*" Ed's voice rose. "Is this that street punk you been mother-henning? Is *Buzz* the genie guy?"

Oh, shit! "No. No, he's not."

"Heiss, have you been protecting one of your strays? Because I will fire you. I really will."

He means it. She saw herself cleaning out her locker at the department. *I've pushed too far. Messed with the boss's marriage—messed with his affair—got him yelled at by the chief attorney—couldn't get his money back— let the con artist wiggle out. Now he's losing Nina, he's sick of having me around, why should he keep me? I remind him of what he's losing.*

Over an empty feeling in her chest, she said, "I'm not protecting him. I know how to find him. I'll take the genie and the Drambuie away from him and it'll be over."

Ed was revving up. "How many times I have to tell you? There is no genie. Isn't. Don't talk about it. It don't exist. Just catch it. Suppress it. Delete it. Make it go away. Stick it in your overworked hoochie and make it go where old boyfriends go," he said unforgivably but with fresh originality, even for Ed. "What I'm paying you for, to stir up trouble or keep it under control? It's your job, protecting the city or protecting some nitwit moron dipshittical goddamndumb feebleschmeeble dope of a homeless criminal? Well? What'm I paying you for?"

She faced the summer sun, squinted, and counted to ten. "My mission is to protect consumers and business owners from unfair marketplace practices."

He pounced. "Exactly! And that means keep the hinky stuff out of sight!" She didn't see that at all, but they both knew Policy. "And what the fuck are you doing? Playin' Lady Mother Teresa Florence Nightingale Go-

diva with a fucking juvenile delinquent and catching genies in bottles of Glenlivet!"

"Drambuie," she said faintly. Ed in full hissy was over-
powering.

"Whatever. What the fuck is that, anyway?"

"It's a sweet Scotch liqueur."

"Christ. Sounds like something my wife would drink.
Maybe she'll drink the genie and he'll turn her into a bottle of Scotch. That I could use."

"Ed," she said reproachfully. *Turn his thoughts before
he bursts a blood vessel.* "Please. You're talking about
my friend. Why don't you talk to her? She loves you. She
wouldn't have gone to a sex therapist unless she wanted
to make herself more acceptable to you."

She was way overstepping the employer-employee
boundary, but after what happened yesterday, she had
new respect for boundaries. As in, less.

"Mind your own goddam business," he grumbled, but
she could tell from his tone that she had got through.

"So I'll get back to genie-hunting and then I'll, uh, contact Clay Dawes again. See what I can find out for you."

"You do that." He hung up.

She found feathery shade under a locust tree and
punched up Clay's number. "Please don't tell me," she
muttered as the phone rang, "where you fenced the cameras from Field's." She wanted to sit but a bum lay across
the whole bench. She settled for standing under the tree.

"Jewel," Clay said cheerily. "Tell me your naked friend
is lost in the Art Institute. Got my eye on a Cezanne, my
connection says he can find a buyer. And I'd appreciate it
if you could make your buddy Nina stop calling me."

Jewel watched a pigeon flutter to the pavement in front
of her with an unlighted cigarette in its beak.

"Oh, dear. Pestering?"

"I'm afraid so. I expect to find her hiding under my bed when I come home."

"I'll call her."

The pigeon pecked at the cigarette. On the bench, the bum stirred.

"Thank you," he said, sounding sincerely grateful.

She hung up, took a deep breath, and thumbed speed dial.

The bum rolled halfway off the bench, stretched his arm, and ignited a cheap lighter.

"Nina? Jewel."

"Hello, Judas. I was beginning to think you'd erased my number from your little black book."

"Not until after Sunday dinner." Jewel tried to sound hard-hearted. The pigeon stopped pecking and bobbed, setting one pink foot on its cigarette. "Did you know Clay Dawes has been accused of fraud?"

"Hah!"

"That wasn't nice, Nina. Ed's all yellow and purple like a dead chicken, and the chief attorney is threatening us in his super-nice way, and my job, such as it is, is on the line."

"Hah," Nina said again with real pleasure in her voice. "Next time, the commissioner."

"No. Please. I'm begging you. It's not about me and Clay anyway, is it? It's about you and Ed. Why mix us up in it?"

"He mixed you in it himself. He's mad at me for bringing home strays, citing you and all the trouble you make. And I'm not so sure he isn't right," Nina said darkly.

The pigeon stepped in a circle around the cigarette, keeping its round eye on the bum the whole time.

Jewel swallowed. "Can we talk about you and Ed for a moment? You can't fix this unless you deal with him. Have you considered marriage counseling?"

"Hah."

Don't dump your strays, Nina. At least, not this one.
"You're not ready for a divorce."

"You're right about that. I haven't made him suffer enough. He's screwing that little blonde bitch at the office, isn't he?"

Jewel crossed all ten fingers. "Not that I know of."

"Sure he is. Don't lie."

"Okay, have you considered going downtown and threatening to gouge her eyes out? You're scary, Nina. Don't waste it on me and Ed, use it where it'll do some good."

Silence over the phone. *She's thinking about it.*

The pigeon picked up the cigarette in its beak.

"It wouldn't matter if I did. He doesn't love me anymore." Nina sounded so mournful, Jewel wanted to gouge out Ed's eyes and skewer them with Britney's in a dry Stoly martini with a twist. "I have another plan."

Jewel said, "Please leave Clay alone. He's out of business. He doesn't have the bed anymore."

Silence again. "I'm not gonna tell you my plan. You're right, you're in the middle, that's not fair." Uh-oh. When Nina sounded rational, she was gestating something wack. "You're still coming for Sunday dinner."

Jewel closed her eyes in relief. "Oh, yeah."

The pigeon stepped closer to the bum and his cigarette-lighter flame.

"Love you, doll," Nina said, sounding tender and forgiving. *Forgiving for what, goddammit?* She couldn't know that Jewel had hidden Clay's bed. " 'Bye."

Jewel called Clay back. "Listen, I just got off the phone with Nina. She's cooking something insane in her noggin. I thought I'd better warn you."

"Interesting," Clay drawled, so she knew he was nervous. "I just got off the phone with Nina, too. I've also heard from four of my other clients. Nice normal women who need sex therapy. They're not fraud cops and they're not Nina. I can't think of a single reason not to sell them a treatment except—" She heard his fingers snap. "Except, oh yeah, how could I forget, you've got my brass bed hidden someplace. Let's discuss this."

She covered her eyes with the heels of her hands, pinching the phone between her ear and her shoulder. On the bench, the bum leaned closer to the pigeon. The flame in his hand shook.

"Your scam worked because you had a sex demon in that bed. I know because he's screwed me silly four times since then."

"So you don't want your money back."

"Dammit, don't you get it? Randy isn't in the bed anymore! Your scam will collapse as soon as you get the bed back."

"I don't see that."

The pigeon took two more steps closer to the flame.

"Because Randy is with me, you dope!" she howled. The bum shushed her. Technically Randy was at a video arcade with her jarful of laundry quarters, because she couldn't watch him and get any work done.

"We agreed that your naked buddy has nothing to do with me."

"He was in your bed," she hissed.

Delicately bobbing its pinky-purple neck, the pigeon stuck the end of its cigarette in the flame of the bum's lighter. When the cigarette was alight, it backed away, pivoting nervously.

"You'll have to prove that to me," Clay said with finality.

"Okay. Well." She spoke slowly, trying to collect her

thoughts. "If your customers aren't satisfied—I mean, *if* you resume business and *if* they don't like the treatment anymore and *if* they want their money back—will you cease and desist?"

They're bound to be dissatisfied. She couldn't imagine anybody confusing a Randy romp with a three-hour nap.

"I don't do business if it doesn't make money," he said.

The pigeon walked in little circles as if it were trying to keep its pinhead in the stream of smoke floating off the cigarette. The bum rolled back onto his park bench and sniffed deeply.

She said, "If Nina ever finds out I impounded the bed—"

"Oh, she figured that out already."

"What?"

"I told her."

Jewel's heart clutched up. "What! When?"

"Couple of days ago," he said, sounding way too relaxed. "She wanted to buy the bed, and I told her I didn't have it anymore, and she said, and I'm quoting her, 'That scheming bitch.'"

"Oh, shit." Jewel looked at her watch. "How soon can you meet me at the Drake?"

"What's the fuss? If I can't get it back, she can't."

"You don't know Nina."

"I beg your pardon, I know Nina. I've had to assign her number its own ring-tone."

"That's nothing," Jewel said with authority. "You think you're a pro—" That made Clay sputter, and she said hurriedly, "I'm sorry, sure you're a pro. But Nina is totally other."

"Yeah, she's pretty persuasive," he said, sounding unconcerned, the dope.

"So meet me at your hotel room in twenty minutes."

He sighed. "Jeez Louise. If I get my bed back, sure."

"If your bed is there anymore," she said grimly.

"Now you're freezing my blood."

"Finally."

CHAPTER 25

Glumly Jewel hung up and watched the bum suck secondhand smoke. She was about to get her car when she spotted Buzz across the skating rink with a Drambuie bottle in his hand, talking earnestly to a portly tourist.

Sprinting around the rink, she came up behind Buzz.

He said to the tourist, "I can make change."

She flashed her badge behind Buzz's shoulder. "Sir, this man has no peddler's license," she said to the tourist, but she might as well have screamed, *Homeland Security, you're under arrest for thought crime!* The tourist's eyes got huge and he waddled away, elbows pumping.

Buzz twitched like a wild thing.

She grabbed his arm. "Relax, it's me. Gimme the backpack."

"Officer Heiss, you're so harsh! C'mon! I only got one bottle left." He pretended to pray to her.

She tugged on his arm. "Gimme. You want to go to the penitentiary for robbing a bank?"

He looked scared then. He handed over the backpack.

"Hey," she said in a softer tone. His scrawny arm felt like a toothpick in her grip. "I'm going to a friend's house Sunday night. She cooks enough for ten people. Want to come with me?"

He jerked free. "You just feel guilty for wrecking my livelihood."

Clay had accused her of the same thing. She took a deep breath. "I want to keep you out of jail. My boss wants you arrested. He may fire me if I don't." *And if I bring you to supper, he'll bust you and fire me. What am I thinking?*

Buzz hunched his shoulder. "Forget it."

Okay, if not Nina's, maybe she could buy him lunch.

"Do you live alone?" she burst out. In two years she'd never asked him where he lived, never asked any personal questions. She hadn't wanted to know. He was so obviously the last puppy in the shop, the littlest rat in the shoebox.

He turned lewd, challenging eyes on her. "Do you?"

"Yes." Oops. Except for a sex demon. "No." *Don't give the kid ideas, girl.* "I have a guy. Roommate."

"Shit." He spat on the sidewalk. "I'm just, like, one of your crows that you feed. You don't actually want me, like, in your house. Underfoot."

She heard echoes in his voice of some other voice, someone out of his past.

Her eyes stung for him. "Look, I'm sorry. I don't want to wreck your efforts at—at independence." She shouldn't be saying that. She should be saying, *Sure, come live with me, I'll feed you and keep you safe.*

Great, the Wisconsin dairy-farmer's daughter said in her head. *He can sleep on the couch and Randy can sleep in your bed.*

He grumbled, "You want me to be independent but you want to control me."

She thought of Nina yelling at her daughter and laughed shakily. "Hey, if you had parents, they'd act the way I do."

He narrowed his eyes. "Guess I'm lucky then, huh?"

"Look, I don't mean—" She swallowed a lump.

"Smug charity lady. You won't give charity to humans because it bites you in the ass," he said, every word a punch in her gut. "So fine, fuck you, have a great day and God bless."

He hunched both shoulders and mooched away.

She watched him go, feeling stunned and helpless.

She found a different bench under another tree and sat, holding Buzz's backpack on her lap. Her throat was hot and tight. Rollerbladers zipped by in the skating rink. Kids splashed in an inch-deep reflecting pool. Tourists fed such pigeons as were not too busy ruining their lungs.

Everybody came in pairs, in flocks, in families, whole Cub Scout troops, and softball teams. *I'm alone*, she thought.

Her best friend was gunning for her boss. She'd muffed the brass bed case to the point where she was now semipermanently haunted by a sex demon. She'd betrayed Buzz to Ed, who would fire her for not busting Buzz, and Buzz would go to jail for cussedness in spite of her lame efforts to reach out to him. Even fluffy-bunny Britney was mad at her. Jewel blinked away acid tears.

And what should she do about Clay?

He was too venal to blow town while there was money to be made. She could give the bed back and let Nina finagle it out of him. And if he kept it, he would learn it was useless without Randy. So maybe that would work out.

And Jewel would have Randy.

In spite of her recent urge to shoot him and stuff his body down the garbage chute, she knew she wanted to keep Randy.

She could feel her claws curling.

She couldn't forget the avarice in Nina's voice as she said, *I need it. I deserve it.* Like Randy was an *it.* The two of them had wrangled over him as if he were a sweater at a sale. She felt sick. "Nobody should own anybody," she said aloud.

Don't leave me, Randy had said, his eyes so big.

Nobody should own anybody.

She felt breathless and exposed under the pitiless sun. She pressed speed dial on her phone. Crap, it was show-time.

"Ask Your Shrink, you're on the air, caller."

"Hi, Doc, this is Ruby," Jewel said hoarsely.

"It's good to hear from you, Ruby. Are you feeling better?"

She drew a shaky sigh. "I feel like my life isn't my own."

"Many of us struggle with burdensome obligations, Ruby."

Her heart sank. The doc was gonna tell her to bite the bullet and cope. Ask Your Shrink, Queen of Denial.

"That guy I called about before? He's moved in with me. He gets into my dreams, Doc."

"Have you tried sleep aids? Nonprescription antihistamine?"

"I don't mean I dream *about* him. He's there. Visiting my dreams. It's hinky. He's actually in my head."

"Mm-hm."

"I mean, I don't mind being helpful to somebody in trouble, but there's a limit." God, there it was, like Buzz said. She couldn't freely give anything to anybody. She was too tight, too selfish. She laid her head on the back-pack and let tears fall.

"Ruby, it sounds to me like you have intimacy issues."

"Oh, please. I'm calling you on the air!"

"*Exactly. It's easier than meeting face-to-face,*" the doc said, and Jewel didn't have an answer. "*What you think of as a hinky experience is this man's praiseworthy effort to reach out to you. My advice to you is to let him in. You'll find it isn't as scary as you imagine.*"

Jewel hung up without answering. She wondered where she could go for a nice private cry.

Her cellphone rang. Automatically she answered, "Heiss."

"Ruby?" Your Shrink said with sympathy, "Do you want to talk more? We're off the air so we're not violating Policy."

"Thanks, Doc." Jewel sniffed and hesitated. "I have— I may have two boyfriends. One of them makes me totally crazy. They both drive me crazy. In different ways."

"There's nothing hinky about that," Your Shrink said warmly. "Young girls have so many options, so much pressure. You don't know who you are yet," she said as if Jewel were fifteen. "You aren't ready for commitment. You don't want to get close to any one man, so you split yourself in two."

"But I never had one who—" She bit her lip. *Don't say it.* The doc would probably have to hang up on her.

"Trust your instincts, Ruby. On some level, you know what you want."

She thought of Randy's eyes, black with desperation, and the ambulance moving slowly through snow. "Everyone who loves me dies."

Your Shrink was silent a moment. "I think you'll find that's an exaggeration."

Jewel's brain felt like it had been stirred with a weed whacker. "I have to hang up now, Doc."

"Call back anytime."

She stuck the phone in her pocket.

Bottles clinked in Buzz's backpack. She flipped the backpack open. One bottle looked pristine. The other was plastered with half a dozen of those "sultan's seals" Buzz had boasted about. She lifted that bottle and held it up to the sun, trying to peer into it, but the glass was too dark.

Maybe I can wish for Ed and Nina's marriage to be fixed. Then she could keep coming over for Sunday dinner, and Nina would boss her forever. *I'm like Randy. I'm the last puppy in the shop. I'd do anything to be owned.*

Pain welled up in her throat. Impulsively she grabbed the bottle by its seal-gummed-up cap and pulled.

The cork came out with a !pop.

Iridescent smoke fountained up.

She dropped the bottle. Her head tipped back and her mouth fell open.

The genie billowed up, towering over her, its turban-jewel winking in the sunlight, its mighty arms folded.

It bowed.

"I just don't want to be alone anymore," she blurted.

The genie bowed again.

A cymbal crashed in her ear. Something hoisted her high into the air. She shrieked. Instantly, the plaza in front of her filled with people and flashing metal. A brass band whomped into a Santana song. She cowered, shrinking around Buzz's backpack, as a parade filled the plaza and poured down onto Michigan Avenue, carrying her with it. Taxis swerved, car horns honked, trombones sawed the air and blatted, brakes squealed, and hordes and hordes of sticky, yelling, flag-waving people crowded into the street. A paper cone of red-white-and-blue cotton candy fell on Jewel's bare arm and stuck there. To her horror, she saw she was sitting on a gold-sprayed plastic chair on a pouffy white float. She put one hand to her head. Yup. A crown.

Cars and buses, apparently displaced by the genie, sat on the sidewalk on Michigan and on the pavement and the lawn of Millennium Park. One car was stacked on top of another next to the Bean, both drivers still inside, honking and screaming.

A police siren snarled once, then went into its whoop-whoop.

Jewel climbed, teetering, on top of her gold plastic throne. She screamed up at the genie, "Stop it, stop it, that's not what I meant!"

The genie looked down at its handiwork with an expression as haughty as any of Randy's, as if to say, *Who are you to question my work?* Its huge turbaned head bobbed in time to the whack-a-boom of the bass drum, and it smiled on the crowd jammed around her float. In every direction, human bodies jostled and yelled and waved flags and tooted horns. Her flesh crawled.

Hands shaking, she popped open the last full bottle of Drambuie.

The genie's head whipped around.

"I mean it," she said, so quietly she couldn't hear herself over the racket of the parade. She put her thumb over the bottle's mouth. "Fix it. Or no booze."

The parade popped away with a sound like the cork coming out of the bottle.

She felt herself falling. The genie grabbed her in its giant hands, carried her through the air, and set her down on her park bench. Down on the plaza, streamers fell to the sidewalk, along with ice-cream cones, cups and cans full of soft drinks and beer, rally caps that proclaimed, "I ♡ MY ▆," and smoldering cigarettes. A swooping phalanx of the park's pigeons descended on the cigarettes.

Slowly the cars crawled out of the park and off the sidewalks. Traffic on Michigan straightened itself with much horn-blowing, and the squad car siren stopped.

Jewel clutched the Drambuie bottle tightly. The genie's nose twitched. Breathless, her heart pounding, she took her thumb off the mouth of the bottle.

Instantly the genie's long sparkly contrail dove into the bottle, like an elephant's trunk plunging into a bag of peanuts.

She heard a hooting, sucking sound, like someone blowing across a bottleneck at the same time as they sucked up the last drop of milk shake with a straw. Genie smoke rushed past her face, but she turned her face away and kept a tight grip on the Drambuie.

Then the genie was gone. She shoved in the cork. Remembering Buzz at the bank, she rummaged in the backpack for more of his homemade sultan's seals and plastered them over the cork and neck of the bottle.

She stuffed the bottle into the backpack and clutched it to her chest, then slumped, panting.

"Holy gazoony. That was a close one."

Then she realized that every single tourist in sight was aiming a cellphone at her.

She ran for the State Street subway.

Limp and sweaty, Jewel emerged at Grand and State and pushed through pedestrian hordes toward the arcade where she'd parked Randy.

Traffic was even worse on the Near North Side. She spotted Officer Dobbs at the intersection in front of the Hard Rock Café, wearing white gloves and looking cross. "What up, D?"

"Move, move, move! Oh, hi, Jewel." Poor Dobbsy's face was running sweat. "Not bad enough we got Taste and Blues on the same weekend, fuckin' Pan American parade detoured onto South Mich and back." He lowered his voice. "Plus, here's the hinky part, the parade ain't s'posta be until tomorrow morning. Downtown's a total clusterfuck." He stepped away, gesturing big. "Okay, move it, move it!"

Feeling horribly guilty, Jewel ran for the video arcade.

What had she done? *Ain't until tomorrow.* What would happen tomorrow? Had the genie fixed it when he took the parade away again, or had he just magicked everybody into limbo? Hyperventilating, she threaded her way to Rush Street amid heavy tourist foot traffic, muttering a rosary of disasters.

In a cavern of cacaphony, Randy was playing some

superlatively tacky and violent game while a bunch of excited 'tween-aged boys hung over his shoulders.

Another crowd. She breathed deeply, willing herself calm, and pushed forward.

"Nobody's ever made it past level fourteen," one kid told her when she loomed up behind her sex demon.

"Randy."

He ignored her. The room was deafening with bangs, pings, sounds of simulated battle, roaring engines, and the screams of video victims.

"Whoa, look at that!" her informant squealed.

She forced herself through the press of smelly adolescent bodies to look. A cartoon commando guy in fatigues ran around a fake desert, blasting people wearing black—she looked closer—that was weird, they seemed to be wearing antique clothes. Here was a guy with a three-cornered hat like the Quaker Oats guy. And a guy with lace cuffs and tights and a wig. And a woman with a haunting face, wearing a long, froufrou peignoir. They looked human, as if live-action movie actors had been introduced into a cartoon. When the commando shot them, they bled and screamed with horrific realism. Ooh. Now the commando looked like Randy, rabid dinner napkin and all.

Creepy. Randy must have done something to the video game.

It crossed her mind to wonder what prolonged contact with Randy might do to her.

Yet another reason to set him free for real. Out of the wreck of her life, maybe she could do this one decent thing.

Randy's audience cheered. She flinched. *I hate crowds*.

"Randy, it's time to go." She moved around the machine so she could get his eyes.

"No one's ever made it past level fourteen," Randy said, his brow furrowed in concentration. In the sea of zitty faces, he looked dangerous, the predator unleashed.

She sharpened her tone. "If you ever want to have sex again, you'll leave with me. Now."

Two of the boys actually looked up when she said that. And looked up again, when they realized she was taller than they were by a head. One of them tapped Randy on the arm.

"Uh, dude. If you don't want her, I do."

Randy looked up amid a chorus of groans.

She smiled at the kid who had graduated to girls. "Thank you." Reaching past him, she attached herself to Randy's wrist. "I'll bear that in mind, if I ever dump this sex demon here." She yanked. "Let's go. I think Nina might be planning to steal that brass bed. We have to stop her."

"Yes." Randy scooped up the pile of quarters by his elbow and shoved through the crowd. "Let us return to the bed."

"Way to go, dude!" her new fan called as they left.

When she and Randy knocked on his suite door at the Drake, Clay was as close to a state of anxiety as she had ever seen him. "You're late," he said.

"I was detained." She sighed. "It's been a bad day."

He didn't bother to sound smooth. "Where's my bed?"

She hesitated. That bed was her only leverage with him. Give it back and she could kiss goodbye any hope of recovering Ed and Nina's money.

He took her hands in his. "Are you going to go against your promise and prosecute me?"

"No."

"Do you have any evidence—or witnesses"—he

arched his eyebrows in Randy's direction—"that could convict me?"

Hide the hinky stuff. "No."

"Do you hate me enough to put me through false arrest and a trial and my ultimate vindication?"

She licked her lips. "I can't arrest you. It would be a hearing in front of the hearings officer."

"So you hate me a little bit? How much, Jewel? Did I rub your feet the wrong way?" His lips pooched out as if to say, *I'm being serious and you're being mean and silly*.

She shut her eyes. "I don't hate you." To shut out his voice, which was crawling inside her ears and down into forbidden territory, she listened for her Wisconsin dairy-farmer's daughter common sense.

Wisconsin wasn't talking today, apparently.

Oh, well. He was right. Ed would have to live with it.

She pulled her hands free and lifted the house phone. "Security, please. Yes, this is Jewel Heiss with Chicago Department of Consumer Services, I'm up in Clay Dawes's suite. Oh, you remember me? Good. I'm, uh," she said and turned to look at Clay. "I'm sending down a guy named Randy to pick up the bed and bring it up here. Where should he meet you? Uh-huh. Okay, thank you."

Clay sent her a pained look.

She signaled to Randy. "Meet the security officer on duty at the front desk," she whispered in his ear. She said to Clay, "I guess your credit card must still be good, because they're giving you back your bed."

"Are you safe while I am gone?" Randy growled.

She rolled her eyes. "Yes. Beat it."

Randy left, eyeing Clay with suspicion. *Oh, hell. If he's gonna act jealous, I don't know how much I'll be able to enjoy the next ninety-odd orgasms.*

"Glass of wine? Cabernet, right?" Clay said, and she was so tired of excitement, she said, "Sure."

They sat side by side on the edge of the big cushy sofa in his parlor.

"What's bothering you, Jewel? You can't decide whether to bust me or not. We've agreed that's a dead issue."

"I know." She accepted the glass he offered her, sipped, and let her head fall back against the sofa. "My boss wants me to make you give his money back. Nina hasn't told me how much it was and Ed's been too furious to say."

That was funny, now she thought about it. If Ed was so all-fired mad about the money, he would have mentioned it with every breath. And he hadn't.

Which meant Ed didn't care about the money.

"Huh," she said. *It's Nina after all.* Jewel's heart expanded. *He still loves her.*

She smiled and turned her head to find Clay watching her.

"You're a mixed-up person, Officer Jewel."

"Back off," she said lazily. "You want to talk, talk about yourself." The wine soaked in and she began to relax.

"Who, me?"

"You. I'm done with your needling. Tell me about the poor little lonely rich kid and the gorgeous women."

"Oh, him. He's not very interesting." He was drawling again, which should have made her nervous. What was the worst he could do now? After last night she felt she'd had her capacity for embarrassment traumatized out of her.

"Tell me anyway. Tell me about your father."

Clay remembered their first interview. What were her trigger words again? Risk, love, hope.

"My father's in the same business, only he's ten times better," he said, and felt a ripple of shock at the sound of truth coming out of his mouth. "I think it's because he doesn't actually give a damn about risk. Or love."

There. Her pupils dilated, then shrank. She turned ever-so-slightly closer toward him.

"Some guys, they live for the thrill. Me, too, I guess. Not Virgil. He likes a safe con, and he never falls in love, and he gets out at exactly the right moment. Maximum profit, minimum risk."

Her lips parted.

Wow. It was like pressing a button. That Randy moron might have something going on with her, but Clay knew how to get her hot with three little words. He put his wrists between his knees and leaned toward her, signalling his complete interest in their conversation, plus sexual attraction controlled by boy-next-door-type virginal restraint.

She leaned closer. "You're conning me, aren't you?"

He blinked. "Only a little bit."

"Tell me something. When we were in Field's last night, did you set us up to get caught by the security guard?"

He stared. How did she do that? One minute he had her, the next, she had him. A laugh jumped out of him. "Yeah."

Turning pink, she said, "You did."

He shrugged. "Guilty."

"Show-off."

Risk, hope, love. *She's got my kinks.* He laughed again. "Just reminding you who your friends are."

Her eyes glittered. "So, how are you like your father?"

Clay felt on top of the world. "He trained me." *Let's try word number three.* "He gives me no end of shit for caring. I guess he's right. I'm a fool to hope that anyone's going to love me after I take them." He looked away, then down at the wineglass in his hand. "But I always do."

"Always take them, or always hope?" Her eyes were huge.

Bingo. Risk, love, hope. In that order.

"That's why this job has been special for me. I deliver what I promise. Yes, there's always the risk somebody will ask me for her money back. Nobody has so far. They love me. It—" He paused and watched her lips part. Slowly he put his spread hand over his chest. "It feeds that fool inside me who still has hope."

She's gonna blink and say huh in six seconds.

Five.

Four.

Three.

He leaned in and kissed her, open-mouthed, and she took him and raised him fifty. Something hot pinched him in the shorts. What the—? He realized that he had actually forgotten his erection for a few minutes. *Spooky,* he thought, and let her push him back onto the couch and pin him there with her knee between his thighs. She went for his belt buckle, then his fly, eating him alive the whole time. He put his hand between her breasts and pushed gently until she lifted her mouth off his.

"You're not teasing, are you," he said reproachfully. "Because that wouldn't be ni—"

That was all he said before she pounced on his mouth and ripped his zipper open at the same time.

Jewel felt as if every nerve in her body had waked up at once. *He's off the suspect list, I can screw his brains out if I want.* Behind her, her fears and self-doubts pursued her on fast-beating tiny wings, but she was pulling ahead, and when he finally put his hands on her butt, she rocketed into orbit.

It wasn't as easy as with Randy. It wasn't as scary. They wrestled with her pants, and he got hopelessly tangled in the clasp on her bra, and she laughed at him trying to kick off his loafers when they got stuck in his chinos, and she was ridiculously turned on to find out that he did not, in fact, wear underpants. He didn't magic her away to some full-body illusion of flying or having sex on horseback. He was just a guy with hot hands and a hot mouth who knew, amazingly, how to make her wait, knew enough to put off the moment of penetration until she had begged, howled, grabbed it in her fist to *show* him, dammit.

Normal sex, in fact. What a relief.

Dizzy with lust, Clay heard the suite door open. He glanced over her shoulder.

The streaker Randy stood there, his mouth agape, his eyes bugging out. A security guy blinked next to him, holding a key. *Master key. I underestimated Lord Jaybird.*

Clay signalled *scram* with his eyes.

The security guy bolted out the door. Randy wavered and crumpled to the floor. Fainted, the wussy. Clay hoped he'd have the tact to sneak out quietly when he woke up.

Clay got back to business.

She threw her head back and let Clay's talented lips do fabulous things to her right nipple, the underside of her breast, her ribs, her navel, mmmm, while his hands kneaded her buns slowly, so hot and slow that the room whirled. "Ohmigod."

"That's good, right?" he mumbled against her flesh.

"Mmm." His hands kneaded her buns. His hands slid over her wrists. His tongue teased her clit. His tongue tickled her ear. He was warm on her belly, hot on her back, and she opened her mouth to kiss him and felt his cock slide into her mouth, silky and smelling a hundred percent male. *This is the best sex*, she thought, *in the universe, and it's mine, You're mine*, said the voice in her head, *I know every single desire you've ever had and I will make you come screaming*. "Yemmm!" He bore down with his cock, with his hands on her wrists, his hands on her buttocks, his mouth on her pussy, tangling her legs in his, whispering, *Scream, Jewel, beg, Jewel*, and she wanted to, but her throat was full of his cock and his tongue drove deep into her pussy and she came so hard that shock waves zinged from her center out her arms and legs and snapped sparks out the tips of her fingers and toes.

He slid his cock out of her mouth and kissed her lightly. "Thank you."

She opened her eyes into Randy's. Somehow he was lying under her, and yet he'd—his cock had been—how did he do that?

Gasping for air, she lifted her head.

Down between her thighs, Clay raised an astonished face. "You!"

Both of them.

They didn't look pleased to see each other.

With some difficulty Jewel disentangled her legs from the naked men on the sofa. Every inch of her skin burned with humiliation and residual lust. She slid to the floor.

"Uh, I gotta go freshen up."

She ran for the bathroom.

Clay found himself alone with Randy the Evernude. "You!" he said again. "Jiminy freakin' Christmas, don't you have any tact? You don't move on a guy's girl when they're in bed."

Something was so wrong. He took in Randy's position, recalling that she had been lying on the bottom. "How the heck did you get in—get into—no."

She was always going on about this guy being, like, magic.

"No way."

Randy looked at him with his usual superiority, as usual totally ignoring the fact that his ding-a-ling was hanging out. "Way, I fear," he said smugly.

Clay pulled on his chinos. Whether Mr. Barebutt knew it or not, clothes were power. Clay tried to feel more powerful facing a guy who could materialize *under* the woman he was doing.

"So it's true," he said, struggling for composure. "You've been—?"

"Trapped in that bed by a curse for two hundred years." Randy raised his eyebrows snottily. "I thank you, by the by, for procuring all those women these past few weeks. You greatly truncated my term of imprisonment."

"Think nothing of it," Clay said. He felt sick. So it was true. Here he'd been thinking they wanted him—he'd told Virgil so—all this time, all those repeaters—he sat down on a chair, nauseous with realization. He'd thought all those women loved him. He'd thought it was him Nina wanted. Sure, she was nuts, but love's love, he'd learned to take it where he could steal it.

He hadn't even cured their frigidity. *This* was what they kept coming back for. She'd dragged him half the night through Field's for *this*.

He heard Virgil's scornful voice. *Believe your own malarkey.*

Pimping. For *this*. His heart felt like lead.

Clay said dully, "If the curse is broken, why are you still hanging around?"

"Jewel Heiss rescued me. Several times."

"Yeah, yeah, I know." She had talked him into helping. Some of his best work, wasted on *this*. "So why are you still here?"

"The terms of the curse were that I satisfy one hundred women." Randy paused. "But I suspect a sting in its tail."

It was the first visible crack in his self-satisfied armor. Clay paid better attention.

"I believe," Randy said reluctantly, "that I don't stay rescued." He leaned forward and put his elbows on his knees. "I satisfy her and I am freed—for a time. Then something happens, perhaps my free time runs out, and I am trapped in another bed."

"So? Satisfy some more women, if you're so darned good." Clay felt two inches high.

"I have tried. You brought that woman to me two days ago, remember?"

"Jewel?" He blinked, feeling stupid.

"No, a dark-haired woman."

Clay tried to remember that far back. It had been a hectic two days. "What'd she look like?"

"I don't look at their faces. I look at their souls."

Jeez, what a cheesy line. Wasted on Clay. *Must be working for him, though, 'cause Jewel sure bought it.* Reluctantly Clay realized he might have something to learn from Randy.

"It was the last day you hid money in the bed," Randy said.

Clay turned his head and narrowed his eyes. "You keep clear of my stash."

"I don't need money," Randy said loftily.

"The heck you don't. You steal my clothes. Who'll keep you in Thai food? You gonna get a job now?"

"Jewel will provide for me," Randy said.

Clay rolled his eyes. He didn't say, *You'll never steal her love. You don't want to know her.*

Randy said quietly, "When I am truly free, I will recover my title, my lands, my funds. Then I will be able to repay her."

Clay was so disgusted, he looked him in the face so he could explain the facts of life. He saw the truth there.

Randy was afraid.

More factoids penetrated Clay's self-centered fog.

The guy was big, muscular, not bad looking in a sulky way. Sometimes he sounded like a genuine lord. He couldn't keep clothes on. He believed that Jewel was, like, his savior.

Finally, Clay bothered to look at Randy as a mark, closely, selflessly. "What happens if you miss an installment on your get-out-of-jail-free plan?"

"What?" Randy said.

"If Jewel doesn't find you and—" Clay gestured at the couch. He thought of what could have been happening at the exact moment he'd been going down on her, making her moan. Was it even him making her feel like that? Ew.

Randy shook his head. "I don't know. Perhaps I will spend another two centuries satisfying women. Trying to find another one whose happiness matters enough."

This struck a note like a gong deep in Clay's gut. He thought about Virgil hopping from cheesecake to cheesecake, dumping Clay with them so he could run his cons, and about little boy Clay charming the girls into putting up with Virgil as long as possible, so little Clay could have a mommy. Then, inevitably, starting over again when Virgil left them.

"So that's the big deal?" Clay said softly. "It's this curse thingy, isn't it? You can't afford to stay away from her."

"She has no reason to permit me to stay."

Clay examined him carefully. If Randy's story was true, he had no money, no skills, no home, no legal identity. He didn't know the century or the country. He didn't sound American. If he couldn't get Jewel to let him mooch off her, he was not only screwed for eternity, he was on the street.

Clay felt like a king by comparison. He rubbed it in. "You always been able to satisfy a woman in less than three hours?"

"No." Randy looked him in the eye. "That took a great deal of practice. I am useful for only one thing."

Clay thought about that one for a minute. "I'm amazed you don't hate women."

Randy sat up. "I can't afford it."

"Never had the option to switch to men, either," Clay guessed, and caught a flash in Randy's eyes.

"I like women more, now, than I ever did when I was free. I know how they think. Without them, the past two centuries would literally have been a blank. When she is in my bed, you might say I can read a woman's mind. Though her secrets are not written in words, nor am I seeing her thoughts. I see deeper. I know what she wants better than she does."

Holy crow. The perfect con artist.

"Then you should be able to get Jewel to give you what you want. Clothes, Thai food, roof over your head, clean sheets—"

"I am not a doxy," Randy said sharply, and Clay was pleased that he'd needled the guy at last. "Circumstances have made a whore of me. Once, I had a place in the world. I fit in."

"As a lord," Clay said with scorn.

"Lords had their uses," Randy said.

Clay reined in his jealousy with a start. *He's been working me! The perfect con artist. After two hundred years, he knows stuff about the mark that would take me a lifetime to learn.* This led to the thought, *He has something I want.* And then, *I have something he wants.*

"That's what you want me to do. Make you—useful."

Randy's eyes were big. *My God, he's been playing me all this time and I bought it.*

"I once had an abundance of clothes," Randy said wryly, making a tiny opening gesture with his elbows and hands.

Naked! That's my trigger word for this guy. And he figured it out. "Are you reading my mind?" Clay blurted, sounding like a mark. He felt stupid but relieved. Virgil used to play him relentlessly until he could defend and attack at the same time.

Randy shook his head. "I can't teach you that. It's part of being a demon."

"A demon," Clay said breathlessly. *I thought he could*

*teach me to read minds. What am I saying, Virgil taught
me how to read minds when I was five.* "A demon who
wants a job."

"And an identity. Some skills outside of a bed. I have
known that since Jewel took your credit card away from
me." The bitterness in his tone startled Clay. "I shall
need a false past."

"Driver's license," Clay murmured.

"I should first learn to drive," Randy said drily.

*He's got me bought in. I'm hooked. Now he'll ask for
the big one.* Clay swallowed, as curious and breathless as
any mark.

Randy cleared his throat. "What is Stockholm syndrome?"

"What?" Funny thing to spend the big one on. "It happens to kidnap victims and hostages. They fall in love
with their kidnappers because they turn into, like, little
kids and they're totally dependent on the bad guy for
their needs." To take back some power, Clay said, "Who
told you about that?"

"Jewel." Randy murmured, "She is wise."

Clay stood abruptly. *You don't know her.* He walked
to the window and looked down on Michigan Avenue. "I
don't need you to teach me anything about women," he
said over his shoulder.

Silence.

Randy said, "Are you quite, quite sure?"

The bathroom door opened.

CHAPTER 28

Ten minutes earlier, in Clay's suite bathroom, Jewel had parked on the commode lid, trembling all over. Waves of shock and knee-weakening lust raged through her.

That was the biggest thrill of my life, she thought. *Can I die of embarrassment now?*

It was too much. Too much. Sex with Clay had felt so good, so normal, he was merely an ordinary, cuddly petty criminal like the kind she saw every day. Of course he wanted something, but she was used to that, that felt normal, too, so she was perfectly happy to let him deliver his brand of soothing, mark-cheating, womanizing comfort. And he was, frankly, very talented.

And then Randy. He was so darned sneaky. She hadn't noticed he was there until she counted the hands. Or was it when he was messing with her head, saying *scream, Jewel, beg, Jewel,* when he was halfway down her throat and she couldn't breathe.

She shuddered with sexual aftershock.

She wrapped herself in a towel as tightly as possible. "That is never, *EVER* going to happen again!" she rasped.

Probably.

It was that uncertainty that upset her the most. She'd thought she was actually getting better. Randy actually seemed to be helping to get her unscrewed. Okay, he was a sex demon, but she'd lost interest in the Nathans and Chads.

Then he does this to me.

Worse, it turned out she was as corkscrew-kinky as ever.

Because she'd loved it.

Jewel pulled the towel over her face.

There was only one solution. She had to swear off sex with Randy. Put him in a hospice for the terminally arrogant. Send him back to Wales, where he could look for his roots.

Piss him off so he would bop into a bed somewhere, and then forget about him.

No. She wasn't mean enough for that. However freaked she was at this minute, she knew she couldn't condemn him to sexual slavery for the rest of whatever. Even if she'd known he was in that sofa, she couldn't have left him there.

He needs me.

She shut her eyes and banged her head against the sink. *You need him, you slut. Headline: Tables Turned On Office Slut.* Every guy in the department would be high-fiving Randy if they knew what had been happening to her.

She took a slow shower, using every single one of the hotel giveaway toiletries in Clay's bathroom. She did her hair. There was a big, fat puffy bathrobe on the hook and she put it on.

Maybe one of them has left by now. I can't face them both.

Fat chance. When she came out into Clay's sitting

room, they turned to look at her as if she was interrupting something.

"Okay, I'm back," she announced in a shaky voice. What if they were discussing how to get her to do it again? What if they liked sharing?

Clay sent Randy a look and went to her, taking her hands in his. "You okay?" For once he didn't look sly or teasing or provocative or criminal.

"Fine," she squeaked. She cleared her throat. "I see you've, uh . . . That is, I assume Randy has convinced you, uh."

Clay looked as if his world had crumbled.

She felt guilty, though how the hell any of this could be her fault she couldn't fathom. "I'm afraid that brass bed won't be much use to you anymore."

His expression darkened. "So I gather." She remembered Randy jeering, *The poor fellow fancies himself the sole origin of all his customers' delight.*

"You'll come up with something else," she said brightly. Then she remembered who she was talking to. "Or not. Something legal."

"At least I got paid," Clay said, sunk in gloom. The phone rang. "Yeah?" he said listlessly. Then he jerked upright. "What!" He hung up, his face a mask of shock.

Randy said, "I fear the bed has been stolen. That was what I came to tell you." In high lordship mode, he looked down his nose at Jewel. "And found you in flagrante delicto."

She flushed.

"When? How? Who?" Clay sputtered.

"Now, just before I came in. A woman put the bed into a van and the van drove away with it," Randy said calmly.

"My money is in that bed!" Clay howled. He scrambled into his shirt. "How could you let them steal my bed?" he accused her.

"You don't seem too upset," Jewel said to Randy.

"I've seen enough of that bed," he said.

"That's fair."

"Oh yeah?" Clay said, breathing hard as he shoved his loafers on. "Try this on for size. I can't pay my credit card bill without that bed."

Jewel whistled. "That's a big bill."

"You never intended to pay," Randy said.

"Of course I intended to pay," Clay said crossly. "And now I've got to stick around helping you," he said pointedly to Randy, to Jewel's puzzlement.

Randy frowned. "I see," he said, sounding reasonable. "Yes. Pity."

"Did you see who was driving?" Clay said.

Jewel was on top of that one. "Nina. Bet you a million dollars. I warned you not to underestimate her." Her heart sank. She threw off her robe and started yanking on her pantsuit. "The hotel could prosecute her for theft. Ed will stroke out. Where's my purse? We'll get the car and go after her, we'll catch up with her, I promise," she assured Clay.

Randy turned pale. "That isn't necessary. Perhaps— perhaps she'll return the money if she has the bed."

Clay and Jewel gave him identical scornful looks.

Jewel said, "You don't have to come with us."

Randy looked from her to Clay. "Yes, I do. Please," he said, as if the word were extracted from him with forceps.

"What's his problem?" said Clay.

"Nina," Jewel said. "She wants to get her hands on him."

Clay raised his eyebrows offensively. "Jealous?"

"No!" She sent a silent appeal to Randy. "It's—"

Randy said, "If Nina has the bed—if I get close to it—"

"He's afraid he'll zap into it and she'll keep him forever," Jewel finished.

"So? You two are buddies. You get into her house and bingo, he's free again," Clay said sourly.

Jewel shook her head. "She would never let me in her house again if she thought I knew she had Randy." Tears leaped to her eyes. "God forbid she ever finds out what I—what happens when I sleep on one of Randy's beds."

"So don't tell her," Clay said, as if that was easy.

She dashed away the tears. "I think I know where she'll take it. I used to take her boys to see her old auntie on the Northwest Side. The auntie left Nina the house. It's a cinch that's where she's headed. Randy, get dressed. Unless you want to wait here." She punched speed dial for Nina's cell.

Nina tapped her fingernails on the steering wheel of her rented van. Her phone sat beside her like a bomb. Ed had called twice. He'd ordered her to come home and she'd told him to stuff it. Her ears still burned from the sound of his fury.

But she had the bed. She tried to remember how good it made her feel, but her head was full of Ed, roaring over the phone. She'd been so mad at Clay for holding out on her. Mad at Jewel for hiding the bed. That didn't feel good, either. Poor screwed-up Jewel. Maybe someday when things quieted down, she would bring Jewel out here and let her use the bed.

No. I need it. What if Jewel insisted she give the bed back? *What if she steals it from me?*

A nasty dark hard place tightened in her stomach.

I don't like me like this. She wiped a tear off her cheek with her forefinger.

The phone rang. Nina jumped. She didn't dare pick up again. Ed was wily as hell when he wanted something.

Too bad he doesn't want anything but his supper on the table and his shirts pressed.

She checked the phone to see who was calling, but it had stopped ringing.

Between rush hour and some kind of festival in Olive Park, traffic sucked. She crawled up Lake Shore Drive, got off at Irving Park Road, and crawled westward. As she passed under Edens Expressway she saw a haze of pink in the air. Nina held her breath. She actually knew somebody who had disappeared into the pink eight months ago. What did that woman say on "Ask Your Shrink"? *Think happy thoughts.* Nina tried to think happy thoughts about visiting Aunt Onofrio's house for a little nap.

Twenty minutes later she was sitting in the van in front of her aunt's house, wondering how to get the bed inside, when her passenger-side door opened.

"What the fuck are you doing?" Ed said furiously. Her heart stuttered. He climbed in, reached over, and yanked the keys out of the ignition. If she'd had a gun at that moment, he'd have been dead.

"How did you find me?"

"I went over to the Drake. Found the security dicks panicking over a missing brass bed belonging to your friend. Called the credit card company, found out you'd rented a van. Put two and two together. Where else would you take him but your aunt's place?"

Her heart started beating again. "Take who?"

He looked her in the eye for the first time. "C'mon, Nina. Your gigolo."

She drew herself up, which was hard to do sitting in a bucket seat. "For the gazillionth time, I am not sleeping with Clay."

"You move in with him, it's over," he warned, and she exploded.

"I am not moving in with Clay! He is just my sex therapist! You get your office bimbos and your late hours and weekends 'working overtime'," she sneered, her voice shaking, her fingers making clawed quote marks at him. "And I don't get sex therapy?"

His eyes slid away from hers. "Bull. Why the van?"

"I'm—moving something for him."

"Don't lie, Nina," Ed said dangerously. He dangled the keys at her. "I can call the cops right now. Maybe if you have to go to night court and explain what you been up to, it'll wake you up. This is serious. You are fucking crazy."

Tears started down her face. "You bastard."

He bore down on her. "Why the van?"

"It's Clay's bed. His treatment bed. I don't give a damn about Clay, it's the bed I want."

Ed stared at her as if she was loony. *I'm sure as hell not gonna tell you more.* "His bed. What are you, a fetishist? How much did it cost?"

"Nothing! Not a nickel, you tightwad! I stole it!"

"You turning into a klepto? Jesus Christ, my wife spends all my money and now she's cracking up!"

"It's important to me, so you wouldn't understand. You don't know what I want and you don't care! It hasn't bothered you for years! I don't see why you're making such a stink now."

"Get out. Take the car home," he said. "I'm driving."

She wanted to push him in front of a bus, but he was bigger and stronger and he had the keys. Instead of getting out, she moved to the passenger seat. "Why, where are you taking my bed?"

"Back to the hotel." He made a disgusted sound in his

throat. "Stealing. For Christ's sake, what next? No," he said, "fuck, I'm not taking it back to that gigolo, what the fuck am I thinking? It's going to the dump."

She shrieked. "No!" She grabbed his arm. "Don't," she pleaded. "You can't!"

"Hell I can't. Bob's Parts and Car Crusher Service, and bing, straight into the hopper."

All the blood drained out of her face. "If you do this, I'm divorcing you. What do you care if I have a good time? You and your sluts at the office." She said in a vicious, throaty voice, "I'd like to kill you. But I'll take you for everything first."

Ed looked pale but he didn't stop driving. He threw her hand off his arm. "So divorce me," he said, but he swallowed.

She caught her breath and rubbed away her tears. Her hand came away smeared with mascara. "Bastard," she sobbed. Her phone rang. She snatched it up. "Hello?"

"Nina! Jewel."

"Oh, Jewel, thank God, thank God you called, I'm at my aunt's house, it's Ed, he's with me and he's driving—"

Ed batted the phone out of her hand without glancing at her. "Shaddap."

Jewel hung up. They were frighteningly far behind Nina. All the buses had been full, so Jewel had led Randy and Clay on foot from the Drake to the Corncob Building, retrieved her car, then fought north and west through rush hour traffic, working her way toward the Kennedy Expressway.

Now she handed Clay the phone. "Keep trying speed-dial two. She's at her aunt's house with Ed. She said, 'he's driving' and we got cut off. Either he's driving her crazy or he's driving that van Randy saw. Knowing the two of them, I vote crazy."

"I vote van," Clay said, "because I want it to be true."

"I agree with Clay," Randy said.

"But if her husband has caught up with her—" Clay said.

Jewel laid on the horn. "What is your goddam problem?" she screamed through her windshield at the traffic. "Why is this street always like this?"

Clay turned on the radio. "Relax. We'll catch up with her."

"*Lake Shore Drive is stationary and the entire Mag Mile is totally gridlocked. A parade detour and a genie-*

*sighting are blamed for the holdup. Back to the news-
room. Lewis?"*

"*Dave, we have a positive ID on the woman who turned
a genie loose on Millennium Park this afternoon—*"

Ohmigod. Jewel smacked the radio preset to change
the station. She was doomed. This would definitely cost
her her job. Some protector of the city dat woiks, she
was.

I'm going back home to the farm and eat some worms.
Except, oh yeah, she'd lost the farm, too.

From the radio, the cultured voice of the doc from
"Ask Your Shrink" said, "*Go ahead, caller.*"

"*We should shoot all the pigeons. They're filthy. And
now they're suicidal. Twice now, a pigeon stole a butt
right off my lips. I hadda use mouthwash. They could of
gave me cooties.*"

"*Don't you mean,*" the doc said gently, "*that you are
suicidal? Denial can be an enemy as well as a friend.
Isn't smoking a form of self-destruction?*"

Jewel killed the radio with a trembling hand. "She
drives me nuts."

"I don't smoke anymore," Clay said, looking out his
window.

"Why," Randy said from the back seat, "is there so
much magical oddity all over your city?"

Jewel's nerve broke. "What are you talking about?
Couple of little hinky things here and there. Nothing
major. We cope." Her voice shook. *And it's my fault,
this time.*

"Yet you complain that you must pursue magic—"

"I don't pursue the hinky stuff. It pursues me. I don't
need to do this stupid work. Chicago works. It works
great. People cope. They take it in stride."

How many people had been hurt in the panic at the genie's bank heist? Who had had their pocket picked while they gawked at her, enthroned in her parade? And how screwed up was the world after the genie had moved an entire parade twenty-four hours out of the future? Her insides twisted and her head ached.

"Like finding guys materializing in beds where they weren't invited," Clay said, still looking out his window.

Jewel turned on him. "Magic is not all over this city. My whole career is sidelined trying to keep magic in this city under wraps. It's guys like you pimping magic to innocent women who make my job suck."

Drawling slower, Clay said, "That radio shrink is only half right. You probably shouldn't buy into denial too much. 'Specially if your job is dealing with magic. Lie to the public if you have to, but not to yourself—Ruby."

She sucked in a horrified breath. "I do not lie!" *Why's he being such a jerk?* "My job is not about dealing with m-magic. I'm getting out of Hinky Corners real soon now and Ed's giving me a real assignment as soon as I get you wrapped up and busted."

Clay said in that maddening drawl, "Ruby's more honest than you are. She admits that Lord Randy Sans-Culottes here obsesses her. I'm merely incidental to your sex life."

Her breath caught. *He's jealous.* That startled a laugh out of her.

"Jewel!" Randy announced in a surprised voice. "You must have found the djinn merchant." She looked in the mirror and saw him holding the sealed-up Drambuie bottle.

Oh, God. She put on the parking brake, killed the engine, and lunged over the seat back. "Give me that."

Clay said, "Hey, a genie bottle, cool."

"Leave that alone!" She snatched the bottle out of Randy's hands and stuck it under her seat. "That thing is never, ever, ever getting out of this bottle again."

"That's a little harsh," Clay said. "Never is a long time."

"Shut up," she suggested, starting the car again. In the mirror she saw Randy's face, white and thoughtful.

Nina clenched her jaw as Ed inched up the ramp onto the Kennedy Expressway. The air was already going pink. He said nothing. He cranked up the air-conditioning. She wondered if the pink stuff could come in through the glass, or if they could keep it out with the windows rolled up. She caught herself holding her breath. Her blood hammered angrily in her ears.

He cursed under his breath. He leaned on the horn, gunned the van, screeched up to the bumper of the next car, and slammed on the brakes, over and over and over. Every driver out here seemed to be doing the same. The yelling and horn honking escalated. The air got pinker.

She stood it as long as she could. "Let's get off the road."

"Hey you! Yeah, you! Fuck you! Fuck off and die!" her helpmeet screamed through the driver's side window. "Tried to cut me off."

The car behind them pulled out onto the shoulder and roared past, honking continuously.

"Please, Ed. I'm afraid."

"Shaddap." Traffic slowed again, then stopped. "This is your fuckin' stray's work, that fuckin' Heiss. She let a genie loose on South Mich. Tied up traffic all over downtown." Pink fog rose around them. He said savagely, "Tomorrow I fire her fuckin' ass back to fuckin' Wisconsin and I never want to see her fuckin' face at my table again."

She counted as cars ahead of them disappeared into it, five, four, three.

Ed didn't seem to notice the pink stuff. He was lost in road rage. Half rising in his seat, he leaned on the horn and kept leaning. *Beep beeeep beeeeeeeeep.*

The cars in front of them faded into the pink. Two. One.

She tugged his arm. "Stop it. You're making it worse!"

"Fuck you, too!" he screamed at her, and she felt the van lurch forward toward the bumper in front of them. She covered her face with her arms and turned her head to the side.

Everything went silent. The horns and yelling voices disappeared. The van's engine died. Her throat stopped up with fear, and she uncovered her eyes.

They were floating in the pink. She couldn't feel the tires meeting pavement anymore.

Ed's eyes popped in astonishment. He was still leaning on the horn, but it made no sound.

"What's happening?" she gasped.

He gaped through the windshield, then through her side window, his side window, and into the mirrors.

"Ed, I'm scared." She shrank into her seat.

She watched his color slowly fade. "Fuck me," he said in dumb amazement. "What happened?"

She said in a small voice, "It's like Ask Your Shrink keeps saying. If you drive in a bad mood, you make pink stuff."

He shook his head. "No way. Whole city would be swamped."

"So where's the city? Do you see it out there anywhere?"

She remembered that he no longer wanted her, that he was taking her treatment bed to the dump. *I'm going to die and go to hell like this. A wannabe adulteress with a trashed marriage, scared out of my mind.*

"What's going to happen to us?"

"Beats the shit out of me."

"Sometimes people disappear into the pink."

He turned toward her at that. "I'm aware of that. I've heard that. You don't hafta tell me that."

She heard fear in his voice. Scared, he looked halfway human. *I don't want to go like this, with somebody who doesn't love me.*

He turned away as if he had stopped seeing her and stared out the van windows once more.

She put her hand on the door handle. She could jump out. If it was only fog, she'd land between cars that weren't moving. Wouldn't she?

And if it wasn't fog?

Ask Your Shrink's catchy little phrases came to mind. Anger vapor. Atomized road rage. If rage made pink stuff, it surprised her the van wasn't full of pink.

I don't want to die mad.

"Ed?"

"What?" he said hoarsely. He was looking at her again.

"I don't want to die mad."

He stared at her. "What if we don't die? What if we're going—someplace?"

"Where?" She looked out the windshield fearfully. There was nothing to see but pink.

"I been listening to that show, the one you said."

"Ask Your Shrink? She makes sense, kinda."

Horror crept into his voice. "If she makes so goddam much sense, how come people still disappear outta their cars? How come cars go into this shit and never come out?"

Nina stretched one finger to touch his forearm. "Ed. I don't want to die mad at you. I have so much to say to you."

He looked away and then, as if unable to avoid her eyes, looked back. He said gruffly, "What."

He thinks I'm in the wrong. He thinks I owe him an apology. Well, she did. If she waited for his apology, she might die waiting, and real soon.

She said breathlessly, "I've missed you. I didn't want sex therapy. I wanted you."

"Nuts."

"If you work late, I don't sleep until you get home. I pretend. I don't give a damn if I look good unless you think so." She was on a roll now. Her voice shook. "If you come home for lunch, it makes my whole day. Even when you're m-mean to me."

He stared. "For real?"

She nodded. "Tell you something." She swallowed. "When I take my sex-therapy naps, I dream about you."

Color rose in his face. "No lie."

"Even when I don't want to." She twitched a smile, swallowing tears. "It's you."

Slowly the darkness cleared from his face. "I thought you were gone already," he said.

Her head wavered, *No.*

She smelled his sweat change. "Oh. Oh, baby." He touched her face. "You're, like, the queen of my heart forever. I don't want nobody else for the rest of my life on a day-to-day constant basis, twenty-four-seven, three-sixty-five. Every morning." His rough thumb stroked her cheek. "Every night."

She squeaked.

He was bright red. "Always."

She gulped, but no words came out. Her heart was full.

"Do you still want to kill me?" he said, his eyes narrowed, like he didn't want to see if she hit him.

"I never wanted to kill you, you asshole." She sniffled hard. "I want my husband back."

He nodded like he was thinking. "Want him for the next two minutes?"

She squeezed his hand and he squeezed back. "Love you, Ed." The pink rolled past the windshield in waves.

"Love you, baby."

She heard him sniffle.

Then her ears filled with deafening honking.

The Kennedy Expressway stretched out in front of them, bumper-to-bumper.

Ed restarted the van and made it crawl forward.

What a firecracker I married, he thought. She was like this twenty years ago, only less, if he could believe that. Her eyes were still big and bright. A sigh came from the passenger seat. Crap, she was crying again.

She said, "I still love you. In spite of all those bitches at the office."

"I still love you, in spite of the bitches at the office," he said, feeling oddly light.

"I never screwed Clay."

"I screwed a lot of bitches," Ed admitted, "but I was only half there. The other half of me was wondering what you were thinking."

"I guessed," she said, and he felt both foolish and a lot less shitty. In a thoughtful voice she added, "That's why it threw me when you got so possessive. I never expected that."

"I know, confused the shit outta me, too. When I saw those charges I figured I knew what was happening, and I realized I had to have you. An' I looked in the mirror and I saw a fifty-five-year-old guy with a bay window who wants to own his wife. What the fuck is that? Who am I, thinking I can do that, at my age?" He risked another look at her. "You're worth hanging onto." He had to bite his lip.

She turned impulsively toward him. In a breathless voice she said, "Ed, I think I'm changing." His blood ran cold. "I'm turning into—"

"Yeah?" he said roughly. Here it came. He'd been dreading he-didn't-know-what.

"Into me," she said in a surprised voice.

He put his hand out and wiped tears off her chin. "You're scaring the shit out of me."

She sniffled hard. "Situation normal, then."

"Wouldn't have it any other way," he croaked.

He drove holding her hand in silence for another half mile.

"Ed?" she said in a small voice. "Do you have to wreck the bed? Let's give it to Jewel. She needs it more than me."

He gave it some thought. Something about this bed set Nina off, no lie. Jewel was putty in Nina's hands. He wished he could have at least punched this fucking gigolo. Or, why couldn't he have come out and said, *Stay away from my wife*? That's what you did when guys moved on your woman.

He couldn't remember how he'd slid from tough guy into bureaucrat, the way his chest had slid into his beer gut.

He glanced in her direction.

She looked pretty good in the fading afternoon light. And for some reason she still wanted him.

"Where are you going? Downtown is that way."

"Bob's dump," he said.

"Now, that would be a waste," she said. She groped on the van's floor and picked up her cellphone. "Hello, Jewel? Meet us at Bob's Car Crusher Service. It's in Des

Plaines, off 90. Yes, it's in the van right now. Oh, and hey, don't take the Kennedy, it's solid pink."

Ed drove. The phone quacked in Nina's hand.

"Don't be mad at me," she said in a persuasive wheedle. "We're still having bread pudding Sunday."

Ed sucked in a long, hot, shaky sigh of relief. *Doing a number on Jewel. Situation normal.*

When she hung up, she said cheerfully, "We're in trouble now. She's meeting us at the dump with Clay. He could prosecute."

"He wouldn't have the balls."

"Both of us, since I stole it but you're driving and you won't take the bed back to its rightful owner."

"That's Jewel talking. We don't know what this guy wants."

Nina laughed. "Guess we'll discuss it at the dump."

If I get it into the car crusher before they arrive, there's nothing to discuss. Ed stepped on the gas.

CHAPTER 30

When they found Bob's dump, Jewel noticed with foreboding that all the lights were off, but the chain-link gate stood wide open. Something about that said *Nina* to her. Beyond the gate, rows of junk cars stretched into a darkness unrelieved except by a string of bare light bulbs hanging from the tip of some distant tall machinkus.

"Okay, we go in, we find them, we get the bed. Randy does not talk. I'll deal with Nina. Clay, it's up to you to make Ed give up the bed."

"Piece of cake," Clay said. He sounded cocky again.

She sent him the evil eye. "Don't piss me off. For two cents I'd hand you over to Ed. He might punch you instead of resorting to the law." She turned the evil eye on her demon. "Did you get that, Randy? No talking."

Randy's upper lip twitched. "As you wish." He was gonna be such fun to live with.

She said, "We don't want Nina guessing who you are."

He lost his huffy look. "No."

"Right. Let's go."

A god-awful growly machine-noise started up somewhere in the bowels of the dump. Jewel drove toward the noise, weaving through snaggly aisles of junk cars. She pulled up next to a rental van next to a yellow machinkus that looked like a giant toaster oven with teeth. It was festooned with light bulbs. A crane brooded like a waterbird over stacks of neatly crushed car-bricks big as kitchen stoves. More bare light bulbs shone at the crane's foot. The oily-smelling ground was covered with cinders, shards of colored plastic, and millions of sparkly bits of windshield glass. When she spotted Ed and Nina standing close together, Jewel parked.

The machine noise was overwhelmingly louder here.

"This is it, guys," she said, raising her voice but trying not to attract Ed's or Nina's attention. "What do we do?"

Clay's eyes glittered. "I'll distract Ed. You distract Nina. Randy goes after the bed. Only, I don't trust him with it, because he didn't want us to go after it in the first place—"

Jewel interrupted him. "Randy. What do we do?"

Randy said in a hard voice, "You keep Nina away from me. Clay tells lies to Ed. And I go about getting out of your life."

Up in her face again.

"How you gonna manage that?" She was pretty fed up with his attitude. He never seemed to notice when other people were having a crisis. "Look, buster, I wasn't exactly wishing on the good-fuck star for this particular mess to fall into my lap, but I am trying to keep you from ending up in Nina's clutches for the next forty years." God, he could be a pain in the ass. "Unless that's what you want."

His face fell. "No."

"No is right," she said, ashamed of bullying him.

A metallic screeching added itself to the roar of the machine. Jewel whipped her head around.

Clay screamed, "My money!" He ran ahead, totally not to plan.

Jewel saw three things at once: Ed and Nina locked in a clinch kiss, the big yellow machinkus slowly smashing the brass bed in its jaws, and what looked like confetti flying through the air. Biggish confetti.

Clay slapped a big red button on the front of the car crusher and darted forward, snatching at the air like a lunatic. Deafening silence fell.

Her boss and her best friend didn't seem to notice. They kissed like the end of the world.

Behind Jewel, Randy gripped her shoulder.

She spun around. He looked walleyed.

"Oh, no. Don't be flipping out on me now." She grabbed his arms and glared into his eyes. "That would be a really, really bad idea. You have to stay calm."

He looked freaked. The whites of his eyes showed, his fists clenched and unclenched by his belly, and his chest heaved.

"Stay with me for a minute, okay? Are you getting this? Randy?" Her voice rose in panic. "Can you hear me?"

He nodded, his horrified gaze on the car crusher. The brass bed was a tangle of bent and split tubing. No one could ever sleep on it now. Behind Ed and Nina, Jewel saw the big red button and, under it, a Frankenstein switch. "Randy, let it go!"

Nina peeked around her husband and sent Jewel a thumbs-up.

Out of the corner of her eye Jewel saw Randy marching toward the brass bed. Her heart jumped into her throat.

"No!" She bodychecked him. "No. You don't need that bed. It's not important anymore. Will you stop and think?"

"I understand now," he muttered. He reached out and threw the Frankenstein switch.

The machine roared to life. The bed made spang! and spung! noises, and money flew out of the split-open tubes.

Clay ran up and smashed the red button again, sending Randy a dirty look.

Jewel looked for Nina. She was leading Ed around back of the rental van.

Jewel ignored them. "What do you think you're doing?" she said to Randy when she could hear again.

"You're right, I don't need it," he said slowly. "I've been thinking. I don't belong here."

"Never mind about the bed."

"I must. I am ruining your life, Jewel. If I am trapped again, at least you may be free of me." He touched her face. "There is no need to make a prisoner of you as well."

She swallowed. "It's okay," she faltered.

He shook his head. "You never asked for this mess," he said bleakly. Her conscience stung her. "I know you suffer from my constant presence. You didn't like me invading your dream—"

"I love when you come into my dreams!"

"—About the ambulance in the snow."

She licked her lips. "Okay, that freaked me. But I don't know if I didn't like it."

As if he were delivering bad news, he said, "Jewel, Clay Dawes explained Stockholm syndrome to me."

Puzzled, she said, "And?"

"You were wise to think I suffer from it. I see that I have become like a hound, trained in a kennel, never let loose except to do my duty. I have never been truly free in spirit."

He looked at the remains of the bed, and then past her into the darkness of the dump. "You freed me. Yet I felt unsafe in the world. Prison though it has been, bed is my haven, my kennel. Like the hound, whenever the world confounds me, or when my mistress is displeased with me"—he looked her in the eye, and she felt pierced with guilt— "I flee to my kennel." He took a deep breath. "Also, I have used it to test you, to test your commitment to me."

"Look—" she began.

"You never asked for this."

"No, but I wanted it anyway! Randy, I'm no better than Nina! I wanted a sex slave, and that's wrong. Someday you'll figure out how to get out of a bed without me."

He stepped closer and took her in his arms. His lips touched her temple. "Someday," he whispered, "the good-fuck star will reward your generous heart. Until then, the best I can do is to free you from the prison of my love."

She blinked. He couldn't mean that. He said himself it was Stockholm syndrome.

He looked at the shattered brass bed and beyond, to the limits of the circle of the streetlight. Clay was out there, picking up scattered bills like a demented hen pecking corn. Beyond was nothing but dark rows and rows of wrecked cars.

"Randy," she said, a warning in her voice. "It's all smashed up. You can't go back."

She felt his thumb on her lips. He whispered in her ear, "I don't have much time."

She turned to meet his mouth, throwing everything she had into kissing him.

No going back, she thought, and threw the Franken-stein switch. The machine roared awake.

He turned to mist in her hands.

"*Randy!*" she screamed.

He was gone.

She spun around, tripping over his empty clothes in time to see the brass bed disappearing into the jaws of the crusher, squishing smaller and smaller. Something blurred past her and the roaring ceased again.

Eventually she heard herself screaming and stopped.

Clay stood bare-chested beside her, his pockets stuffed, his Hawaiian shirt tied into a bulging sack. "Can I get a little cooperation here?"

He looked disgusted and, for Clay, tense.

"He's gone." She tingled with shock.

"Did you see which way your boss went?"

"I don't know where he went," she wailed. "He disappeared!"

"Ed," he said patiently. "Your boss. Nina's spousal unit?"

"Oh. They're in the van." The van was rocking rhythmically. She touched her face and sniffled. "I think he's busy."

"Do you think I could ask you for a little help?" Clay said with studied patience. "There was over a quarter of a million dollars in that bed, in fifties and hundreds." He hefted the shirt sack. "I've got some, but I haven't had time to count it, and it would be lovely to have something to tip the concierge with tomorrow and not leave it here for the rats to eat."

Where did he go? Where, where?

Behind Clay, the bed was a cube of smashed metal. Out there in the dark were rows and rows and rows of dead cars.

With back seats. Hm.

"I have to find him. Soon. Before all these cars are crushed."

"He's only doing it to get attention."

She approached the nearest car, a Camry with its doors missing. It smelled. Not an appetizing way to meet the world's finest stealth fuck.

Clay sensed her hesitation. *This is where I get rid of that guy forever.* "Jewel, no. Don't do this."

She didn't even look at him. "I have to."

"You hate clingy guys."

That made her glance up. "You're not exactly helpful."

"Hey," he said, wounded. "What about breaking you in and out of Field's in the middle of the night? Doesn't that count?"

She was getting steamed, but she wasn't looking into the wreck anymore. "Listen, you. When I told you I was an orphan, you—you snubbed me. What the hell was that? I didn't even want to tell you all that; you weaseled it out of me. And then you made fun of me. Randy's there for me. He's in my nightmares, holding my hand," she blurted.

"You don't want my sympathy. You hate whiners."

She gasped. "So now I'm a whiner!"

Clay thought fast and talked slower. He put up his hands, placating. "You're right. It was all my fault. I thought you were tough. I—I guess I wanted you to be tough." Good grief, he was telling her the truth again.

Her eyes narrowed at him.

"You hate clingy guys," he repeated. He was losing. *Shut up before you mess up worse.*

"I know." She softened up. "But I know what alone feels like, too. If I don't go find him, he'll be trapped and alone in some junked-up car until the day they smash it. And probably afterward. How long does it take for a smashed car to crumble? Will that set him free?" Clay saw her backbone stiffen. "Yes, he drives me nuts. Frankly, you drive me nuts. But I'm going after him."

Jewel stared at the wreck in front of them for a long moment.

"I hate rats," she said, and crawled into the wreck's back seat.

Clay counted to ten. That didn't do much good, so he sat down in the shattered-glass-studded dirt and counted fifties and hundreds instead. When he was done, he felt a lot better. Only a little more than five percent of his cash was lost out there in the dump, or was still smashed into the brass bed. With this dough and the money in the bank, he could pay off his credit card and pay Virgil and have something left over.

The bed, however, was a total loss. He fiddled gingerly with the car crusher's controls and got it to release. The bed was a block of metal spaghetti. One short length of split brass tubing stuck forlornly out of the block, like a hand waving for help. Clay tried not to think what it would mean if Randy had zapped back into this, his old home, and not into one of those raunchy, ripped-up, rat-riddled back seats in the dump. Clay needed all his sympathy for himself right now. There were scratches all over the tube, one, two, three, four, and a slash, five, all along the tube, until it vanished into the spaghetti. *Poor naked loser*, he thought. *If Randy's in here now, he'll never score again.*

Something pale stuck out of the tube. Paper?

"That's not money."

Clay pulled. It was big, whatever it was. He kept pulling until a roll of thick, funny-textured paper slid out. The tattered remains of a ribbon were wrapped around its middle. He brushed the ribbon aside and unrolled the paper. A lot of curly handwriting covered it.

My poor Randolph, he read by streetlight. *My heart mislikes my hand as I make plans to bespell you.*

He looked up wildly. Jewel's feet were still visible, sticking out of the back seat of the Camry. "Wow."

He ran his eye over the rest of the writing, lips moving, until it turned to gibberish. *Agol togayesh* something, not Latin, but what? He'd have to ask Virgil.

Or not. No way could he explain to Virgil how his newest collector's item, rented by his son for the dumbest scam he ever heard of, had been possessed by a sex demon. Or how Clay had played pimp to Lord Randy, thinking the whole time he was such a master at the lonely-hearts scam that he could make a woman come when he wasn't even in the room. He shut his eyes.

When he looked again, Jewel's feet were kicking wildly.

What a waste. Knowing her, she would rescue the bare-butt king, and he would encourage all her worst hang-ups, and her boss would yell at her for a situation she had no control over.

She would blame Clay, too. No matter how annoying the streaker got, she never blamed him, oh no.

It was Clay who could always put his finger on her last nerve.

Slowly, he smiled.

One of these days he would have to get her in bed without a kibbitzer.

Nina's van stopped rocking.

Deliberately Clay rolled the scroll up again and stuffed it into his makeshift bag with his money. He dumped the bag into the back seat of Jewel's car.

Then he went and tapped on the driver's window of the van.

"Go see who it is," Nina said, just to hear her husband groan.

Ed groaned. *Good to have you back*, she thought.

"Baby, you're killing me."

"I knew you'd love that. Want to try something else?"

He grunted and rolled off her leg. "Somebody's knocking on the window." He thrashed around on the blanket pads. "My pants. Where are my fucking pants?"

She sighed luxuriously. Reaching up, she turned on the dome light.

"Augh, ack, now I'm blind!"

She picked up his pants and put them in his hand. He grumbled and groused his way into his pants and shoes, then clambered out the back of the van. Before he shut the door on her nakedness, he stuck his mug in and leered at her.

"Stay right like that," he said, and wiggled his eyebrows.

Her heart melted.

She put on her clothes and then laid her ear against the side of the van. It sounded like Clay out there.

"—getting her to recognize her own deep desires without her ever verbalizing them," Clay was saying in a professorial voice she didn't recognize.

"Without?" Ed pounced on that word. "You say she never talked about—about sex?"

"She didn't verbalize at all, beyond 'nice weather we're having.' Once she was deep in therapy, she came in, she paid, she went into the treatment room and did her own work. I'm proud of her. She's probably my most successful patient," Clay said, and Nina warmed to the sincerity in his voice.

Silence from Ed. In the van, her ear on the cold metal, Nina held her breath.

"Mr. Neccio, without being indelicate or violating a client's privacy, I think I can say that Nina's deepest desires, perhaps not fully understood by her, are involved with her partner. That is to say, with yourself, sir."

Ed grunted.

"She's very compatible with my treatment model. From the beginning she insisted on guarding the privacy of the marital boundary, and yet the only person she ever referenced, however putatively superficially, was her husband." *Gee, Clay, that's some sentence*, Nina thought. "After witnessing the degree of her commitment to you when we arrived this evening," Clay said and coughed modestly, "I would say that my work here is finished."

"Damn right it is," Ed said, sounding less grouchy than he could have. "Now that your fancy bed is—"

"Now, Jewel," Clay interrupted, and Nina's ears pricked up. "I wish I could work with Jewel further. I'm aware she only visited my office in order to protect her friend, but we did progress to a certain point."

Whoo-ee. Nina's eyes widened. *We are way overdue for some girl-talk.*

"No shit," Ed said, sounding interested.

"Of course, she's well defended."

"Ain't it the truth."

"And probably, in view of the pressures of her job, she may feel it isn't safe to submit to self-examination. I understand she works alone on sensitive cases."

"Has she been talking about her work?" Ed said in a

dangerous voice. "She's already suspended. I oughta fire her."

Nina began to see where this was going.

"No, sir. You seem particularly capable of inspiring discretion in your associates. About Jewel, you know, my work, with trained observation, and the degree of intimacy which we achieved in our short time together—"

Nina had heard enough. She slipped out the back of the van. "She hasn't had a partner in a year. None of the guys at the office will work with her."

Ed frowned at Nina. "I never said that."

"She said it," Nina said, putting out her tongue at her husband. "It's because she dated 'em all and dumped 'em all. They're scared of her," she said to Clay. "You have to admit, she packs a wallop."

"Oh, I think you exaggerate," Clay said smoothly, but she could see him pokering up underneath. He began to redden.

"It ain't Jewel," Ed said surprisingly. "Truth is, no-body wants to work in Hinky Corners. Shit spills across division lines, there's no commendations, no promotion, no media fuss if you bust some bad motherfucker. It's the fuckin' *X-Files* ghetto."

Clay said, "I'm surprised she tolerates it."

"She thrives on abuse," Ed boasted.

Clay said, "We worked together successfully over the past few days. Perhaps I flatter myself, but I believe she enjoyed it."

I have got to hear this story, Nina thought. With one eye on her husband, she gushed, "I'll just bet she en-joyed it!"

Ed took her by the arm and pulled her against his side.

Clay looked at Ed and said, "How hard can it be? Harder than psychology?" Nina held her breath.

Ed stared. Nina heard the wheels grinding in his head. She realized, *They're conning each other! Clay's wiggling out of trouble and Ed's getting Jewel a partner. Why, the foxy paisano bastard, he's been angling for this all along!*

Ed said with studied scorn, "What makes you think you can hack it?"

Lips pursed, Clay cocked his head to one side. "Well, I was the one who stopped the genie from robbing the bank."

"You were?"

"Ask Jewel, she was there. She backed me up with some excellent undercover work. As for the confidentiality issue, I think I can prove my discretion. No one has ever heard a word about me or my work with clients—from me." He wasn't looking at Nina, but she felt her ears burn. "And although my other clients will be mystified and disappointed, I believe I can keep the fate of my treatment bed under wraps. Of course, I'm not responsible for anyone else who may know."

Meaning Jewel. With a start, Nina realized she hadn't thought about sex therapy in hours. Maybe Clay was right about her priorities. She made a mental note to find out what Jewel and Clay had been up to, once Clay was done working her husband, and they had closed the trap on Clay. Turning her face against Ed's side, Nina grinned.

Ed's arm tightened around her. "If my wife's name is mentioned anywhere," he announced, "somebody is gonna get bruised."

"So can I assume this arrangement works for you?" Clay said. His psychologist voice was slipping as he got more smug.

Ed said nothing.

Nina squeezed Ed around the middle. When he looked down, she smiled. "Somebody needs to keep an eye on her."

Ed chewed on nothing, eyeing Clay.

Nina got sick of the pussyfooting and applied the clincher. "The other guys'll be pissed, because she's finally out of circulation."

CHAPTER 31

Lying in the dark on the Camry's mildewy upholstery, Jewel considered the problem. She had zero interest in trying every junk car in the dump. She'd rather risk multiple lacerations getting laid on the mangled wreckage of the original brass bed.

There has to be some pattern. Twice she had found Randy in a bed not his own. *Let's see, the first time he wigged out and wound up in my bed. Second time, we were in Field's, on the escalator. And he ended up in the beds department.*

He'd compared himself to a hound in a kennel. She smiled. He may have run back to his kennel, all right, but he was perfectly capable of yanking on her that way. *I tested you.*

The question was, where was that bed at Field's, relative to the escalator?

If she'd wanted to, she could have called out to Clay and asked him, but—she lifted her head and squinted out the doorless Camry—he was talking to Ed and Nina.

Now didn't seem to be the moment.

No matter. She had a strong hunch the Field's bed had been the closest. Not closest to where the escalator let passengers off, maybe, but closest as the crow flies. *As the demon flies.* She started to giggle hysterically. She felt like yelling, *I'm looking for trouble in the back seat of a junk car in the middle of the night in a dump!*

In front of your boss? her conscience whispered. *For shame.*

"I wonder how many people have had sex in this back seat?" she said aloud, and giggled harder.

Seven.

"Wait a minute, that's one too many. Unless the owner of the car had six boyfriends."

Or six girlfriends.

"Or there were two owners, but one of them cheated. Or if they all cheated," she realized, counting.

Or they did it after divorce or widowhood or before marriage. What a criminal mind you have.

What had Clay said? Cops and criminals were all in bed with each other. "We need each other to make our lives interesting."

Or perhaps three of them did it together.

She shivered.

She felt rather than heard his sigh of triumph. *Leave it to me,* he said. *Leave it all to me.*

"But I'm not—" *asleep,* she started to say, and fell backward endlessly, turning over and over in a cloud-filled night sky. Her skin heated up from the inside, so that the mist cooled her and made her slick all over with cloudbelly water.

Why in the air all the time, she wondered as her heart expanded in her chest with excitement.

Because it excites you. You told me you are afraid of heights. I can take you to the place where you are afraid because you are aroused. Or aroused because you are afraid.

She flailed out at that. *Where are you?* Her hands felt nothing but cold damp air.

Right here. I am always a breath away. A thought. A dream. He clasped her waist from behind while they plunged. She somersaulted backward, hungry for him, but he was always behind her, warming her back, touching her nipple, her belly, her throat, her pubic bone, making her feel open and yet very secret.

Do you dream what I am dreaming, then? she asked. She felt a hesitation in him. *Tell me the truth.*

I dream what you desire. And then I make it happen for you.

Wow. She tingled at the thought.

You teach me. I grow with you. I had no idea I could do this, before you asked me to do it for you, he said, and at the word "this" their plunge through the clouds accelerated and he wrapped his arms around her, his big hands clasping her face, throat, breasts, and belly, warming her mound with his hand, sliding around her until he seemed to face her as well as warm her back with his naked torso. His legs tangled hers, locking, his thighs prickly with stiff hairs. She felt him kiss her behind her ear, then her mouth, then his lips nibbled her nipples. She was sandwiched between him.

How? she began.

Probably it's best you close your eyes. Then he shut her mouth with his mouth, at the same time entering her from behind, kneading her breasts and belly with his hands, hoisting her to a new angle, oh, impossible, impossible. She opened her eyes, and instead of a close view of his face, she saw, as if looking down from a height, their two bodies locked together, plunging through clouds.

No. She looked closer. Three bodies.

Panicked, she closed her eyes. Her skin was a mass of friction, front and back, inside her mouth, inside her pussy. *I can be two men for you,* he whispered, *if that is what you desire. I can be all the men you will ever need.* She felt him slide a finger into her anus, and then his tongue thickened, and with a shock, she realized he had penetrated her with two cocks. *Want to know how that feels to me?* he said impossibly, his jaw locked over hers, the cock in his mouth shoving against her tongue, into her throat. All at once her tongue was alive with sensitive heat. She clenched all over, throat and pussy, and felt the squeeze with a sexual charge as alien as it was unmistakable. *I feel nothing unless you feel,* he said. *No one else can say that.*

Somewhere in the back of her brain she thought, *He's jealous.* Weirdly, that turned her on even more, as if he had become human finally, a real guy in her arms, in her mouth, stuck up inside her, and grappling every inch of her skin, trying to steal her for himself. He would stop at nothing to convince her.

With that thought, she came, a low slow rumbling explosion like a mushroom cloud falling in on itself and getting bigger in some deep dimension, hissing out of her pores and fading into the darkness, leaving her mind-whacked with smelly upholstery under her butt and a big sweaty guy on top of her.

He sighed, and she realized she was stifling. "Up, big boy."

"Did you bring my clothes?"

"I'm not your butler."

He licked her neck. "Valet. You're not my valet."

"I can't breathe." They sat up beside each other in the back seat of the wrecked Camry. "I hope it isn't a hundred orgasms you have to give me. I hope it's a thousand. Ten thousand."

"Perhaps it was only the one," he said. "Perhaps I deceive myself about the sting in the curse's tail." His tone turned gloomy. "Undoubtedly the curse was designed to exploit my character."

She thought about that one. "Don't tell me your ex-girlfriend knew about Stockholm syndrome."

"Perhaps. I know now that without my collusion, she could not have trapped me."

"How do you figure?"

He looked down into his lap. Son of a gun if he didn't have a boner again. Already. "She used my pride in my appetites. I may have lacked skill but I was a lusty fellow. In bed, attuned to the lusts of women who slept there, I could not help but learn what she meant for me to learn. Once I had satisfied the first woman, pride forced me to continue until the hundredth."

She scratched her head. "Let me get this straight. She used your own horniness to keep you stuck in the spell?"

He turned dark, glittery eyes on her. "As I use yours to bind you to my needs."

"Okay, that's too much information." She scrambled out of the wreck and hunted up her clothes and put them on. Then it felt funny to be dressed with him naked, so she fetched his clothes after all. Her Tercel was empty. "Did you see where Clay went?" She handed him his clothes.

"Your employer took him away."

Poor Clay, busted after all. Her brain hurt with tiredness.

Randy clambered out of the Camry so he could zip up his jeans. He looked bigger dressed than he did naked, more arrogant or something. Looking into his bossy black eyes, she knew she had bitten off a big chunk this time.

For one thing, she could kiss her privacy goodbye.

Yeah, but he can't ever leave. Her heart heated. "I think we need to establish some ground rules."

"Ground rules. Not for when we are in the air?"

She shivered. "Rules for living. Coexisting. Like, you not using my credit card and stuff."

"I need my own credit card," he said seriously.

"And a job to pay for it."

He nodded. "Clay will teach me how to manage."

"Clay?" She stared. "He would do that for you?"

"Yes." *Boy. What does Randy have on Clay that would make that work?* "I need to become a fully functioning citizen. If I am ever to be free, I must begin repaying your kindness now." His voice lowered. "So that you don't tire of me." He looked down and brushed the knee of his jeans. "No one should be useful for only one thing. I don't know what it will take to prove myself to you, but I promise to make this easier for you. Your rooms are small."

She was touched. "It's okay, we'll cope. Do—do you have any plans?" Mortifyingly, she hadn't given a thought to Randy as a free citizen. All she'd thought about were her hundred orgasms. "What else do you want, long term?"

His head came up and his eyes got bright. "I want to recover my name and rank. I want to repossess my home. I should like to discover Lady Juliana's fate—she who bespelled me—and if possible, at the least, find her grave and do something unpleasant to it." She smiled. "I know." He smiled back. "Perhaps I ask for the moon. Most of all I want to be entirely free of her curse. No more sting in the tail. No lingering bondage to you, nor for you to me."

That hurt, though it was something she wanted, too. Her chest tightened.

"Sometimes," she admitted slowly, "it does creep me out. The lingering bondage part." *And if I ever get tired of it, you can shoot me, 'cause I'll be sexually dead.*

Cripes, she needed therapy, stat. "Though I benefit in other ways."

"Indeed." He looked intrigued. "You benefit in ways other than sex? I should like to be more useful to you."

"The losers I've been dating. You've seen some of 'em. I guess I've had every single man at the office. And a lot of others. Morons, maybe, but I worry sometimes that I'll be attracted to some total creep for a stupid reason and wind up dead." With a weak smile she said, "I haven't given them a thought since I met you. Maybe someday my screwed-up libido will get unscrewed." She laughed uneasily. "At least you'll want me alive. Until your hundred orgasms are up."

In the dimness of the dump, his eyes glittered. "I'll take care of you."

CHAPTER
32

Jewel woke up late Saturday morning with a sex hangover. Every joint in her body ached, and her skin felt abraded in unusual places. She felt like a puffy plush toy of herself.

Randy brought her coffee in bed.

"You're still here," she croaked. She shut her eyes and breathed carefully, weighing options. "That's good." Waking sex with Randy had turned out to be as wild as his dream performance. The tendons on the insides of her thighs felt like sore wet noodles.

"You are a famous person!" he announced. "Look!" She squinted. "Your likeness is on the front page."

Her brain hurt. "What did we do last night?"

He put the newspaper on her lap. "*Voilà.*"

And there she was. She unfolded the *Tribune* and stared at a grainy full-color picture of herself standing on a park bench, a liquor bottle and a backpack in her hands, her mouth ajar. She was looking up. The phone-cam had caught the genie in the act of coming out of or going into the bottle, distorted into fluid, swooshing, smoke-bending curls.

The cutline under the photo identified her as "allegedly a city employee."

In a photo inset a pigeon was setting fire to some confetti, amid fallen cotton-candy cones, spilled soda, and pom-poms.

She scanned the article. The Pan American parade, apparently, was still on. She didn't know whether to be relieved or worried.

In despair she said, "Any messages?"

"Edward Neccio telephoned twice. He was most insistent. I assured him you would speak to him when you arose."

She nodded dully. That hurt, too. "He's in the office on a Saturday? Guess I'll go in, too, so he can fire me."

She staggered to the bathroom and cranked up the hot water. She dressed in maudlin mood, and put on the red pumps that poor old Clay had stolen for her from Field's. She hoped he was making out okay in stir.

An hour later she sneaked into the evidence room at the department. The Drambuie bottle full of genie was sealed with every one of the sultan's seals she'd taken off Buzz. For good measure she had put the bottle in a paper bag, taped the bag up tightly, and labelled it POISON. She was tagging the bag with a fake case number when Ed caught up with her.

"There you are, Heiss. I been looking all over for you."

She jumped. "For God's sake, don't make me drop this."

He looked at the bag. "You poisoned your lunch?"

"Depends if you fire me before noon or after." She tucked the bag way back on a shelf behind some boxes dating from the early 1980s. As she dusted her hands off she said, "I know it's bad. But I corked up the genie yesterday. It's gone forever. And I hear the Pan American parade went off okay."

"We gotta go talk to the chief attorney." Ed didn't seem upset. Not necessarily a good sign.

"Taylor's in on a Saturday?" she squeaked.

"Everybody's in. That big identity-theft case."

Thanks, Ed, rub it in. "Is he mad?"

Ed made a *meh* face. "Depends on your report. C'mon, we're gonna be late."

The air conditioning in Taylor's office was so strong, her sweat-soaked armpits felt like ice. The chief listened stony-faced through her debriefing about Clay's sex-therapy scam. Every now and then he looked at Ed, and Ed stared doggedly at Jewel, as if the whole thing had nothing to do with him. She did her best to imply that.

Skimming like mad, she said, "I met with the informant at The Drake Hotel, obtained an introduction to the suspect, and, uh, conversed with him at length. On several occasions. I came to the conclusion that he was skating close to the law, but in fact he never made any claims to offer medical service, nor to cure any diseases, disorders, or psychiatric conditions. The most you could say was, he offered a kind of faith healing."

That wasn't a hundred-percent lie. A sex demon was imaginary, so if somebody thought she met one, and he helped her fix her sex problems, she must have had faith in him, right?

"Ultimately I let it go. The suspect had no record and I had no material evidence." Her face burned with guilt.

"And the hinky part?" the chief attorney said.

She sat up straight. "Suppressed, sir." She met his stony stare head-on. "You've heard the last of this one."

"You're positive?" Taylor looked at Ed, who darkened.

"Positive," Ed croaked.

"How about the genie seller?" Taylor aimed his eyebrows at her. "It seems you got pretty close to it yesterday."

"Captured it, sir," she said. "Sealed up and forgotten."

"He won't sell any more?"

"There was only one genie, sir, lured from bottle to bottle."

"Sounds like fraud."

She swallowed. "Hinky fraud, sir."

They got out of there somehow. Taylor talked to Ed alone for a few minutes and then she and Ed went downstairs.

Can I get fired and go home now?

"I'm glad you got all this experience," Ed said heavily, towing her into his office. "The chief has some suggestions." He shut the door. "First being, you're suspended."

She eyed him warily. "You suspended me two days ago."

Ed looked stuffed, which meant he was putting one over. "Also, you're promoted. You are now a new division under my supervision. You get all the wack cases."

"What? I already get the wack cases!"

"Now it's official. This containerizates the hinky stuff in one accountable spot."

"And what exactly does 'accountable' mean?" she said, though she knew.

"God forbid there's a leak, we fire you, let it blow over a week or two while you go to the Bahamas, and when you come back all tanned, you're on the job again. Like now, you with the genie in the news," Ed reminded her, and Jewel slumped. "Twice. It ain't suspension for real." He showed both hands. "It's paid leave. Time to get to know your partner." He waved all ten fingers. "I never told you this, by the way."

She gaped like a gaffed salmon. "I don't have a partner."

"Yes, you do." He opened his office door and signaled to someone outside.

CHAPTER 33

Clay Dawes sauntered into the office.

She blinked. "I thought you were in jail."

"Shut the door, Dawes."

"Aren't you glad to see me?" Clay murmured. He had on an actual suit, nothing designer-schmantzy, just cheap enough to match the anti-style of her polyester and convey the unbribable probity of a public servant. He still looked hot. And his hair still wanted cutting.

Her stupid face wouldn't stop grinning. "You were busted."

Ed ignored that. "You're a good investigator, Heiss, one of my best, but you suck at undercover. The way this job is, you need some coaching. Little psychological counseling—"

"He's not a psychologist. And he was busted."

"Far from it. I have a job now," Clay said.

"I mean, psychological advantage," Ed said hurriedly. "We talked at length after that other business. I was impressed with his insights. You could use some street savvy on your team."

She tried to wrap her head around this new Ed goofiness, but she was so happy to see Clay, it took her edge off. "Wait a minute, he's my what?"

"We aren't having this conversation, did I tell you that?" Ed said, skating serenely over her interruption.

"Naturally not," Clay murmured.

"Here's a little deli file. You two can work the kinks out on this case, do some normal stuff for a while until the you-know-what hits the fan again."

Flinching at "kinks" and "do some normal stuff," she looked from Ed to Clay.

Clay smiled. "Nice shoes."

She looked down at her stolen red pumps and flushed. Then she glared at Ed. "I can't believe you did this to me. After I fixed your marriage."

"I'm sure we coulda got along fine without. By the way, you're both coming to Sunday dinner." He opened the door. "Now giddodda my office."

His door shut behind them.

Everybody in the outer office stood up and applauded. It seemed as if the whole department was here. Caught in the spotlight, Jewel protested, "Guys."

"Woo hoo! Heiss got a partner!" Merntice sang out.

"Everybody can relax!" Tookhah yelled.

"Three cheers for Heiss!"

Sayers produced squeakers and handed them around. Jewel felt herself blushing crimson. Her coworkers were actually high-fiving each other.

"Hey, what's your name?" Britney said to Clay.

Clay told her, looking aw-shucks and totally comfortable, holding Jewel's elbow like a fucking bridegroom or something.

"Three cheers for Clay Dawes!" Britney shrieked. Clay bowed for his three cheers.

"To Clay Dawes!" Digby toasted with his styro coffee cup. "He nailed Heiss and got her promoted!"

"Excuse me?" Jewel demanded. Her ears felt so hot, they felt like they might fall off. "He did not!"

"Aw, give it a rest," Ed murmured in her right ear, and Jewel jumped. "You blush an' look guilty when you tell the truth, and when he lies, nobody can tell. You're a perfect team."

Jewel rounded on him, but Ed only grinned. He raised his voice. "Here's a fifty!" He held the bill up in the air and Lolly snagged it. "Go get yourselves a beer! Be back here by noon!" He withdrew again, chortling, into his office.

Lolly flourished the money. "Dick's!"

"To Dick's!" everybody yelled.

"Are we bonding?" Clay murmured in her ear as he hustled her down the stairs with the rollicking investigators. "Cool."

"You put him up to this," she said through her teeth.

"Didn't have to. And aren't I getting some insights on my new partner!"

"Grrrr."

"Hold my hand, officer, and we'll face the music together."

In Dick's, they crowded up against the bar, and Jewel heard Lolly say behind her, "I give him two weeks. Ten bucks."

"God, I hope so," Britney said. "You're on."

What did I ever do to deserve such pals? Jewel squeezed Clay's hand, and Clay squeezed back. She felt better.

In the men's room at Dick's, Clay bonded with the guys. Sayers, the guy with the whisky nose, threw an arm over Clay's shoulders. "You should know something about Heiss," he wheezed. " 'Fore you get in too deep. Haw."

"Haw," Clay said obediently. "This should be good."

Sayers held up a finger. "She don't stay innersted. N'am sayin'? Only, only you got to stand by her annahaw."

"Haw?"

"Because that hinky shit is dangerous."

Clay eased out from under Sayers's arm and propped him against the men's room wall. "I believe you."

"The rumdum's right," the guy named Digby said. "We worry about Heiss."

"'Sright," Sayers said. "Little girl lost, our Jewel."

Clay blinked. "Six-foot Jewel? Eyes-like-razors Jewel?"

"The same," Digby said.

"Hi, I'm Jason," said a male model type. "Okay, she's a tart, but we—" Digby clouted the side of his head. "Ow!"

"We take care of her. So will you," Digby finished for him.

"Otherwise," said a so-far-silent man named Finbow.

Clay waited. He raised his eyebrows. "Haw?"

Finbow leaned forward and drove a fist into Clay's solar plexus.

Clay folded up, gasping. He backed away, but Finbow seemed to be done. "Gotcha," Clay wheezed.

Finbow looked thoughtful. "No. I gotcha."

Clay considered nodding and didn't. Finbow went out. Digby and Jason got Clay standing and Sayers offered him a nip out of a flask, which Clay accepted. *That wasn't so bad.*

"Come on," Sayers said gloomily. "We gotta let the women at you sometime."

They led him back into the bar.

Clay spent thirty minutes watching Jewel and fending off come-ons from her female coworkers. *Holy scary harem*, he thought. Apparently he'd underestimated the job: Getting her into bed was the easy part.

But however crowded the bar, however many well-wishers Jewel seemed to have here, there was no sign whatever of Lord Randy the Underdressed.

Excellent.

"What you want with our Jewel, hm?" one of the women said.

Wish I knew. "I hope she'll teach me everything she knows."

"Better hope not," she said. "I'm Merntice. I put your paycheck through." Another gotcha.

In fact, it didn't go so badly at all.

"So, Virgil, I see you cashed my check. Do I win the bet?"

Saturday afternoon, Clay sat on a bench on Oak Street Beach, watching half-naked yuppies play volleyball in the sun. He felt odd. Solid and safe and in control. Not like himself at all.

Virgil grumbled, which his son took to be a yes.

"That's the good news, then."

"Okay, let's have the rest."

"Know that brass bed I borrowed from you? Uh-huh, well, I have some bad news, it's been crushed into a club sandwich."

"My antique?" Virgil's calm broke. "I rented that bed to you. I didn't give it to you so you could crush it! That thing was a piece of history!"

"Virgil, it wasn't the Celestial Bed and you know it. You only told that guy he had Hamilton's bed so he would think he was gypping you in a swap for that phony Ming bowl."

Virgil sniffed. "It could have been the Celestial Bed."

"But it wasn't." Clay hurried on. "And you know that fraud cop I told you about? I have some weird news. I have a job."

"Not another lame con. What now?"

"No, it's a regular job, like, a paycheck and benefits and taxes taken out and everything. So I'm her partner now—"

"What?"

"It was a plea bargain, Virgil."

"She busted you! I knew it."

"Nope. Nopers. In fact, the plea was on the other foot."

"*What?!*"

"Are we square over the bed?"

Virgil sighed. "At least you got some work out of it. You'll be able to live on the profits for a while."

Never tell the truth. "Oh, yeah, the money. Okay, remember the club sandwich?"

CHAPTER 34

"Why may I not dine with you?" Randy said again, while Jewel pawed through her closet for day-off clothes that didn't say "slut."

"Because," Jewel said, exasperated, "you're not invited?"

"Clay Dawes is invited. You go everywhere with him."

"He's my partner now." For the second night in a row she'd had no sleep. She pulled on a scoop-neck, black, silk top. Would Clay get the wrong idea from this top? She'd never worried about any man's opinion before a con man got permanently in her hair.

Randy pouted. "I know what 'partner' means in this century. It means 'mistress.' But you are with me." Clingy, clingy, clingy. Just because they'd spent thirty-six hours in bed.

"I need a work partner. Department rule. I haven't had one for a while, and I didn't have one when I met you, but it was inevitable, Randy," she said, hearing the wheedle in her voice and hating it. *See, this is why I never get serious with a guy.* "Believe me, I'm not happy either."

"A week ago you thought he was a criminal."

"He's still a criminal." And at the first wrong step, she would have no hesitation turning him in. She hoped.

"This top is too low." She pulled it off and threw it in the laundry.

"The man is a born prevaricator."

"Whereas you learned lying when you became a sex demon." No red, definitely no spaghetti straps. How had she come to own an all-slut weekend wardrobe? It would have to be navy polyester. "Ugh."

"So if he's no better than I, why may I not go?"

She sighed. *How am I going to stand having this big baby in my life? He's bratty and clingy and he's driving me crazy. Thank God, Clay's my partner. I don't think I can take much of Randy unchaperoned for long.* Shocking thought.

"Please."

She hated when he said "please" because he was so god-awful bad at it. She confessed, "I can't deal with the antler-clashing."

Randy studied her. His brow cleared. "Antler—oh. I see. Very well. I promise not to dispute with Clay."

She rolled her eyes. "Groovy. Now can you promise Clay won't dispute with you?" The navy polyester was hideous. That was why she wore it to work. With a sigh, she shucked it.

Randy looked at her through his lashes. "I possess self-control, as you are aware."

"Well, I'm losing mine. Nina doesn't know who you are. She was too busy canoodling with Ed to take a good look at you at the dump, but if you're at her supper table she will look. She will know. If she ever finds out how the curse's sting works, how long do you think before she starts scheming to get you stuck in another bed?"

He blinked. "Surely she is reconciled with her husband."

"So? I have multiple sex partners. Ed's had affairs for years. Do you believe in Nina's self-control? 'Cuz I don't."

He scowled. "Hm."

"Am I getting through to you now?" *God, I'm a harpy. I own this guy and I love it and now I'm getting savage about the competition.* She slid back into the black, silk, scoop-neck top and a pair of tight stretch jeans and looked in the mirror. Slut.

But Randy looked thoughtful. "Yes. Yes, I see."

"Good." She sucked in a long breath and held it. *Some guys like a woman with a stomach.* Uh-huh. Couple of quick twists and the hair was up in a French knot.

"Be careful what you tell Nina," he commanded.

She crossed her fingers. This was Nina they were talking about, who needed no thumbscrews to extract information. "Yup."

"And when you come back we will discuss this matter of multiple sex partners."

With her keys in her hand and the door open, she eyed him. "You're still a lord in there somewhere, aren't you."

He looked down his nose. "But of course."

"Well, welcome to the twenty-first century, bub. You don't own anybody and I don't own anybody, spell or no spell. I intend to make you acquainted with all the horrors of feminism."

On the last word she shut the door and scrammed.

She picked Clay up at the Drake. He tried to kiss her.

"Behave, you," she said halfheartedly.

"Sorry. Got carried away. That's some shirt you're almost wearing." He squeezed her shoulder and she pushed him away.

"These are my weekend clothes. When I want you to maul me, I'll tell you."

"God, I hope so."

That was easy, she thought. If she could organize Clay, she might enjoy having him around.

A kid on a bicycle was crossing Michigan, heedless of traffic. She stopped the Tercel with a screech. "Buzz!"

"What the—?" Clay said.

Buzz looked over his shoulder and blushed. "Officer Jewel."

Jewel scrawled and tore a sheet off her dashboard pad. "Here."

Buzz squinted at it. "Your digits?" He leaned closer and looked down her low-cut top. "What is this, like, a pass?"

She rolled her eyes. "As if. I'm practically your mother. I'm giving it to you in case—in case you need help." Any day now, he could be busted. It was a miracle the law hadn't caught up with him. "Put it in your pocket."

What am I doing?! she was screaming inside. *I can barely stand having Randy around, and now I have a partner, too! I don't need more strays!* "Gotta run. Call if—if you need to."

She gunned the Tercel and peeled out, leaving Buzz staring after her with his zitty trap hanging open.

"Interesting. More prayers against homelessness?" Clay said, and she ignored him. She was figuring out that she liked having strays. She just had to be picky.

Nina was enjoying an ecstasy of domestic bliss. She fluttered from kitchen to dining room at warp speed. The boys played video games. Her daughter actually helped Jewel and Clay set the table. And Ed, her wonderful, glorious, pain-in-the-butt husband, watched TV from his lounger in the living room. She filled another bowl with homemade Chex mix and brought it to him.

"Supper in fifteen minutes," she said.

Ed's gaze was locked on the screen. His hand went to the fresh bowl of Chex mix. "How 'bout another beer."

So that's how long the sugar lasts. Nina picked up the dirty bowl and turned to leave, trying not to feel bitter.

His arm snaked out. He grabbed her around the waist and yanked her into his lap. Then he mashed her, long and slow. When she came up for air, his eyes were gleaming.

She sighed happily. Her mouth tasted like Chex mix and horny Ed. " 'Nother beer then?"

"Wanna tell you something," he said.

She settled deeper into his lap. "What."

"Know that night in the van?"

She smiled. "I remember." She wriggled against his boner.

He squeezed. "Why I did it in the van like that? It's because, I know how you and Jewel talk. Girl stuff. She's, I mean, everybody says she's, uh, you know, adventurous. Of course she needs fuckin' therapy, but you got your head screwed on straight." He took a deep breath and put on his "hero" face. "So. I thought. A red-hot sexy firecracker mama number like my wife, she needs some stimulating fun unique new adventurous—different— type—unusual thing. Things. If. If you like that stuff."

She laughed out loud.

"What." He sounded all, *I don't have to take this abuse.*

She put her forehead against his. "I loved it." She kissed him on the nose. "Any time. *Any* time."

Her spouse looked relieved. "How about that beer?" he said hoarsely.

She snickered and struggled out of his lap, making sure to press on his boner.

"While you're up, can you check is that taxi still sitting out front?" Ed had a horror of being followed home from work by a disgruntled taxi driver. She guessed he met a lot of them.

"But it's Sunday." She went to the window.

Across the street, a taxi idled. A passenger sat in back. When she pulled back the drapes, the passenger's head turned, as if he had been watching the house.

"I'll go," she said.

Hackles up, she banged out the front door and marched across the street. She'd beat up anybody who bothered her husband.

"Hello?" she said aggressively. "Can I help you?"

The passenger shrank back. The whites of his eyes showed.

"Do I have to call the police?"

He shook his head. Damn, he looked familiar. He said in an English accent, "There is no cause for alarm. I'm waiting for Jewel Heiss."

All of a sudden Nina got it.

"You're him."

She went hot all over. *The guy from the bed!* Holy crap. Jewel must have done something, who knew what, and got him out of there before Ed smashed the bed into a pretzel. Count on Jewel to save the baby and throw out the bathwater.

Nina grinned.

He bent his head toward her and frowned. "I am whom?"

Don't spook him. "You're the guy Jewel said was coming later," she said. She opened the taxi door for him. "Why didn't you ring the doorbell? Come on in, we're ready to eat."

He hesitated. "I was not invited."

"Sure you're invited, I'm inviting you, what am I, chopped liver? You can't wait out here all evening when I got a houseful of food, come on, come on, come on, come on."

He got out and bowed real nice and she jollied him into the house.

"Who the fuck is this?" Ed said.

She shepherded the bed guy past him toward the kitchen. "He was in the taxi waiting for Jewel. You know her," Nina muttered in her husband's ear as they passed. "Always picking up strays."

He stared at the bed guy. "Oh. Yeah. You were her cabbie that day at the office."

"Supper's almost on," she said.

Whatever other thoughts Ed was having, he seemed to forget them. "Well it ain't like she can't feed you." He turned back to his ball game.

CHAPTER
35

Clay's eyes popped when he saw Randy waltz in with Nina. Randy smirked. Jewel looked staggered.

Nina was a whirlwind. Clay helped, bemused, while she organized table-setting and flower-arranging teams, tossed out orders, passed dish after dish after dish to go on the table, harried her kids to wash their hands, yelled for Ed every three breaths to come and eat, and kept up an effortless flow of conversation with Jewel.

It was like being in a *Brady Bunch* montage, fast forward.

Before he knew it, Clay was sitting in front of a big, clean plate, bowing his head.

"Clay, would you say grace?" Nina said. He peeked at her. She winked.

Oddly, he felt at home.

"Dear Lord," he began. Jewel's head came up and she stuck her tongue out.

A warm feeling spread through him.

"Lord, they say you can't pick your family, but you can pick your friends. As we sit at a table loaded with your delicious-smelling bounty, let's remember that everyone comes to your table a beggar, a stranger asking for a handout. Everyone is a lost soul with no past and no future, if not for your grace."

Randy's face came up scowling, and Clay eyed him steadily until he bowed it again. Jewel giggled silently.

"Thanks be also to our hosts Ed and Nina, without whose great strength and generosity we would not be here today. Amen."

Voices murmured, "Amen."

"Pass the gnocchi," Ed burst out.

"Are you from England?" That was Nina's daughter Lexy, fifteen going on twenty-slut, sulky in goth makeup and simpering at Randy.

"What cab company you say you were with?" Ed said aggressively to Randy.

Randy looked walleyed and a little snotty, as if he wasn't used to being accosted by vulgar people. Clay smiled to himself.

"He's independent," Jewel said.

Randy's glance flicked from Jewel to Ed to Nina. He said to Lexy, "I'm from Wales, originally."

"You're not a wildcat or nothin' are you?" Ed said. "We can't have that. You gotta have a medallion. You get my drift I hope."

Randy's nose went higher. "I assure you—"

"He doesn't work the street, Ed. I ask him to drive me sometimes," Jewel said.

"I'm Jewel's boyfriend," Randy blurted.

Ed's round, red face lit up with comprehension. "Ooh. Okay."

Jewel sent Randy a terrifying glare.

Clay gloated. "Great lasagna, Nina." The lasagna was a revelation, cheesy and fragrant with oregano and thyme and tomatoes that tasted extra tomatoey. "What's in this sauce?"

"Port wine," she said. "The secret is, you use the good stuff. Cheap wine isn't worth cooking with."

Ed looked at Nina. "You said he was in that cab outside."

"He was," Nina said, unconcerned. "He was sitting in back."

"More strays," Ed muttered around his gnocchi.

Jewel shot Nina a searching look.

Nina swigged her wine and smiled at her husband.

Clay fingered the parchment in his pocket. *Piss him off, then buy him back.* "You been away from Wales long, Randy?"

Randy focused on Lexy. Clay noticed he kept his face turned away from Nina. "Yes, my entire life," he said.

Lexy said, "You don't sound Welsh. You sound English. It's cute." Ballbusting and flirting at the same time—good grief, she was Nina's daughter.

Clay could see Ed reddening and stepped in again. "Yeah, Randy, I've been meaning to ask you, how can you tell a low-class English accent from an upper-crust accent? Is it, like, the difference between a lord and a wildcat cabbie?"

Randy turned a withering look on Clay. "The signs of good breeding are unmistakable."

One of the twins belched. "Great 'zanya, Mom."

Nina leaned over and kissed her son on the ear. "Well, it's a cinch I don't have any good breeding signs," she said happily.

Randy bowed. "The signs are unmistakable," he repeated.

Jewel kicked Clay on the ankle. He guessed it was meant for Randy and passed the kick along. Randy frowned and Clay eyed him steadily. To his surprise, Randy nodded.

Nina didn't take offense. "I bet those nobility-type girls in England don't wear an inch of makeup," she said.

Lexy pouted.

"They did not when I lived there," Randy said. "But youth can afford to dress badly. Youth itself is beauty," he said, smiling at Lexy, and she lit up like a little kid.

"Boys, you should listen to Randy. You might pick up some tone," Nina said. Her eyes danced at Clay.

She knows, he thought. *Oh, boy. We're in for it now.*

He watched Jewel's eyes go deer-in-headlights as she, too, figured out what Nina knew. He said, "My dad always claimed that a genuinely classy person never lets anybody feel like they're inferior. Not even a garbage man or a cab driver. That's how aristocrats recognize each other."

"Or criminals," Randy sniffed.

"Pop says criminals and cops are all in bed with each other," Matt said, and Ed shushed him.

"I'd say it takes one to know one," Clay said.

Randy raised his glass. "Point taken."

Jewel kicked Clay on the ankle again. "Tell us about Wales, Randy," she said warmly. "It's part of England, right?"

Randy looked down his nose and started to lecture.

Clay asked Nina for the marinara sauce.

Passing the marinara, Nina said confidentially to him, "I can tell you where you're going wrong."

"Please don't."

Nina raised her eyebrows, but she shut up.

After dinner, Ed stumped back to the TV to watch the game.

Clay didn't want Nina's advice but, out of consideration for Jewel, who must be dying to tell Randy to stop acting like a dick, he lured Nina into the kitchen.

Nina said in a low voice, "I don't care what my husband or Jewel says. You did a very important service for a lot of women, and speaking for all of us I say, Thank you."

He looked over his shoulder. In the dining room, Jewel was shaking her finger at Randy. Clay smiled.

"Shucks, ma'am, I didn't do anything. It was all Randy."

Nina handed him a dishtowel. "You're jealous. You feel inadequate because he was in the bed all along. Well, forget it. You did the talking. Believe me, where sex is concerned, talking is ninety percent of the game. Well, you know that."

She's so clumsy. Her technique is a battering ram. You see it coming and it still works.

Jewel stormed through the kitchen and stomped out the patio door. Randy followed.

Nina blew smoke and grinned into Clay's eyes. He braced himself for a Nina drive-by.

"Siddown, I'll get you coffee."

That guy could be such a prick! *Arrogant pig of an aristo.* Jewel stomped outside to get some fresh air, hoping to get away from her lordly shadow.

But, oh no, here he came, following her.

"Very well, your point has merit," Randy said to her back. "I will be more gracious to your friends Ed and Nina. Whether or not they can return proper courtesy."

She turned to give him a glare. "They are not going to call you 'my lord.' This is America."

He stood stiff and tall in the late summer dusk. "Understood."

"And you'll find a way to deal with my multiple sex partners and Clay being my partner at work."

Randy threw his head back and held it as if thinking. He

really was beautiful. She could see how some English mistress might have put up with lousy sex to look at that face.

He's a peck of trouble, the Wisconsin dairy-farmer's daughter whispered in her head.

He said, "I shall contrive."

While she had him in a compliant mood she may as well shoot for the big one. "Plus—"

He stepped closer, until they were nearly chest to chest. "In addition?" he said huskily.

"Yeah, okay, in addition," she said and pulled in a big breath. "We need to work out if you can, uh, give me an orgasm more discreetly."

It was getting really dark in the garden. A gardenia bush was blooming nearby, smelling like Field's perfume counter. Jewel thought she saw him smile.

"An interesting concern, for a woman with multiple sex partners."

"Let that go," she said sharply. "I mean this. I don't want a repeat of that horrible experience in Field's anytime soon. I could have gone to jail, Randy. And then where would you have been? Back on Field's eighth floor in some couch or other. Or in the rear seat of a passing taxicab. Forever."

He said nothing. In the silence between them she heard Nina, in the kitchen, say, "—Stay forever. But there it is."

Jewel frowned. She went to the patio door and looked in.

"If I didn't know better, I'd think you were trying to get those two together," Nina said.

Clay said, "They're already together."

She put coffee cups on the counter and sat on a tall stool across from him. "But you're in love with her."

Clay winced. "You know that Randy was in that bed all that time. Do you know why?"

That diverted her. "No, but I'm dying to find out." She lit a cigarette and dragged avidly, cupping her elbow with her free hand, her eyes sparkling. He filled her in about Randy's curse, explaining how Jewel was number one hundred, but he left out the part about the sting in the curse's tail.

She said dreamily, "Talk about dumb luck. Coulda been me."

"Probably not. I had a lot of new clients in the two months we worked together."

She waved smoke away. "Aw, Jewel needs him more than I do. I got Ed," she said, her face turning toward the living room with an expression that squeezed Clay's heart a little. "Which brings me to you and Jewel. You want her."

"She's my partner. There's a lot of Jewel to go around."

Clay knew that, even if Randy didn't. It was his biggest advantage. Clay respected Jewel's craving for personal space.

Nina said, "I like you, Clay. I feel responsible for you." A warm feeling spread through him. She leaned forward. "What I'm telling you, one of these days you won't be afraid to make a move. Then what? By then she and Randy will be old marrieds. And, trust me, it's darn near impossible to come between old marrieds, I don't care what they say about the divorce rate. She needs to believe the guy's not gonna up and leave. Randy won't leave her. I can see it when he looks at her. You've got 'sayonara baby' written all over you." Nina stubbed out her butt in a silver-and-crystal ashtray. "I hope you won't take this personally, I hope you stay forever. But there it is."

At that moment Jewel came to the patio door by herself. Clay's pulse kicked up.

Nina got up and assembled a trayful of frosty beer bottles. "Talk to Clay, honey, I wanna neck with my husband. Sing out when you're ready for dessert." She sailed into the living room.

Jewel sat down in Nina's seat across from Clay.

Looking in her face, he realized Nina was right. He'd been moving too fast. That's what everybody at the office was trying to tell him.

I've got to buy some real estate on Planet Jewel.

Quickly, he revised his plans.

Clay looked mellow, so Jewel knew he was guilty of something. "What are you up to now?" she said, feeling tired.

"I'll explain in a minute." He called out the patio door, "Lord Pontarsais, would you kindly join us a moment?"

Clay being polite to Randy? Now what?

Randy came indoors.

Clay was all business. "Read that." He threw a rolled-up paper on the kitchen counter and sat down on a stool, looking expectantly from Jewel to Randy.

Randy unrolled the crinkly old paper. Jewel craned her neck, but she couldn't see anything. Randy's lips moved as he read. He sat heavily and read it again. "Where did you get this?"

Clay said, "It was stuffed into a tube inside your brass bed. Didn't you know it was there?"

Randy stared at the paper. He looked as if a foxhound had bitten him. *What on earth?*

"Show Jewel."

Randy passed it over and Jewel squinted at the handwriting, calligraphically elegant and totally illegible.

Clay folded his hands on the counter. "Tell her, Randy."

"It's the spell. She had it planned." He seemed stunned.

"You can read it?" Clay said.

Randy picked up the paper. " 'My poor Randolph, my heart mislikes my hand as I make plans to bespell you. I will give you all the powers of an incubus save one, the power to steal a soul. Yet might you not break a heart?' " He swallowed, looked at Jewel warily, and read on. " 'She who frees you will have reason to hate me"—his voice cracked—"if you enter her innermost thoughts and learn her desires, only to disappoint. It is not enough to know a woman's wants, Randolph. You must also love her, flaws and all.' The rest is heathen bibble-babble." He tossed the paper on the counter, looking agitated. "She planned it. She knew we would—she expected me to—"

Jewel felt herself go hot all over. With a pang for her lost hundred orgasms, she said, "What does that mean? Is she telling you how you can break the spell?"

Randy locked his gaze with hers.

He loves me. He has to love me, or the spell isn't broken.
Or did he not love her yet? She couldn't decide if that was
good or bad. Lots of guys fell in love with her and they
were a hundred-percent pain in the rear end. She herself,
thank goodness, was a healthy animal and never mistook
lust for love, the way girls like Britney did. The number of
guys she slept with, that would make her a total schizo.
Look how strongly she reacted to both Clay and Randy.

Randy blinked first.

She blurted, "Your mistress was being unreasonable.
Nobody could expect you to really fall in love in—in this
situation."

"Most unreasonable," Randy agreed in a low voice.
He turned to Clay. "Why did you show me this?"

"A gesture of good faith." Clay seemed dead serious,
so of course Jewel was suspicious. "Just showing I can be
a team player."

Jewel rolled her eyes.

Randy scowled.

Clay said helpfully, "So really it seems to me like you
two need to set up some nice, tight, scientific experiments. What makes Randy disappear into a bed? When
you fight with him? When he's scared? When he wants to
teach you a lesson?"

Her breath caught. Randy's eyes were glittering. "This
is kind of our business," she began.

Clay burbled on, "In a situation like the Field's home
furnishings department, does he have a choice of beds? Is
it the nearest bed, the biggest bed, the most antique bed,
the bed with the red satin sheets? How can we test this
without getting busted?"

She didn't trust Randy's smile. She felt sandwiched
between them, in a good–bad way. "Uh, I think we can
handle that part of the experiment thing oursel—"

"On the contrary," Randy said with authority. "Clay's assistance should prove invaluable."

Jewel was puzzled. Randy was such a control freak. Why would he want to share secrets about his magicalness with Clay?

Clay said, "Oh, and if we can get him to disappear into, like, a front-row seat in a theater or something, we can test whether he can give you an orgasm without all that screaming and throwing your clothes around." When Jewel turned a shocked face to him, he pulled something out of his pocket. "Your stockings, I believe. You left them in my treatment room."

She looked from Clay to Randy. They wore identical faces of helpful innocence.

Something was definitely up.

It had to be Clay. He'd conned Randy into some kind of alliance. No problem. She had the key to that picture. She could organize them because they both wanted her. Okay, it was like herding cats, but there were only two of them. She just had to figure out where they were headed and she could be the boss. For the first time in months, a deep peace filled her.

"You guys are all heart." Inside, she was full of glee. *I'm undercover in my own life. And I love it.*

Half an hour later, when the dinner dishes were in the dishwasher and they'd sent all the men into the TV room, and they'd opened a new bottle of Ed's homemade dago red, Nina said, "What were you and Clay and Randy being so serious about?"

Jewel thought about Clay's oh-so-helpful suggestions for scientific experiments, and Randy agreeing just because she objected, and laughed again. "Wouldn't you like to know?"

Nina wiggled her eyebrows. "You'll tell me eventually."

Jewel smiled into her friend's eyes. "Yeah, but think of the fun you'll have getting it out of me."

She drained her wineglass and held it out for another refill. She felt a whole lot better. Clay was behaving beautifully. If she could get Randy this well organized, she could have some serious fun with *whatever* her life had become.

"You're smiling," Nina said.

"You sound surprised."

"Not me. You've been getting laid. I'm happy for you."

"Are you really?" Jewel looked seriously into her friend's eyes. "Because I can't stand that we weren't getting along. Now that Randy's living with me—"

Nina waved a hand. "Pff! That stuff's not real."

Jewel raised her eyebrows. "You committed grand theft to get him."

"That was before I got my husband back." Nina stuck her tongue out. "If you know what I mean."

Jewel tried to imagine anybody swapping Ed for Randy. "Really?"

"Oh, honey," Nina said with pity. "You've never been with the same guy more than three dates, what am I saying, but listen. When the guy you've been schtupping for twenty-two years suddenly notices you—I mean, like, he turns a corner in bed—dammit, you know what I mean—"

"No." Jewel honestly didn't get it.

Nina's brown eyes were bright with tears. "What I'm saying is, it's a big thing. You wouldn't understand."

Jewel actually felt a twinge of envy. Nina was happy. With Ed! "I'm glad for you." Ed, of all people, to be somebody's grand passion.

Nina sniffed, flicked a tear away with a flash of diamonds, and tossed her hair back. "So what's up with you and Clay?"

"He's my partner," Jewel said primly. "I'm not gonna screw up a working relationship over a nooner."

"*Working?*"

To Nina's lewd look, Jewel said, "Yes, working. I need a partner so I can get some decent cases from your pig-headed husband. And I know what you're thinking, that Clay is a criminal. Well, if I catch him trying to use his job to set up another scam, I'll send him to prison."

Nina blew smoke. "That's not what I'm thinking, Jules."

Jewel narrowed her eyes. "What." When Nina wouldn't say, she burst out, "He's conning you! He conned you before. One thing I'm not falling for is any m—any of his gigolo stuff."

Jewel shrugged. "In the meantime, he can keep Randy under control."

Nina's eyebrows went up. "This should be good."

"Already Randy's too possessive." Jewel shuddered. This part of the future worried her. No matter how much of a jerk Randy became, could she punish him by leaving him trapped in a bed? *It won't come to that*, she hoped. "Clay sends Randy up a pole. He can make himself useful that way."

Nina smirked. "And you're not still hating yourself—?"

"For what?" Jewel flushed.

"Well, doing two guys at once."

"I told you, I'm not doing my partner," Jewel said, going hot all over. *She can't know about the hotel room couch*. "Sheesh! That would be a perfect way to lose my shot at ever getting out of the Hinky Division." *She can't know what Randy did to me in the dump*. "And what are you *smiling* about, you goddam sphinx?"

"I'm just thinking Clay's got a shot, too," Nina said innocently.

"Well, of course," Jewel said, mystified. "That's why they call it partners." She let out a belly laugh. "You should have heard Randy flip over that word! He thinks that means I'm Clay's mistress."

Nina made an uh-oh face.

"I told him I was gonna introduce him to all the horrors of twenty-first-century feminism."

Nina beamed. "That's the Jewel I know." She refilled both their glasses. "Missed you, babe."

Jewel touched her glass to Nina's and heaved a deep sigh. "And no, I guess I don't hate myself."

"You guess?"

"Well. I know I wasn't made for abstinence."

"About time you figured that out." Nina got up and hugged her. "Let's feed these men dessert, and then we can get snockered."

Acknowledgments

Those who have been wonderfully helpful in getting this book to happen and in more-or-less chronological order: my husband, Rich Bynum, the nicest man alive; Nalo Hopkinson, so often the wind beneath my wings; Betsy Mitchell, an officer and a gentlewoman; Don Maass, wisest of his breed; Professor Loren Pankratz, who knows everything about frauds; Dr. Gina Ogden, who advised me about sex addiction; Ysabeau Wilce, Laura Moore, and Farrell Collins, for brainstorming; Julie Kistler for early encouragement; "My Balentine" for insider dope; Julie Dreese Griffin for her graphic genius; Jill Purington, Heather King, Victoria Corby, Gin Jones, and Elizabeth Powell, for French translations; Todd VerBeek for cold-water swimming advice; Cat Eldridge, for wonderful support; The Squad, for continual advice and encouragement; and my long-suffering roster of readers, including: the ladies of Chicago-North RWA, Kate Early, John and Pam Nikitow, Pam Telfer, MJ Carlson, Lisa Laing, Barb Partridge, Marianne Frye, Sylvia Halkin, Cynthia Harrison, The Chocoholicas, Ted Halkin, Simone Elkeles, the City News Broads, Barbara Monajem, Jackie Wallis, Nnedi Okorofor-Mbachu, Kari Hayes, Bev Long, Martha Whitehead, Yvonne Yirka, Margaret Gettings, and Mindy "She's So" Fine.

Here's an excerpt from
Jewel's next adventure!

The Velvet Chair

Coming from Ballantine Books

Britney put her head close to Jewel's. "Tell me about your new partner." They both glanced at Clay, who seemed to be deep into his computer.

"He's weird," Jewel whispered. "You know every guy I work with hits on me."

Britney grunted. "I can't believe that one isn't after poontang. Those eyes. You look so pooped, I figured you two—"

"It's not that. I think he wants to know me better."

Britney gasped. "You mean he doesn't want sex?"

"He probably would if I said yes. But I think he wants to get under my skin."

"Don't they all. Honestly!" Britney sounded exasperated. "Where have all the brainless horndogs gone? Now Digby wants to get all, like, serious. After three weeks! 'What makes you tick, Britney?' Like I want to bare my soul 'cause we've done it. What if I just want to get laid?"

"Exactly!" Thank God for Britney, who made sense.

At this point Randy himself sauntered into the staff room with a garment bag over his muscular shoulder. Tall and dark, with hot black eyes that could see through women, he really didn't need to be magical, too.

Before she could chew him out, Clay beckoned him over. The staff room was filling up with investigators dumping their day's paperwork. She took the thick psychic-spa file to the copy room.

When she got back to the staff room, Clay had moved to the conference table. He had playing cards in his hands and he was surrounded by investigators. He seemed to be teaching a class.

"So now Randy signals to me what he's holding. Don't look at me, Randy, look at somebody else. Good. So you've got two aces and a king?"

"Queen," Lolly said, looking at Randy's cards over his shoulder.

"That's the other eyebrow. Okay, good. Wait two beats, *then* look at me." Clay turned his head. "Now I'm looking away so I can signal my hand. What have I got? Not you, Randy. Someone else tell me."

"Uh, three hearts?" Sayers blurted.

"Very good, Sayers. But what's wrong with that interpretation? Three hearts is a bridge term. What card is high? I'll give the signal one more time," Clay said.

"Lemme try," said Finbow the monosyllabic.

It was miraculous. A dozen contentious, competitive, bad-mannered investigators reduced to a schoolroom.

"No cards in the staff room!" Ed bellowed from his office door, and everybody got up fast.

"You were supposed to stay with the car," Jewel told Randy.

"I grew bored with the automobile." Randy sat in Jewel's chair, looking smug. "Did we earn anything?" he said to Clay. Clay slapped some money in front of him and he pounced on it.

"Would you mind not corrupting this man?" she said.

Clay was looking in his wallet. "Honey, you have no idea how corrupt this guy is. He must have been born with a deck in his hand."

"Very nearly," Randy said, stuffing money in his pocket.

"If you've been teaching him—"

Clay's voice dropped. "Okay, here's how I think we should handle this. You chase after the street vendor."

"Now, wait a minute—"

"Then you two check out the spa while I go to Thompson's and wriggle into the woodwork. You and Randy show up after I'm in."

"Randy is not on this team," she stated. Randy looked up with a wary expression. "How about the background check?" Her tired heart was dancing. *Undercover!*

Clay tossed some printouts on the desk. "Complainant is a former Jersey showgirl. Her brother, the millionaire, collects antiques, crackpot stuff. Newage." He pronounced the word to rhyme with sewage.

She smiled. "Real, or fake?"

"The machines are fakes. The gold digger looks like the real thing," Clay said. He tapped a picture. "And she's got the right bait for her mark. This here is a well-known piece, been in several private collections over the last century. Keeps disappearing."

Jewel took the picture. "What is it?" She turned it upside down. "Is this a chair in the middle?"

"The chair is Hepplewhite. Valuable antique itself. This unit here," he pointed to a chunky box covered with dials and frankenstein switches, "is the CPU, if you will. The tubes and wires probably do something like convey mystic vibrations to the subject. The straps, I'm guessing, keep him from flying out of there like a scalded cat when the current comes up his rear end."

Yowch. "Did they even have electricity back then?"

"Sure. Remember my brass bed? The one you wrecked for me? Many devices of that vintage favored the juice."

Randy took the picture from Jewel. "Hamilton's

Celestial Bed was electrical. Built in 1795 to treat impotence in men."

"So this guy collects swindling machines? Kinky."

Clay shrugged. "This is the Katterfelto Miracle Venereal Attraction Accelerator Apparatus, otherwise known as the Venus Machine. It makes you irresistible to the opposite sex."

"What's it worth?" she said, studying the picture.

"Maybe half a million dollars. If it's stolen, we can bust this gold digger tomorrow. Won't even have to infiltrate."

"Not so fast," she said. "Check the stolen property angle, Mr. Underworld Connections. If this is the real thing, then who owned it before her and did they part with it voluntarily? If not, she's holding stolen goods. If it's still in somebody else's possession, we've got her on counterfeiting antiques."

Randy pricked up his ears. "We are investigating a lady?"

"That's no lady," Clay said, tossing Randy another picture.

"*You* are not investigating anyone," Jewel told Randy. "You're my driver."

"But you don't let me drive." Randy took the picture.

"Hey, he could sleep with her, read her mind, and tell us all her secrets," Clay suggested. "Save time. That the new suit?" he said, indicating the garment bag Randy had draped over Jewel's chair. "How's it look?"

"I made them replace the buttons," Randy said.

Distracted, Jewel squinted. "How did you pay for it? Oh, no. You didn't use my credit card again, did you?"

"I have my own credit card, now. The shop offered me one."

Uh-oh. "What did you use for a job reference?"

He drew himself up to his full height. "They didn't ask."

She slapped her head with one hand.

"And a social security number?" Clay said, sounding amused.

Randy waved that away. "I made one up. Why? Is it important?"

Jewel slapped her head with both hands. "Argh!"

"Is this the suspect?" He picked up the Sovay picture.

"Don't change the subject," Jewel said. "You do not 'make up' a social—"

Randy ignored this. "What is your parlance? She appears to be 'hot.'"

Jewel rolled her eyes. "You are such a horndog!"

"No, seriously. He can, like, read women's minds in bed, yuh?" Clay looked innocent. "Our secret weapon."

"I should like to be a secret weapon," Randy said.

"By boning suspects? I don't think so. We need a new angle on this spa," she said.

"You puzzle on that," Clay said. "Let me take the point on the machine. I'll go in undercover. Then you come in after me."

"We'll meet in the morning and talk it over then."

Clay cupped a hand at his ear. "Sorry, I didn't catch that." He pooched out his kissy-face lips at her and his blue eyes crinkled.

"*Nyet, nein, non*," she said. "You don't go in alone."

He cocked his shaggy blond head. "You're just saying that."

"I am your senior partner and I say we go in together." She felt her blood pressure rising to almost normal levels. God, what she wouldn't give for a full night's rest.

Clay said, "You know, if you got some sleep, your judgment wouldn't be impaired. I know Randy didn't do anything but nooky for two hundred years, but can't he spare you shut-eye time?"

"I am present," Randy said stiffly.

"Dude, you're *omni*present," Clay said, squaring off with her glowering incubus. "Look at this woman. Dark circles under her eyes. Her hands shake. Her hair's a mess."

"Hey!" Jewel said. "I am present."

Clay shook his finger at Randy. "You may not remember what being human is like, but a person who misses sleep loses judgment, endurance, mental acuity—" Jewel swiped at him and he ducked "—and her reflexes go. This isn't about finding the hundredth woman to make you human, is it?" he sneered. "It's your ego."

"Sh!" Jewel flapped her hands. "Don't talk about it here!"

Randy inflated his chest, his long black hair bristling. They were the same height, but Clay was actor-slim. Randy looked like he bench-pressed taxis.

She began, "Can you two please—"

Randy said with sinister softness, "Jewel is your senior partner. She chooses her own bedmates."

"So you'll leave her alone tonight?" Clay said offensively.

They were nose to nose.

Randy looked like thunder. "She did not choose you."

Jewel picked up the files and headed for the car. They would knock it off when they saw their audience was gone.

Probably.